T0017262

ADRIEN BOSC was born in Avignon in 1986. He is the founder of Éditions du sous-sol and the magazines *Desports* and *Feuilleton*, and works in Paris as a publisher. In 2014, he received the Grand Prix du roman de l'Académie Française for his first novel *Constellation*.

Outrageous Horizon

Adrien Bosc

———

Translated from the French by Frank Wynne

This paperback edition first published 2022

First published in Great Britain in 2021 by
SERPENT'S TAIL
an imprint of Profile Books Ltd
29 Cloth Fair
London EC1A 7JQ
www.serpentstail.com

First published in French as *Capitaine* in 2018 by Éditions Stock
Copyright © Adrien Bosc, 2018

Translation © Frank Wynne, 2021

Extracts appear with permission from:
Martinique, Charmeuse De Serpents by André Breton. © Pauvert, département
de Librairie Arthème Fayard 1972, 2000. Frank Wynne's translation.
Tropiques, 1941–1945. © Nouvelles éditions Place (Revue fondée par Aimé Césaire).
Wifredo Lam by Max-Pol Fouchet / Éditions Cercle d'Art.
Look, Listen, Read by Claude Lévi-Strauss, translated by Brian C. J. Singer, © 1997.
Reprinted by permission of Basic Books, an imprint of Hachette Book Group, Inc.
Tristes Tropiques by Claude Lévi-Strauss 1955, translated by John and Doreen
Weightman 1973 © Librairie Plon 1955, Atheneum Publishers 1974, Penguin Books
1992, Penguin Classics 2011. Reproduced by permission of Penguin Books Ltd.
*Écris-moi à Mexico. Correspondance inédite 1941–1942 de Victor Serge et Laurette
Séjourné.* © Éditions Signes et Balises. Frank Wynne's translation.
Notebooks 1936–1947 by Victor Serge. Published in English by New York Review Books.
Translation copyright © 2019 by Mitchell Abidor and Richard Greeman. All rights reserved.

1 3 5 7 9 10 8 6 4 2

Typeset in Tramuntana Text by MacGuru Ltd
Designed by Nicky Barneby @ Barneby Ltd

Printed and bound in Great Britain by CPI Group (UK) Ltd, Croydon, CR0 4YY

The moral right of the author has been asserted.

All rights reserved. Without limiting the rights under copyright
reserved above, no part of this publication may be reproduced,
stored or introduced into a retrieval system, or transmitted, in any
form or by any means (electronic, mechanical, photocopying,
recording or otherwise), without the prior written permission of
both the copyright owner and the publisher of this book.

A CIP catalogue record for this book is available from the British Library.

ISBN 978 1 78816 274 6
eISBN 978 1 78283 561 5

MIX
Paper from
responsible sources
FSC® C171272

For Hugues and Victorin,
cabin mates

*Italicised passages are drawn from writings, diaries and accounts of this
journey by those who took it.
All sources are indicated at the end of the book.*

Articulating the past historically does not mean recognising it 'the way it really was'. It means appropriating a memory as it flashes up at a moment of danger.

Walter Benjamin, 'On the concept of history'

'But, Captain,' said Lieutenant Henri, 'they say you have travelled far, and seen much of the world. Have you not been to the Antilles, to Africa, to Italy, to Spain? But see, here comes your lame dog!'

Victor Hugo, *Bug-Jargal*

Prologue

—

We cannot know the taste of pineapple
by listening to travellers' tales

ONE NIGHT, LONG AGO – I don't quite remember when – as we left a bar, a tipsy friend said with feigned gravity: 'We cannot know the taste of pineapple by listening to travellers' tales.' We were standing in the middle of an alley somewhere between the rue de la Grange-aux-Belles and the rue Saint-Maur in the tenth arrondissement of Paris, a little the worse for wear, and I remember I stopped, I laughed, then I walked on towards Belleville. I was living in a building on the corner of the rue de la Fontaine-au-Roi and the rue du Moulin Joly, at the point where the tenth and eleventh arrondissements meet. The building faces a derelict multi-storey car park; there is nothing on either side of the courtyard, so, from a distance, it looks a little like an ocean liner. A rented apartment we had been handing down from brother to brother for about ten years without the lease or the rent ever changing. The first handed on to the next, leaving his place to his younger brother, and so on. The two-room apartment was furnished with oddments randomly gathered during peregrinations, and marked by home improvements undertaken for the band of brothers – a library in the hallway, a chest mounted on the ceiling, a leather armchair nicknamed the *pocket-emptier*, a clothes-shop mannequin with no clothes, a tricolour stolen from the entrance to a town hall, a neon sign from a Chinese restaurant with every other letter missing. From the window, we suspended a pink tricycle found during a night on the tiles, and this served as a figurehead for our ocean liner-cum-apartment block. I had arrived home late and, before I went to bed, had scrawled my friend's words on a slip of paper:

We cannot know the taste of pineapple by listening to travellers' tales.

I like these pithy phrases that say everything without saying anything, those futile maxims whose hollowness becomes evident the moment they are inverted, the paradoxes pinned over desks. Honestly, this is exactly what I did as soon as I woke up: I pinned it on

3

the corkboard over my desk, between a photograph of Walter Benjamin bought from the German bookshop Marissal Bücher (now gone) and an aphorism by Ambrose Bierce: *A rabbit's foot may bring good luck to you, but it brought none to the rabbit.* I forgot the phrase, but it stayed with me. During one of my moves, I found a brown paper envelope containing a number of Polaroids, postcards and scraps of paper, and there it was. On the reverse, I had noted the date: 12 June 2004.

When I discovered the stories of Nicolas Bouvier, I remember thinking how perfectly the maxim hit home; even the most faithful and inspired account could, at best, offer only a counterfeit of the real, and would stop short when it came to sensation. And yet, one line, one carefully fashioned phrase, gave the lie to the maxim, contradicted it for a moment: *Without this detachment, this transparency, how can one hope to show what one has seen? Become reflection, echo, breath of wind, guest who sits mute at the end of the table before uttering a word.* It was from *The Scorpion-Fish*, and it was luminous. I jotted it down in a notebook, this was in January 2007, and I reread it recently.

In May 2014, a friend invited me to the theatre. A performance, he explained, not real actors, but artists from various disciplines meeting on stage; it was in Vitry, on a Friday at 8.30 p.m. The artist in question was André S. Labarthe, who created the documentary series *Film-makers of Our Time.* I had nothing planned that evening, and I went. Outside the theatre, the title was writ large: WE CANNOT KNOW THE TASTE OF PINEAPPLE BY LISTENING TO TRAVELLERS' TALES. You couldn't make it up. In the programme, I read: *The title, borrowed from Leibniz, reveals all the difficulty but also all the zest of experience.* I was amused that it had never occurred to me to track down the author of this phrase, so convinced had I been that it was just drunken late-night showboating, one my friend had probably since forgotten, a clever throw-away remark. The back of the programme read:

1. *One does not need to be old to tell one's life story.*
2. *To imagine recounting one's life from A to Z is a tangential activity, a manner, by means of fiction, of elevating one's biography to the status of art.*

4

3. *If fiction is me, is non-fiction other people?*
4. *All (hi)story contains an element of fiction.*

If this were a philosophy, I would subscribe to it, especially point three. In the middle of the stage, was an elongated bubble of transparent plastic about eight metres wide, onto whose inner surface videos were projected that accompanied the story being read or played out. Strangely, it was quite funny.

After the performance, I went straight home without staying for a drink, to track down the precise source of the quote and read the whole passage. It was from *New Essays on Human Understanding* – and took the form of an imaginary dialogue between Philalethes and Theophilus, one an empiricist, the other a rationalist, in which Leibniz responds to the theses of Locke. The phrasing was different and the conclusion more astonishing: *We cannot know the taste of pineapple, for example, by listening to travellers' tales, unless we can taste things by the ears – like 'Sancho Panza, who had the faculty to see Dulcinea by hearsay', or like the blind man who, having often heard scarlet described as a blazing colour, thought that it must be 'like the sound of a trumpet'.* I thought, perhaps this is what the novel is, perhaps this is what memory is.

Another apartment, another desk, and above it, pinned to a different corkboard, a photograph – on the high seas, the sun is rising over a number of faces, in the centre is a woman, arms dangling, her expression cheerful, her pose mimicking the lurching of the boat while, behind her, an elegant, neatly coiffed man wearing braces and shirtsleeves is looking away from the camera, staring at some higher point; two hats, one looks to be made of straw, the other is a sort of panama; in the foreground, half out of frame, is a child of two or three dressed in shorts. Alone, on the far left, a man stands apart from the group, squeezed into a heavy artist's jacket with roomy pockets, he is bringing his hand up to his face, to smoke, to shield his eyes, it is impossible to tell. According to the caption, he is Victor Serge. One figure is turned towards the sea, her hand on the gunwale, her dress and her hair bisected by a band of light (at first glance, it is impossible to say whether the negative has been overexposed, or whether it is a broad beam of sunlight); she is Jacqueline Lamba. The two faces are lost, one staring at his feet, the other gazing out to sea.

I look at this photograph taken on the deck of the ship. There are two, and they are the only ones taken during the crossing. Don't go looking for others, I was told, all you will find are snapshots of mist taken from the quay, as for the rest, it is a strange journey devoid of images. A moment of history attested by official documents and by travellers' tales but shielded from film, one might say, in the blind spot of a century of images. The two negatives can be found on the website of the United States Holocaust Memorial Museum; both are credited to Dyno Lowenstein – and they bear the same date: 25 March 1941. Looking at the photograph, I can only dream of sitting down to dinner, of talking to these paper faces who suddenly come to life, talk, answer, offer a true perception of this moment, just one, a fleeting impression that fades as quickly as it appears of being on board, or somewhere above, slightly to one side, or simply else-where. We assemble memories, surround ourselves with an array of archives, tinker with them, move them, twist them, bring them together until the door opens just a crack, you grope your way through a room plunged into darkness and, in a thin shaft of light, a theatre comes to life. You take to the sea, you cast off, you set off on a long voyage and perhaps, when you reach the quay, you will have the taste of pineapple in your mouth and landsickness. I noted the date: 21 June 2014.

Part One

—

Pôvre Merle

We say that for our civilisation the Atlantic is what the Mediterranean was for antiquity, an inner sea.

Victor Serge, *Notebooks*

1

The Squid

———

Hangar No. 7
24 March 1941

Beneath a thick black cape, she moved in the darkness, her face haggard and a little wild. From the rue des Catalans, she took the corniche, crossed the gardens of the Pharo Palace, skirted the bassin de Carenage, balancing on the edge, leaving the sun, the Café Ventoux and Le Brûleur de Loups. When she reached 10, cours du Vieux-Port, she glanced up at the offices of Cahiers du Sud, then continued walking to the bustling warehouses at la Joliette filled with empty, upturned casks. At thirty-two, Simone Weil was this shadow shifting beneath the sunlight of Marseilles harbour; her brother André had left the city in January aboard one of these ships. She was living alone, dividing her time between learning Occitan and reading the *Iliad* through the prism of war. People called her strange, quick-tempered, reckless. On the wall of the apartment at 8, rue des Catalans she had pinned a reproduction of Giorgione's *Pastoral Concert*, she slept on the bare floorboards and often, in the middle of the night, swaddled in thin sheets, she would sit out on the terrace overlooking the shore, cleaning the lenses of her round glasses and straining her eyes as she watched the stars mingle with the sea. In the morning, sunlight would blanket her non-existent bed and the island of Frioul would appear, framed by the window. To the south, the sweeping cove, the Anse des Catalans, and beyond, the vallon des Auffes, the tiny fishing port hidden by the arches of the bridge behind which it nestles; beneath the broad arches, small craft are dragged ashore, hulls scuffed, oars limp; numerous alleyways stretch away towards the headland of Endoume, or to the rocky cove of Malmousque; those who are curious will head northward, towards the memorial, stopping along the way at the Impasse des Beaux-Yeux, which affords brief glimpses of the cityscape. Simone Weil had already lived many lives, in the lecture halls of the university, in factories, on the frontlines of the Spanish Civil War with the Durruti column, where a pot of boiling oil had put an end to her fervour, and soon she too would be on the quays awaiting the departure of a ship, immersing herself in chance encounters, she too would have melted into the maelstrom that jests and sets out its table according to its whim, bringing together the most curious fates, one day a poet, some revolutionaries, one night art dealers, a mathematician, a storm aboard an old tub that has sprung a leak, in the senseless and incessant hiccough of the backwash, in the eddy of events, she will play her role. And the novel is ingenious in that it is formless, its sprawling fields require skilful clearing, it nestles between the multiple strata of history, and once it has accumulated sufficient cargo, the heavy nuggets of anthracite, the engine roars into life, whistles and sends out plumes of smoke, the choo-choo puffs of steam are like the smoke signals of Native Americans: they clear the horizon. Like the dawn steamers on the Mississippi, the sternwheelers, it churns up the river waters, chugging against the current, slapping the snouts of crocodiles, marking time. And it glides between the sun's rays, suspending the breath of time, with every other turn drawing from its folds vast fictions just as algae clings to the steamer paddles, clinging to the rigid structure of truth.

Simone Weil was not leaving on 24 March. Since nine in the morning she had been watching on the quays at cap de la Pinède, near Hangar No. 7, watching the hundreds of men and women of every class who were against the railings of the rusty prow of a cargo ship. Victor Serge knows her and, in his notebooks, attests to her presence: *The port, long wait by the railings. Simone Weil, beneath her heavy loden cloak.*

On 3 December 1940, the city had been transfixed by the visit of Maréchal Pétain. A colossal portrait of the old man stared out over the Vieux-Port and over the cheering jubilant crowds that lined the route of the parade, dressed in their Sunday best, sombre black velvet suits, braid piping, red linings, elegant fedoras or the *chapeaux de Lunel* favoured by Folco de Baroncelli, polished boots made of creaking leather, and Claudine collars for the schoolgirls lined up outside a school that had been hastily renamed the Lycée Philippe-Pétain. Along the route of the parade that set off from the steps of the gare Saint-Charles, people jostled for space as others joined the throng on the harbour quays, thousands of supporters lined the thousands of worn flagstones and the canvas awnings snapped in answer to the tricolours that hung from the windows. The winter had been grim, the snow-covered tarpaulins of the Provençal fishing boats lashed to the piers formed a long powder trail difficult to distinguish from the roiling sea, weighed down by drifts of huge snowflakes, the wispy fleece of a leaden sky. From the balcony of the préfecture, surrounded by a pile of cockades laid in a semi-circle, the Maréchal spoke to the masses, responded to the cheers, throwing his arms wide; his voice, though restrained, rumbled, and his unhinged address stood out against the chaos of the church bells and the parade chants and drowned out the screeching of the gulls above the pylons, the chimneys, the cranes and the narrow wooden jetties between the vessels, far above the skeletal carcasses of boats and the eels twined around the driftwood rudders that strew the depths of harbours. All along the transporter bridge, from the buffet-restaurant by Saint-Nicolas to the newspaper kiosk near Saint-Jean on the far shore, its counterweight bascule of wrought iron winched by machine, a creaking beast of bolts and cable stays, supported by slender steel girders, countless interlocking lines formed a grid soaring to almost eighty metres. Further off, along the breakwater, moored in the coves of la Joliette, Lazaret, Arenc, National and la Pinède, between the hangars of the Société Générale des Transports Maritimes, the ocean liner *Massilia* and the cargo ships *Capitaine-Paul-Lemerle* and *Arizona* had been daubed in red, white and blue, and festooned with banners emblazoned 'Vive

Pétain', stencilled onto reams of canvas, worthy of a village fete – all foreign flags had been removed. At 11 a.m., in the Corniche, in front of the war memorial known as the porte de Poilus-d'Orient, the Maréchal was conversing with his 'fine comrades-in-arms', veterans and disabled ex-servicemen, their faces haggard, whipped by the dry wind, blinded by the winter sun, standing to attention in patched-up uniforms.

At 3 p.m., the disbanded army paraded along the quai des Belges: the armoured cars, the cadets from the military academies of Saint-Cyr and Saint-Maixent, the mountain infantry from Fréjus and Hyères, the cavalrymen of Nîmes, the marines, the mounted riot police, the bicycle infantry, the 43rd Infantry Regiment; an army rendered impotent by armistice, a military farce as powerless as a scout troop at a jamboree.

Around the old almshouse called La Vieille Charité, in the laneways and on the place du Panier, the only rush was that of the whirling wind trailing in its wake the fliers and confetti that strewed the gutters. The day had been preceded by sweeping arrests. The riff-raff had disappeared, people said proudly. The usual suspects – Jews, anarchists, foreigners, gypsies, communists, artists – had all been crammed into hurriedly improvised prisons, four days locked up around the city in storehouses, barracks, theatres and ships with six hundred in the hold of the cargo ship *Sinaïa*. Some knew that these first raids heralded others; the dissidents from the East saw them as an omen; they knew the vocabulary of tyranny, internments, exterminations, deportations, they knew that the persecution, the complicit silence, the blind obedience to orders would steadily increase until the day came when it was too late, when escape would mean life or death. Driven back to a rock or a hard place, to the Pyrenees or the Mediterranean, forced to choose the route across the mountains or the route across the seas. They were witness to the inexorable movement that leads to an impasse, from the agonies of uncertainty to voluntary uprooting.

Can we ever know how a war begins? The first gunshot, the retreat, the pitched battles – they give way to sporadic sniper fire. On a notepad, scribbled in haste, the solemn account of a captured moment, a fleeting lie, a brash strike that turns from a skirmish to a spearhead. We will be surprised to find that the weather was so beautiful, to read about the warmth of a night before battle; the slowly gathering autumnal dusk will frame an artillery emplacement like a wedding party, and at dawn, the sun's rays, drunk in with a cup of coffee, will filter and percolate through the leaves, the eyes, tapping out note after note on the skin, taking on the urgency of a mobilised army. Thunder rumbles, we see a nose pressed to the glass, a striated sky, we count the seconds separating the flash from the rumble, the light from the report. One, two, three, four, five, six seconds, then the sky rolls with heavy, muffled echoes, two kilometres, we calculate. It is from here, safe behind the glass, that the looming chaos is best observed, while in the distance the dark device growls and creeps closer in curtains of rain.

If France in 1941 was a funnel, Marseilles was the slender tube; here people rubbed shoulders, desperate for a way out. A chance meeting was now seen not as a joyous coincidence but a tragic inevitability. The sheer number of stateless people compared to the few cafés and hotels where they could congregate meant that the probability of such encounters, like untold throws of loaded dice, all but abolished the notion of coincidence. To leave France entailed securing a valid passport and a series of visas stamped by the harbour authorities before embarking. Hell had a name: the department of paper pushing. In that waiting room, the arbitrary reigned, proscriptions often disappeared only to be replaced by others, more devious. The vice was closing, each parting ship seemed to be the last, at which point the convicts flanked by the gendarmes found themselves fortunate, the zeal of bureaucrats was understood, even appreciated, when, finally, a scrap of paper was stamped, a hand beating on the cover of the logbook like the gavel of a judge delivering a sentence – this was authority, one it would have been foolish to challenge having come so far – and so people bowed their heads, mumbled their names, announced their destinations, stammered a few words of explanation: 'I'm going to join my brother in Mexico', 'My wife is waiting for me in New York', they presented safe conduct, ticket, transit visas, from country of refuge and last point of departure, grateful that there were no more questions, that another stage of the journey had begun, that there would be many other stages no longer mattered: once aboard, on the open sea, Europe would already be far behind.

A rumour spread across the terraces: cargo ships were sailing to the Antilles. There was talk of freighters laden with tons of bananas and sugar going one way, and with hundreds of people going *the other* – phantom ships plying their trade between two continents, which widened the mesh of a narrow net, opening a route to the Americas through the tropics. The solution seemed too facile, people were suspicious, it might be a godsend or it might be a trap. The maxim of those times: trust to your misfortune and mistrust your good fortune. And discussion of this new situation was in veiled terms, in rushed tones, as a digression from a conversation about the weather: this was how word spread that at the passport office in Arles, the elderly lady at the main counter was handing out travel tickets; that at the Mexican Consulate at the far end of La Canebière in Marseilles, the consul, Gilberto Bosques, was handing out visas and safe conducts; that in January seven hundred passengers had taken to sea aboard the SS *Winnipeg*, the same ship chartered by Neruda in 1939 to transport two thousand five hundred Spanish Republicans to Chile, and spare them certain death in Franco's jails. There was already news from the other side that a number of passengers on an English cargo ship had been forced to disembark in Dakar and were now sweltering in a barracks in the middle of nowhere, and that the SS *Wyoming*, which put in on 24 February, had arrived at Fort-de-France. Since December 1940, the government that had been so keen to discourage those wanting to leave was now facilitating the process; orders had been given. By late January, it was possible to get an exit visa – this document, obtained only through the most extraordinary wiles, by disassembling and disarticulating the cogs of the idiotic system, instantly turned into Monopoly money, people all but laughed when presented with it. This was not generosity of spirit, the true reason behind this volte-face could be summed up in two words: good riddance! The Gestapo had already tracked down and arrested many of the dissident refugees in France, with the complicity of the French authorities who had supplied a list of enemies of the Reich still in the country and denied exit visas; as for the rest – the *rabble* – let them flee and contaminate America, that was the idea. *We could now openly engage in what had all along been our* raison d'être: *emigration,* remarked an astonished Varian Fry at the Emergency Rescue Committee, which had moved its makeshift office on the rue Grignan to the boulevard Garibaldi to give the association an air of respectability. Within a few months, some fifteen thousand people applied to the association and more than a thousand managed to flee. The source of the waters mattered little, what mattered was that the riverbed was wider.

From 1930 until 1939, the Société Générale des Transports Maritimes à Vapeur – the SGTMV – had operated a quarterly freight service between metropolitan France, the Antilles and French Guiana. A fleet of seven cargo ships – the *Mont-Cenis,* the *Capitaine-Paul-Lemerle,* the *Mont-Kemmel,* the *Mont-Everest,* the *Mont-Genève,* the *Mont-Viso* and the *Mont-Angel* – had been laid up after war was declared. From December 1940, the SGTMV's cargo ships were converted into ocean liners. Meanwhile, other companies bought up rusty old tubs and, at little cost, disguised them as gleaming liners. In the wet docks of the étang de Berre, they repainted the tin cans lead-grey, and patched them up with little more than puncture-repair patches and clapped-out engines – and the ships sailed on! Political affairs (even by association) go hand in hand with business affairs: there is not a single law, not a single decree or directive that does not bolster such an ingenious trade. That is the way of the world: even rescue is a commercial endeavour; you have to be a manager to be an altruist. Persecute the refugees, set up a rescue network and you have a licence to print money: visas, guarantees, privileges, second-class tickets, first-class tickets, cabins, berths, deckchairs, provisions aboard, mind the gangway – a thriving business, a maximised profit and a political administration, like a doting father figure, guided by *strict humanitarian rules.* It is possible to be a refugee and pay for one's salvation, the two go hand in glove, in fact, surely this is what is meant by paying tribute.

It is at the foot of the *Capitaine-Paul-Lemerle* that the crowd has gathered on this morning of 24 March, under the watchful eye of armed, uniformed riot police. The cargo that left Cayenne on 28 January 1940 marked the temporary suspension of commercial trading between the Antilles and the old world. A vessel of 4,945 tons and an imposing aspect; when one looked up towards the prow, and the sun shrouded the angles in a dazzling halo, it almost looked the part. And indeed, it was a kind of illusion, at the dawn of a great exodus. An ark, nothing less. Some three hundred exiles, escorted by gendarmes, were emerging from Hangar No. 7, moving along the quays, dwarfed by the hulls of the ships, which, swathed in shadow and newly refurbished, had a certain style. Not far away, the *Carimaré* was in dry dock at la Pinède, waiting to be streamlined and refitted, its huge, dry propellers motionless, arse in the wind, a fat man being washed. All around it, the longshoremen were at work, yelling to each other, calling down from the prow to the walls of the dry dock, like an army of men perched on aqueducts, hauling on ropes, securing the metal hulk like the Lilliputians lashing down Gulliver.

From the *Paul-Lemerle*, the *Carimaré* seemed to have been stripped bare, and an observer saw only a series of oily, shapeless forms, nothing more or less than a heap of rusting nuts and bolts atop a stack of rotting planks. A raft piled with scrap metal, a machine bound for the wrecking yard, like a deboned chicken. It was a joke, a pitiful hoax, a risible framework, a cargo ship worthy only of the scrapyard, the flagship of a pantomime fleet. And yet no one would complain before reaching the open sea, people were willing to pay anything for a ticket, and besides, everyone knows that uncertainty is life's ultimate gamble. In single file on the gangway, the procession of trunks and suitcases stripped the scene of its drama, fleeing Russians rubbed shoulders with exiled Spaniards, ethnologists with poets, KPD activists with Soviet renegades and a ginger tomcat with a little girl. The scene now set, thirty days at sea would transform this floating coffin into a treasure chest.

Victor Serge scanned the quay, searching for Laurette and her red flowers. Standing on a timber frame, he saw her, flanked by Jean Gemähling and Dina Vierny, and watched as, within the first mile, her blue overcoat was engulfed by the great blue of the sea, a point pinned onto the horizon. Aboard, sadness and joy. On the forward deck, a happy Polish family. The father, bushy-bearded, was waving his hands wildly in a parody of heart-breaking farewell and singing 'Oyfn veg' – while his two sons shrieked and whirled. A world turned upside down.

The passengers quickly realised why the *Paul-Lemerle* had been nicknamed *Pôvre merle* – poor blackbird.

They could not help but wonder what would be left of the poor bird after the first storm. Apart from the cabins allocated to the crew, four in number, the two hundred and fifty passengers were astonished to discover that the twin holds had been converted into dormitories, each containing about a hundred bunk beds hastily cobbled together by the company's labourers more accustomed to patching hulls and ships' timbers – caulkers had spent three days in the belly of the ship, busily constructing two levels with salvaged materials, from timbers salvaged from small crafts to planks found lying around the hangar. This was not the ark described as constructed of *shittim wood*, coated inside and out with *pitch*. This was a shack made of odds and ends, a labyrinth of berths with mattresses of straw, in Second Class and First; in fact, class had ceased to exist. With the exception of those who had secured a cabin – paying three to four thousand francs in hard currency at the counters of the Société des Transports Maritimes – everyone had to fight for a bunk in the stifling hold. Once at sea, the passengers made a fuss, harassed crew members – those they could find: the quartermaster, the steward manning the field kitchen – to no avail. The crew responded to the abuse with threats: you're free to disembark at the next stop – Oran, in Africa – and after that you can fend for yourself! People settled themselves in the dormitories, unpacked their kit; sitting cross-legged on one of the bunks, a suitcase on his pillow, a boy was thinking about the long sea voyage, about adventure, savouring the tingling feeling in his belly, relishing the excitement of the moment. They would put the past behind them, in the great cleansing of the journey, crossing the equator, even their names would be forgotten. Up on deck, where the Saint-Étienne machine gun and the 90 mm naval guns once stood, three sheds – four planks of mouldering pitch wood – had been nailed together to serve as washhouses; a standing tap dripped and large tarpaulins strung between posts planted between the shroud lines offered shelter from sun or rain. On deck, all space was now taken up with rows of deckchairs between which squealing children zigzagged, playing tag or cowboys and Indians, threatening each other with bits of wood, firing, falling, dying once, twice, then getting up and racing off again. For this game, axle grease and sump oil could be daubed on faces to create Iroquois warpaint, while the coiled ropes too heavy to serve as lassos became, in their imagination, sleeping boa constrictors, and they were careful not to fall into the coils lest the snake contract. Crates were upended to serve as card tables – clubs and spades overlapped in solitaire. Voices mingled and drowned out the rumble of the engines, and from this ceaseless noise a language slowly formed, composed of exclamations, where Czech merged with Yiddish, French with Catalan and the wails of infants with the groans of old men. Quickly, communities began to form, Spaniards in steerage, mothers on the forward deck, businessmen on the bridge. Up above, around the smokestack, the KPD elite gathered in a circle around a rickety table with a battered zinc top.

In the early afternoon, the crew would distribute mess tins into which stewards would ladle some noodle soup and a cubic centimetre of meat, and hand out a crust of bread and an orange. On the upper deck, the ship's officers would laugh at this farce; the old rust-bucket could sink on the open seas and it would be no great loss. If the British inspected it, the captain would scupper the freighter – and there would not be enough lifeboats, they laughed, or enough lifebelts.

The passengers cursed their fate, and their pet names for the old tub gradually became more contemptuous: *a floating cork – a sardine can with a cigarette butt – a leaky tub rotted to the gunwales – a prison without a porthole*. From *Pôvre merle*, it quickly became *Pôvre merde*.

From shore, the ship was a curious sight, coughing and spluttering, its angular profile softened by washing lines that floated and dangled, off the port of Sète. Night drew in, to starboard were the lights of the pier at Saint-Louis and the fishermen's huts. Breton was holding the hand of his daughter, Aube. He was remembering the gentle jubilation of reunions, and the comings and goings of old friends in the curious phalanstery of Château Esper-Visa in

Marseilles. 'I cannot stay in such a country!' he confided to Varian Fry, begging him to get him a visa for 'anywhere', by any possible means. In February, he had managed to get Jacqueline and Aube visas for Mexico and the United States. Breton's visa had yet to arrive. They had had to wait and, and thanks to the intercession of the committee in March and the financial support of Peggy Guggenheim, they were finally able to embark.

For passengers whose departure was deferred, every second was merely a stay of execution, they were mistrustful, they cultivated a fear of informers and spies. The period abounded with condemned men saved *in extremis*, with those who had cheated death by dint of circumstance, vacillating between blind fate and fatal decisions. Many such passengers found themselves arrested, sometimes at the foot of the gangplank, just when they had lowered their guard.

Alfred Kantorowicz was one such miraculous survivor. When he presented his passport and his ticket at the port office, the customs official, having studied the document before him and carefully compared the name on the visa to the alphabetical list he was scanning letter by letter, seemed to wake up. 'You are Kantorowicz, Alfred, born 12 August 1899 in Berlin?' Kantorowicz heard himself say yes. For several endless, almost timeless seconds, he had glanced sidelong down the hall, the floor tilting, his body listing, the clock stopped at 11.04, the crack at the foot of the oak desk snaking across its top along the veins in the wood, before he had choked back disaster and stared at the customs officer, who had turned, exchanged a knowing look with the gendarme guarding the door, and – proud that this morning he was finally able to use the time-honoured phrase – announced, 'You are under arrest.' Kantorowicz was immediately taken upstairs. It was over. Despite his escape, despite securing an American visa, he was convinced that he would not leave now, that his exile would end here. He berated himself for not taking the risk of crossing the Spanish border, the journey through the jagged peaks he had crossed the other way in 1938 after the fall of Barcelona. The official route was a mousetrap, a fine sieve used by the Gestapo. His name, appearing on the official list of 'enemies of the state' drawn up by the Kundt

Commission and circulated to all ports, was his death sentence – *Alfred Kantorowicz, forbidden to leave France.*

Among the community of German emigrants, Kantorowicz was a name to conjure with. A playwright, theatre critic and member of the KPD, forced into exile in 1933, he had left a bohemian life in the artists' colony of Berlin-Wilmersdorf; his companions Arthur Koestler, Bertolt Brecht, Ernest Bloch, Oskar Maria Graf and Lion Feuchtwanger had also fled. He was a man of principle and liked to define himself as humanist-communist. A member of the German Association of Proletarian-Revolutionary Authors, he had joined the XIII International Brigade in Spain and marched into free Madrid, had fought for two years and returned, defeated, weighed down by a past that had been twice trampled. On his return, thanks to the support of the American Guild for German Cultural Freedom, he wrote a war diary. And yet, his life's work was composed of books that he did not write, books he had saved from the flames and from oblivion, in a gesture of defiance that had doubtless earned him the great honour of appearing on the list of enemies of the state drawn up by the Gestapo. It was in Paris in 1933, together with the members of the Association for the Protection of German Writers, that he conceived the idea of a library of books that had been burned, censored or ignored by the Third Reich. On 10 May 1934, a year to the day after the first Nazi book burnings, Alfred Kantorowicz and Heinrich Mann inaugurated the Deutsche Freiheitsbibliothek – the German Library of Freedom – at 65, boulevard Argo. A committee of intellectuals, led by André Gide, was established to support the organisation, and included Romain Rolland, H. G. Wells, André Malraux, Paul Eluard, Louis Aragon and Henri Barbusse. 'Writers banned by Hitler are establishing libraries in the great capitals of the world' was one headline in the press the following day. Kantorowicz later published a pamphlet entitled 'Why a library of burned books?', contributed to the *Brown Book of the Hitler Terror and the Burning of the Reichstag*, presented a paper at the Congress for Culture entitled 'On the Preparations for War in Germany', and, having been accused of fomenting war, was placed on the list of persons wanted by the Nazi regime and, therefore, at 11.04, in the passport control office of the port of

Marseilles, in accordance with Article 19 of the Franco-German Armistice, was 'surrendered on demand'.

Paralysed by an inertia common to those who know they have been captured, Kantorowicz said nothing, exhausted by the machinations and the dead ends, ready to capitulate. He turned to the officer, as though to confess, but as the commandant was checking the arrest warrant, he whispered something that a friend had suggested he say as a last resort: 'Sir, Colonel Riverdi has spoken to you about us. My name is Alfred Kantorowicz.'

'Ah, so that's who you are.' The gendarme picked up the rubber stamp of the port authority, validated the visa and tore up the arrest warrant. 'Get the hell out of here and find some way to disappear.'

At 1 p.m., as the foghorn of the *Capitaine-Paul-Lemerle* sounded, he felt the deck of the ship judder beneath his feet. Kings have two bodies – the *body natural* and the *body politic* – and are sometimes known to wander with a head tucked under one arm; sitting against the gunwale, one hand holding a forgotten cigarette between the index and middle finger, the other pressed to his ear, his broad brow furrowed, his eyes staring blindly at the water between the piles, Kantorowicz thought about his beloved Victor Hugo and a line from *Castigations*: 'Know this well, shame is the greatest of tombs.' This perhaps is surrender, he thought, to allow oneself to be tossed on a rollercoaster without murmur, to be crushed to pieces and not complain, to survive, to be no longer truly alive, to allow one's life to become a series of thwarted promises, to be shamed by one's missteps, constantly humiliated. He brooded on exile, on what becomes of him who remains, on what remains of him who leaves. And on the figure of the emigrant that had haunted him ever since that night in December 1933 when he stood, frozen on the threshold of his Berlin apartment, key in hand, already lost in the memories of vanished years, and with a last glance at the upright piano in the hallway, the bookcase in his study, the books and all the yesterdays that came before tomorrow, he closed the door for the last time. Surrounded by his people, engulfed by the optimism of the passengers on the ship, he had no choice but to accept his fate, to *make a new life*, to *disappear* further, ever further, or choose to founder, to endure the gibberish of simpletons, of blissful idiots, and sink into a black rage, a dull melancholy, and bitterly contemplate the waste.

Even the terms *refugee, exile* or *stateless person* are not self-evident; to be forced to assume one is to be plunged into a condition that simultaneously compels and constrains. Rather than *refugee*, a word for which he had little appetite, Kantorowicz preferred the term *émigré*. In 1935, he contributed to an anthology of 'camouflaged writings', published by the Library of Freedom and, of the forty-three essays, his was an appraisal of the *émigré* through the figure of Victor Hugo, seen from the present day, which described him as a 'great emigrant' and 'the investigating magistrate of history', banished from the empire, whose writings in exile were a beacon for those times, a lantern from the past to illuminate a dark continent.

We do not like to be called 'refugees': these are the first words of a short essay written by Hannah Arendt in 1943. Kantorowicz could not have read it, obviously, or at least not yet, but let us shift time forward or backward as we see fit. In Sanary-sur-Mer, where German literature was exiled, we meet Thomas Mann, Walter Benjamin and Arthur Koestler as well as Hannah Arendt and Alfred Kantorowicz. Let us wager that they met. Let us imagine, in the noonday sun, over a winter lunch, a conversation, laughter, a common consciousness of loss, the dreams of a tongue weighed down by lead, the urgency and the illusion of exile when, from one side of the world to the other, history is repeating itself. And let us wager that, before they went their separate ways after this meal, taken at a stone table, beneath an awning hung from the bare branches of the plane trees, we might have heard them say: *Hell is no longer a religious belief or a fantasy, but something as real as houses and stones and trees.*

2

The Green Ray

———

The Belvédère du Rayon Vert towered over the fishing port of Cerbère. From the 'stern', to the gangways and either end, the stairwell in the shape of a funnel and the curves of the reinforced concrete, every architectural detail conspired to make the hotel look like an ocean liner that had been washed up on the hill, between land and sea, in the pure Streamline Moderne style so fashionable during the Roaring Twenties. The roof terrace boasted a tennis court surrounded by railings, while in the concrete 'hold' there was a casino, a cinema and a theatre. The flag fluttered from the topmost point of the building, beckoning travellers at the railway station below, offering a rest stop before the Spanish border, a pleasant sojourn suffused with pre-war opulence for well-heeled clients. Moored next to Port-Bou-Cerbère railway station, the Rayon Vert was a superior port of call. People killed time here between trains. The great lobby still welcomed wealthy travellers, but for the most part it was filled with soldiers on patrol, border-zone citizens, Francoist captains, and Germans. Sometimes, while putting the new net up for a game of tennis, one could see the endless procession of emigrants, driven west, ever further west, on the station platforms of this port that was now a revolving door to Europe. From Banyuls-sur-Mer, boatmen guided you through the mountains, taking the smugglers' routes to Port-Vendres, trailing exhausted travellers up steep passes and scree. On the far side, they were left waiting at the border post of Port-Bou to get an entry visa for Spain. To the passengers gathered in the prow of the ship that morning, the snow-capped peaks of the hinterland seemed like a cemetery – all too often, the paths to freedom had become the path to death. One recalled an emaciated cadaver on the Pic de l'Aigle, his every limb broken, finished off with a bullet to the head by his comrades, a casualty of the routed Republican forces whom no one had returned to claim. In the stern, the daughter of René Schickele, who had died a year earlier, was scrubbing laundry in one of the washtubs beneath the tarpaulins while she told Victor Serge how Walter Benjamin had committed suicide in a hotel room in Cerbère.

It was early spring. The plains of Figueres were covered with a mantle of solid green. After a night at sea, this presented a tedious sight to most of the voyagers. The steamboat was following a curious path, it was a rough-and-ready coastal vessel whose passengers had begun to mutter about suspicious cargo. The boat hugged the shoreline, chugging in slow motion, avoided the open sea, staying close to the land. To those thronging the foredeck, the coastline evoked memories and those who strained to listen could hear the story of defeated Spain. For many of them, this was the land from which they had been exiled, after the Catalonia Offensive two years before. In their hasty retreat, they had fallen back to the last stronghold, to the town of Figueres at which they were gazing right now, where Azaña had met with his council of ministers for the last time.

In Marseilles, the port authorities had separated the Spanish into two groups, the women and the men. At the time, no one had made a fuss, no one had worried. The children, barely awake, faces drawn, hair tousled, their clothes rumpled from sleep, held hands as they trailed after the women; they did not talk, they did not sob, they accepted this new arbitrary rule. From the Department of Migration hut where the first exiles waited for their papers to be stamped – 'SEEN AT EMBARKATION' – the formalities had dragged on, people became restless, voices were raised, people began to shout and then they realised: only women, children and the elderly were being allowed to board; all Spanish men deemed *able-bodied* were to be detained on the quay. Orders from the préfecture. As a measure of appeasement in the wake of Franco's visit in 1941, a covert decree had been issued forbidding adult Spanish men under the age of forty-eight from leaving the country, together with emigrants considered 'dangerous' and 'possible anti-German activists'.

A commotion broke out, the women refused to leave, the men clamoured to board, families were ripped apart, promising to meet up again on the far side of the ocean, they had to keep moving ... When they reached their destination, from one post restante to the next, one stopover to the next, they would somehow manage to keep in touch, they promised, unconvinced by their own words. They were bound for Mexico, the country of asylum for Republican refugees, for re-immigration, according to the agreement signed with the Vichy regime. And to the Dominican Republic, a hypothetical refuge governed by the dictator Rafael Trujillo.

At the sight of the plains, the Spanish women gathered on the foredeck. The slanting sun scorched the horizon, the past, whole and entire, reappeared. It was at once a lost land, the country of their parents, the trenches where the battles had raged, the memory of their husbands. In his notebook, Victor Serge wrote:

Waiting for Barcelona, landscapes flying past. Around 2:00, Barcelona. The four smokestacks of the electric plant visible first. The whole city gradually emerges under a light, bright mist, stretched across the length of the gulf. The grey towers of the Sagrada Familia; I remember them as phallic from close up, but from this distance they put one in mind of grieving hands raised in the air. The Christopher Columbus column can be seen clearly, the Customs Palace and the Gobernación near the port, the cathedral, the San Jaime tower. Montjuic in the foreground. The flat lines of the pink brick citadel; the rock, steep when viewed from the coast, appears to be composed of gentle slopes when viewed from the sea. Fog over the background of the city. I believe I can make out the Rambla de Flores, broad and grey, probably trees whose leaves have fallen. The Spaniards look on, tense. Thought of defeated men. Mental prayer. It's here that I must say farewell to Europe, while making the commitment to return. Not adieu, but au revoir. I attempt to write a poem, can't make it work. Too much feeling, too many thoughts; all

deaths appear contemptible. Inspiration missing, I feel hard and lucid, con-
fident as well, all of this clear, neither fever nor joy. (Perhaps a secret joy is
needed to write a poem, even in the depths of suffering?)

  As night falls, we reach the mouth of the Ebro. Somewhere on the heights,
in the sierra, a huge blaze – probably a forest fire. Calm sea, twilight despond-
ency, absences. Thought of defeat.

Off the coast of Majorca
26 March 1941

At dawn, Wifredo Lam left the cavernous dormitory in the hold. He stepped over the coiled, sleeping bodies; in the distance, the first glimmer of day reddened the mountains of the hinterland. What appeared was a scene of ruin, a charred, deserted landscape, a blaze swept down the slopes until it reached the shore, the white pebbles and the shimmering sea. As they neared Valencia, the cargo ship was escorted by a flotilla of small boats, and the fisher-men raised their fists to salute their comrades as they passed. In a loose shirt whipped by the wind, Lam's slender figure fluttered like a wind sock on the foredeck. In the half-light, he looked Cuban, as day began to break, he looked Spanish, and when the sun com-pletely bathed his face, he looked Chinese. Sitting cross-legged, his back to the companionway, he had taken out an Opinel knife and, on a piece of wood no thicker than his palm, was carving the face of a gargoyle whose terror became more apparent with each pass of the blade. On the top step of the companionway, he set down his amulets, including a small metal deity armed with a sabre that glittered in the sun. He set up his Santería family on the boards. His godmother, the Santería priestess Mantonica Wilson, a large doll wrapped in a dress of fine lace; himself, the mixed-race god-child, born to a Cantonese immigrant scribe turned carpenter and the daughter of a former slave and a Spanish nobleman; it had been his godmother who had initiated him into the faith of the galley slaves, a syncretic pagan religion that blended the mythol-ogy of the Yoruba people of west Africa with Christian rituals. One day, Mantonica had grabbed him by the arms, lifted him up so that they were face to face, stared at him, her eyes bulging, her pupils almost white, and announced in a shrill, terrifying voice: 'I grant you the protection of all the gods.' In the village of Sagua La Grande, surrounded by *an ocean of sugar cane*, in the little workshop, while Yam Lam was turning a piece of wood on a lathe, Wifredo would perch on a log and sketch his father's face in pencil, smoothing the shadows with a fingertip, hollowing the bags under his eyes, drawing a fingernail through a layer of graphite on the thick paper to create the undulations of his hair.

1914. Looking out at the two rocks planted in the sea, he learned to sketch, encouraged by his father, who early on acknowledged his son's talent and his right to develop it. So did he pass on his knowledge, treating the boy as his companion, taking him walking along the forest trails. There, he would talk about the seasons, about the stars, about the curious calls of the birds, red, green or indigo birds, that made their home here. He would lay a hand on the boy's nape and, with the gentle pressure of thumb or forefinger, direct his gaze into the topmost branches; he would call him *Lucero*, his light. For his father, seventy-seven years old, these walks had a flavour of childhood. His mother would dress Wifredo in white, a carefully tailored linen shirt, a silk tie, she would shine his shoes. He looked like a slightly gauche Governor of Tonkin, taciturn like old Yam Lam, reserved and attentive. He observed everyone: some were terrified at being stared at by a child; others were fascinated, believing themselves to be in the presence of a sorceress' apprentice, the pupil of La Matronica, a fount of prophecies and of curses. At sixteen, he left for Havana to study at the Escuela de Bellas Artes, exhibited his first canvases, impressed the patrons of the sugar companies, and made a name for himself, the name with which he signed his works: LAM.

1923. Spring. Having arrived in Madrid with a letter of recommendation in his pocket from the curator of the Museo Nacional de Cuba and a scholarship *for a disadvantaged young person of colour*, Lam began studying with one of the masters of portraiture, Sotomayor. He roamed the halls of the Prado, filled his notebooks with charcoal drawings of Goya's paintings, imitating his line only to abandon it, convinced that in contour and movement one earns one's own place. He overwhelmed his imagination gazing at the frescos in the Velasquez and El Greco rooms, quickly burned himself out, allowing himself to be engulfed in certain paintings, sought refuge in the ominous teeming of the northern schools, of a Bruegel convulsed with sin. He still carried the weight of this journey to the West; one might say his inspiration was finding it difficult to adjust to its new moorings. His portraits were those of a good painter from a previous era, and they were condemned, if he continued in this manner, to die with it. Awkward oils from before the revolution, before the joy, before the rapture. Before death, too.

1929. In March, at a temporary exhibition at the Galeria Vilches in Madrid, *Exposición de pinturas y esculturas de Españoles residentes en Paris*, Lam discovered Picasso, Gargallo, Miró and Juan Gris. After spending the summer in Cuenca, where he met Eva Piriz, he married. She gave birth to their first son, Wilfredo Victor (whose name he did not forget to spell correctly on the birth certificate). In the wave of blind joy, mother and son died two years later, victims of tuberculosis. There followed days and months of long hallucinations, yawning graves, seas of boiling blood, bottomless chasms, and always before the dream faded, one of his two ghosts would leap forward, prepared to rip out his heart. He no longer painted, except for the commissions that put food on his table. Another ghost invaded his dreams, it came from a more distant past, brandishing a cauterised stump. He recognised the figure, it was José Castilla, one of his Cuban ancestors whose story his mother used to tell. Castilla, a mixed-race slave who converted to Catholicism in order to gain his freedom. A modest landowner, he had been swindled by a Spaniard. Castilla went to court. While the Holy Inquisition found in his favour, the civil courts found in favour of his rival, in spite of the man's confession. Outraged, Castilla punched the Spaniard, laying him out cold. For this, he was condemned by the Inquisition, his lands were confiscated and his hand was cut off. Nicknamed Mano Cortado – the Severed Hand – he disappeared. And this is what Lam also did. He disappeared for two years, to León. Away from the world, he staged two exhibitions in León, in April and May, some twenty portraits and a handful of landscapes. In León, his forms pulled away from his earlier classicism, he softened the outlines of buildings, rounded out his landscapes and the ovals of the faces he painted on card. His drawing style became more austere, he drew on the broad outlines of his training and amassed many new techniques. He sketched the peasant labourers of León, poor bastards worn down by work, who initially posed in silence and then, whether trustingly or simply out of boredom, recounted the miserable lives of men with no lands doomed to toil for others, to live from hand to mouth on paupers' wages destined to alienate them from the land that was bleeding them dry. In them, he recognised a common suffering, in short, another colony. He set himself the task of painting a *general democratic proposal for all men*, and from that moment he read voraciously, about Africa and slavery, about Cézanne and Gauguin.

1932. Without coffee, there would be no revolution, they say. When Lam returned to Madrid, it was from the terrace of the Café Gran Vía that he witnessed the birth of the Republic. Around the table were Faustino Cordón, the artists Juli Ramis and Mario Carreño, the writers José Martínez Ruiz and Ramón del Valle-Inclán, the poets Miguel Ángel Asturias and Federico García Lorca. Lorca gifted him his volumes of Góngora and an anthology of Iberian poetry and invited him to come to Granada and visit the Alhambra. Like Van Gogh, every day Lam painted the view from a room painted yellow and blue. He had chosen bare, spartan accommodation, a single bed set against the wall of a solitary room, the floor set with ochre tiles, a rustic wooden chair with a straw seat and a circular table in fake marble; all around were piled the writings of Marx and Gogol, Bakunin and Omar Khayyam. His paintings were propped against the walls; in the middle of the room there remained a narrow space, a corridor that led from the door to the window through which spilled the morning madrileña sun. At the Prado, Lam made the acquaintance of Balbina Barrera, an amateur artist who spent her days making copies of old masters. A stubborn woman who sat on the central bench in one of the vast halls and left only when it was dark, having fought tirelessly with her subject matter, she became *his comrade in life and in the struggle*. His art hardened, he became obsessed with painting and repainting the same motif, life lithographs in oil. In his diary for the year 1935, sketches from the ethnographic museum and notes from Carl Einstein's study of African masks vied for space with political issues. Little by little, revolution supplanted art without finding any common ground. On 18 July 1936, the military coup plunged the country into civil war. In Madrid, Lam fought with the Fifth Regiment of the Milicias Populares, and later in the Eleventh Division, commanded by Enrique Lister. He defended the city during the November siege and placed himself in the service of the revolution, designing posters to the glory of the Republican movement. Later, he worked in an armaments factory, where he assembled anti-tank missiles. Handling toxic material weakened his health, and by February 1937 he was in a poor state.

1937. Perhaps it is not permitted to doubt one's art, even if it is guided by one's life. *The revolution changed the way I wrote and the way I painted* – except that he no longer painted. In the spring, Lam was sent to a sanatorium in Caldes de Montbui, in Catalonia in the countryside north of Barcelona. Each destiny is imbued with a similar strangeness in that it takes a roundabout route that, in hindsight, looks like a deliberate series of short cuts and meanders, of illogical detours that make up an unbroken path. Hence, for Wifredo Lam, Spain seemed like a trap at first, a stopover transformed into a destination. He glimpsed the change of direction on 26 March 1941 as they approached Cabo de la Nao; he recognised it in the sky bursting with lilacs, the parched perfume of the cracked clods of earth of Alicante. No longer a charred pasture, but a *trompe l'œil*, here there were hidden memories, the plausible details of a past life. The sun quivering on the sea raced ahead of wavelets, grey-green, blue-green, dove-grey, whose reflections shifted and changed as the clouds skimming the mountains covered the inlet. Lam recalled the month he had spent in the sanatorium, his meeting with Manolo, and how, with a few words, the sculptor moulded his story, recounting his memories of Paris, the surrealist adventures, the trips to Normandy with Braque and Raynal, the mossy path in Varengeville that leads to the headland, the church perched on the clifftop, the graveyard by the sea, the stained-glass windows, and the place some cable lengths away, in the hanging valley of Vaucottes, where, set back from the steep, winding road, there stands a tumbledown manor, its porch in pale peeling timber, and behind it an atelier, where, in winter, an opalescent mist presses itself against the tiles. A pause in the present, these conversations with Manolo, while outside the civil war was raging, seemed absurd, misplaced, a little pathetic; here they were talking about African art, about which Lam knew so little and Manolo so much. And he left, with a letter of recommendation tucked into his inside coat pocket, determined to go to Paris, to the studio of Picasso, whose address on the quai des Grands-Augustins was written on the envelope. He wrapped his paintbrushes in a large kerchief and tossed everything into a canvas bag. He broke his journey in Barcelona, put up at the Ateneo, a sort of socialist artists' commune, where he stayed for several months. There Lam completely changed his artistic style and between September and April painted almost three hundred canvases, among them *La Guerra civil*, a homage to the Republican movement. He had learned much from Manolo, without knowing precisely what, except perhaps the thick outline he now used systematically. In January, he met Helena Holzer, a young German research chemist who, for four years, had been director of a laboratory specialising in tuberculosis at the Hospital de Santa Coloma. They were introduced by the photographer Fritz Falkner in a café on the Plaça de Lesseps. It was a brief meeting, there was much shelling that day. After Franco's major offensive, Lam left Barcelona, where he entrusted his paintings to Balbina Barrera, kissed Helena and, with an army of refugees, entered France one morning in May.

May 22, 1938.
I arrived from Spain at the gare d'Orsay. I walked along the Seine and eventually found a room in the hôtel de Suède, 8 quai Saint-Michel. I had a letter of introduction to Picasso, given me by Manolo Hugué in Barcelona. I set off on foot for the rue de la Boétie, where the painter I so admired lived. I was greeted by a uniformed chauffeur – I later learned his name was Marcel – who said:

'*You give the letter to him in person at 4 p.m., at his studio on the rue des Grands-Augustins.*'

I wandered aimlessly along the rue du Faubourg-Saint-Honoré, there were many art galleries, and I went into the Galerie des Beaux-Arts, where there was a retrospective of French painting. For me it was a veritable feast.

Shortly afterwards, I saw a little man in a gabardine and a hat come in; he was accompanied by a woman. I realised that it was Picasso and Dora Maar, but I decided not to introduce myself. This unexpected encounter, in the middle of a crowd, would have stripped our first conversation of its intimacy.

At four o'clock that afternoon, I found myself standing in front of the door of his studio with another person, of about my age. I didn't dare open my mouth because my French vocabulary at the time was very limited. This man, who would later become a dear friend, was Michel Leiris.

At close quarters, Picasso was imposing. I was awed to see him standing in front of me. His head was round and a lock of hair fell across his forehead. His dark, keen, piercing eyes moved with such sympathetic intelligence that they fascinated me.

Having greeted me, Picasso led me into a room where he kept his African sculptures. I was immediately drawn to one of them, a horse's head. It was placed on a chair. As he passed, Picasso skilfully moved the chair so that the sculpture swayed as though it were alive.

'What a beautiful sculpture!'

'I mounted it to the chair so I can make it move without it falling.' Then he added, 'You should be proud of it.'

'Why?' I said.

'Because this sculpture was made by an African and you have African blood.' Turning to Michel Leiris, he said:

'Teach Lam about African art.'

After a few moments' discussion, he confessed:

'I saw you at the Galerie des Beaux-Arts, and I said to Dora, "That must be the young Cuban who has just arrived from Spain, but I would rather meet him when we can be alone."'

Exactly what I had thought.

We talked about various things then, suddenly, he asked:

'Would you like a drink?'

'Alright.'

He had a bottle filled with a white liqueur. He poured a little into a glass.

'I'm not drinking that,' I said. 'Are you offering me petrol?'

Picasso started laughing. It was Calvados.

Picasso liked to laugh. And he laughed a lot with me, the timid mulatto, who spoke Spanish with a z, and would pronounce Madrid, for example, Madriz. Later he invited me to dinner. He ordered a fat chicken for me, which I ate bones and all, because I was ravenous and had not had enough to eat for a very long time.

Picasso said to Dora:

'He could eat the legs of the table.'

When we took our leave of each other, he was very cordial, as he was in everything he did. He surprised me by saying:
'You remind me of someone.'

Michel Leiris invited Lam to the opening of the new Musée de l'Homme, in the Passy wing of the Palais de Chaillot, where the museum's directors, Paul Rivet and Jacques Soustelle, were unveiling the collection devoted to anthropology and ethnology together with a vast library. Leiris offered a number of issues of the art review *Documents* to Lam – who pored over them, leaving them open on the floor of his hotel room. From now on, he painted others, or himself, from behind a mask.

'I have never been wrong about you. You are a painter. That's why the first time we met I told you that you reminded me of someone: me.'

1939. Lam was struck by the very particular lifestyle that Paris had to offer, between church bells and private views. He met André Masson, Georges Bataille, Oscar Domínguez, Asger Jorn, Victor Brauner and Joan Miró. Picasso introduced him to Pierre Loeb, a *dealer in modern art* by profession, who bought a number of his works and featured him in an exhibition at the Galerie Pierre, 2, rue des Beaux-Arts from June 30 to July 14. Lam set himself up in a studio in Montparnasse, on the rue Armand-Moisant. In January, Helena joined him. November saw the launch of the exhibition *Afrique noire française*, and Leiris secured him an invitation. All too quickly, he became that crank who stands outside gallery windows, bustling about, sketching in his notepad. He cut an astonishing figure, like a featherweight boxer with the hands of a pianist. When not at the Musée de l'Homme, Lam could be found in the hothouses of the Jardin des Plantes, sitting on a folding stool, sketching green snakes and the stout-handled assegais among the giant blossoms. In mid-winter, the glasshouses filled with steam, the light caught in the thick clouds and the damp twigs; and then, masked by the shimmer and the condensation, the hidden jungle would appear.

1940. June. Caught in the lens of Marc Vaux, Lam posed in his studio, like a hunter with his trophies, surrounded by dozens of paintings, some hanging, others in piles, in a sort of retrospective before they were scattered to the winds, a *catalogue raisonné* crammed with two years of work. Lam was wearing a thick wool cardigan tucked into a tightly belted pair of dress pants; behind his back, it was just possible to make out a self-portrait and an invitation to the Galerie Pierre exhibition tucked into the corner of a mirror. Here, where he usually sat to read and listen to the wireless, above a radiator and next to the images from his private museum, a statue from the Far East and a plate taken from the portfolio *Masques Africains*. Helena had been arrested at the beginning of the German offensive and sent to Gurs internment camp. They wrote to each other, nothing vain, no words of love, but words of encouragement, and the promise that they would see each other again soon, beyond the line. In early July, he wrapped his paintings in brown paper, tied them into packages of ten with rough twine and initially stored them in the basement of the building on the rue Armand-Moisant, then – fearing both his neighbours and the concierge – eventually entrusted them to Auguste Thésée, a friend from Martinique who had decided to stay.

On 14 June, German troops had marched into Paris. On the doors of the Musée de l'Homme, Paul Rivet pasted a quotation from Kipling, some passers-by stopped, read the words aloud: *If you can keep your head when all about you / are losing theirs.* Lam left, abandoning his paintings as he had done when he fled Barcelona. His footsteps followed those of the great exodus people called *le débâcle,* whole families lining the roads, unkempt soldiers from routed armies moving in pairs, children perched on their shoulders, all seeking the shelter of an embankment while planes roared overhead, curled up at the bottom of ditches, lying in fields beneath sunflowers or tall ears of corn. He was surprised to discover that a joyous camaraderie reigned; for some it was the taste of adventure, for others a time of possibilities, all the while it moved forward, this motley carnivalesque troupe, moving mattresses lashed to the roofs of stationary cars and suitcases tied to the mud flaps. Equipped with only a notebook and a few sticks of red chalk, Lam sketched this circus, the countless faces grinning beneath the June sunshine, eyes screwed up, heads covered with rags as though in the middle of the desert, men in shirtsleeves turning the starting handles of broken-down cars, water tanks belching steam from the heat and the humidity. Bordeaux proved to be a dead end, where every day brought the war-sick remnants of routed battalions and civil servants fleeing the Vichy regime. When the armistice was announced on 22 June, Lam caught a train to Marseilles.

In November, Lam moved into the Villa Air-Bel. In spite of the worry, the fear of imprisonment or exile, he was surprised to discover in those suspended days the pleasures of being reunited with friends and an intense collective creativity. Never had he felt so happy, or almost never; perhaps the civil war veiled the same forbidden joy, a happiness fuelled by fear. Helena had returned and Lam spent his days drawing in the greenhouse in the garden or next to the frog-filled pond, sketches in pencil and pen that would comprise the bulk of the illustrations for André Breton's book *Fata Morgana*. In March, five copies were published by Éditions du Sagittaire and instantly banned by the Vichy government. Before their departure, an impromptu exhibition, with paintings hung outside from the boughs of trees, brought members of the surrealist community together for a Sunday afternoon in winter. Gathered around the plane trees were Hérold, Ernst, Masson and Itkine. Two gouaches sold to Peggy Guggenheim earned Lam several hundred dollars for the crossing.

9.30 a.m. One after another, the children woke, rubbed their eyes, stretched, padded over to the companionway, gathered around Lam, and watched him, sitting on the steerage steps, surrounded by wood shavings, as he carved the grotesque little man. Lam spoke to the first of them in Spanish, 'Did you sleep well?' he asked, and without answering the little boy picked up one of the amulets on the ground, a gesture mimicked by his brother or his cousin, and the boys quickly improvised a game. The day could begin. Soon after, the whole ship was awake and bustling like a fair; the fashionable people of Marseilles who had been strutting about the night before had been transformed into a group of resourceful travellers, prepared to barter a mess tin of food for a place at the front of the queue for the bathroom. In the bathrooms, at the laundry, over meals, all talk was of the ship's suspect cargo. As they sailed past Majorca, Wifredo slipped his knife back into his pocket, got to his feet and stared at the distant shore – not knowing that there, on the island, that same day, Joan Miró was putting the finishing touches to the sixteen gouaches in the series *Constellations*, which included the oil-on-burlap painting *Woman and Kite Among the Constellations*.

12.30 p.m. As the ship drifted past the bay of Peñíscola, Anna Seghers, who had been lounging in a deckchair, got up and leaned over the ship's rail, staring out at the water as though about to jump. She was talking to her son, who was standing next to her, as she scanned the horizon for a memory, and finally glimpsed it amid the terraced ramparts of the fortress. She told her son the story of that day in July 1937 when, as her chauffeur was driving her along the coast to the International Writers Congress in Valencia, they had stopped in a village. She could not explain why, perched atop that cape, she had sensed a new phase in her life, a turning point. It was as they passed the headland aboard the *Paul-Lemerle*, en route for Martinique, which was sometimes described as a savage place, grim as a penal colony, sometimes lush as the jungles in a painting by Le Douanier Rousseau, that, with a twinge of sadness, she tried to explain that feeling, not a sense of déjà vu, but a premonition: this fishing village was their frontier post. She would glimpse this past again, this time from the sea.

3

A Ginger Tomcat

Oran
27 March 1941

On a loose sheet of paper, in green ink, André Breton was making a shopping list. He painstakingly set down the essentials, in anticipation of the stopover in Oran, where, they had just been informed, only French citizens would be allowed to go ashore. The first hours of the voyage had taught him much about practicalities, and among the lessons they had learned, to their cost, was the crucial importance of a deckchair. Aboard the *Paul-Lemerle*, this humble object – whether the wicker chair seen on ocean liners in the Roaring Twenties or the canvas deckchairs common on holiday beaches – was transformed by the magic of the squalid, over-crowded dormitories into a private room, so much so that, by the first evening, they were the subject of lucrative trading. The Breton family planned to acquire one deckchair each. Victor Serge, when pressed, added another to the order. Hygiene was the other principal preoccupation, so the list looked like a cross between a manual of social etiquette and a doctor's prescription. In the order of its concerns, cigarettes of course, but also the sending of letters.

ORAN
TOILETRIES: *washbasin, soap dish, toothbrush, nail brush, shoe brush,*

shoe polish, 6 face cloths, 2 hand mirrors, soap, comb, 25 paper towels, toilet
paper, 4 towels (2), toothpaste, razor? shaving brush? shaving soap? cotton
wool, gauze bandages, medical soap
EFFECTS: *Overalls Aube, 2 pairs cotton trousers, 1 navy, 1 light blue, cap,*
glasses Jacqueline, 4 deckchairs (3 Breton, 1 Serge), spirit lamp, hot water
bottle, cotton wool, photographic film
TOBACCO: *shag tobacco, Job cigarettes?, green Virginia tobacco?*
LETTERS: *Skira, Bonnard, Paulhan, Péret, Mabille, Denoël, Matta,*
Francis, Tanguy
Deck of cards, Indian ink, fountain pen

The *Paul-Lemerle* coughed and spluttered in the twilight, the engine stalled or raced, the tremors from it were unsettling, it clattered like an old jalopy; with some difficulty, the ship juddered into the harbour at Oran, between two other cargo ships, the *Sidi-Mabrouk* and the *Gouverneur-Général-Cambon*; the foghorn did not boom but gave a shrill squawk, like a cockerel crowing. The passengers next to the gangway were waiting for the ship to be safely moored so they could rush into town in search of coffee, a bed, a crumb of comfort. While still on deck they speculated aloud, toying with thick wads of notes or with the few coins they had in hand, a tall glass of pastis, a beer, a bedroom, a bathroom. A ginger tomcat, seen carried aboard by his master, a Viennese man with a bushy moustache, and later asleep in his wicker basket, rummaged between the large water tanks, now roasting in the sun, which would not be cleaned before being refilled, appeared from between the huts on deck and, frightened by his own shadow, leaped overboard and ended up in one of the stagnant pools next to the quay. With nets and lines, officers tried to rescue the cat, now looking like a coypu, as it writhed and mewled between mouthfuls of brackish water ... Having tried and failed to catch the tomcat, to the terrified howls of its Viennese master, a small fishing boat pushed off from the quay to rescue the animal. According to Ferdinand Sagols, the captain of the ship and commander of the motley crew transporting illicit passengers and cargo, it would be difficult to imagine a more triumphant entry into Oran harbour. A year earlier, in these same waters, the British Vice Admiral James Somerville had mined the entrance to the harbour and torpedoed the French naval fleet at Mers-el-Kébir, north-west of the city – first the battleship *Provence*, which ran aground but did not sink, closely followed by the cruiser *Dunkerque*. Only the *Strasbourg*, after some perilous manoeuvring, managed to reach the open sea. The battleship *Bretagne*, still at quay and unable to return fire, was hit by a British navy shell and sank with the loss of 977 sailors, now buried in Oran cemetery.

> *Only the French go ashore, we are prisoners on board. Reflections on the absurdity of xenophobia in a people with a low birth rate, bled by two wars, which has more than a million of its people in various foreign countries, and at home dependent on foreign labour. A people of heterogeneous origins and which certainly owes the richness of its temperament, the varied aspects of its intelligence, to this composite origin. Reactionary nationalism, the reflexive reaction of decrepitude. [...] Feeling of captivity on this floating concentration camp, with its stinking hold. Absurdity of a motionless boat in the shelter of a harbour. To be outbound, launched onto the sea, justifies all.*

The Story of P. The little old man who throws the scraps of paper from a first-floor window to attract cats. Then spits on them. When he hits one of the cats, the old man laughs.

On the balcony of an apartment on the rue Arzew, Albert Camus, his back to the railing, lit a cigarette with the smouldering end of the previous one, turned, leaned over and tossed the still-smoking cigarette end into the alley. In that barely suppressed smile, one could see the beautiful morning, the joyful toil, and the man oblivious to mute anxiety. Between the history and geography classes he taught at Études Françaises, a private school on the rue Paixhans, opposite the Lycée Lamoricière, Camus wrote a lot and read little, save for books about the history of the great plague, whose margins he copiously annotated and whose chronologies he carefully copied out, the relationship between cathedral towns, the accounts left by writers of memoirs. He was bored by Oran, the city did not interest him, and when he tried to pinpoint his scorn, he talked about *indifference*, the word often came to his lips as though it were self-evident, the right word to reflect the feeling of unease and nostalgia from which he wrenched himself when evening came. He had come back to Algeria and yet everything here frustrated him, he sometimes lunched with a colleague at the Belvedère, a restaurant in quartier des Planteurs, on the slopes of Mount Murdjadjo, near the pine forests, where he indulged in his favourite pastime, reading the newspaper in good company. He battled this *indifference*, he would say, by keeping a diary, writing articles, maintaining his correspondence – with Jean Grenier in particular – and by working with his friend Pascal Pia on the project of launching the literary magazine *Prométhée*. When he went to a café, he brought folders of page proofs to be corrected which he sent back in packets of ten. On 21 February, he recorded in his notebook:

Finished Sisyphus.
The three absurd works are now complete.
Beginnings of liberty.

Francine, his wife, was at his desk in the other room. On 14 January, they had set sail from Marseilles on the *Président-Dal-Piaz*, leaving France to settle in Oran for a time. Camus's family had everything arranged, a comfortable apartment was waiting for them, fresh, clean sheets, a guest room which they secretly hoped would soon be a child's bedroom, a large circular table in pale wood in the living room, and a desk for Albert with a single drawer, a library lamp and an empty bookcase. Francine's mother, Christiane, had done her best to decorate the apartment simply – knowing she should do no more than furnish it. On 3 March, while walking on the dunes along the beach at Mers el-Kebir, Camus encountered a stray dog, threw sticks into the dunes, let it trot along beside him and, when the walk was over, adopted the animal. He named it Proto.

At dusk, Camus would stroll along the quays as far as the bassin Poincaré. He would wander aimlessly, choosing no route, only a destination – a walk to the quays and back – nothing that would hinder his thought processes. The harbour offered a breath of foreign lands, it was set apart from the maze of winding alleyways. Camus would often walk as far as the end of the pier, sit on one of the random blocks and watch ships come and go, then, when it was dark, he would go and sit in the harbour café. If he was afraid of forgetting what was going on in his head, he walked quickly, otherwise he would saunter, as though obedient to some ritual, he would push open the door, settle himself on the left, to the far end of the bar, looking out over the junction, the Bastos tobacco factory, while he scribbled feverishly, filling page after page of his notebook. He would soak up the front-page news, the inexorable advance of chaos, while he planned the writing of his essay on Hitler, 'The Absurd and Power'. He became disgusted with the idea before he even tackled it, overcome by a sense of *Why bother?* which, if not checked, could darken his heart and sap his strength. Only fiction, he believed, could sound this void, this ugliness, wrap everything up in a story, a *pretext*, offer Oran something it did not realise it had within it: a novel. And using the power of his imagination – since nothing here appealed to the spirit – blight the city with disease, conjure plague as a metaphor for evil and for man's inability to respond. *The Plague*: 'Plague or adventure (novel)', he wrote in his notebook. Freed from the writing of *Sisyphus*, he began pushing another boulder up the hill.

During his walk, he watched, half-amused, half-embarrassed, as the old tub *Paul-Lemerle* pulled into the harbour, a curious steamboat, the rumbling relic of a moronic age. How many people were aboard? Three, perhaps four hundred people, so many strangers, a tangle of individual, contradictory stories impossible to unravel, the distillation of a lost world, a shifting microcosm ... the catastrophe and the inherent conflict of possibilities gathered together on the deck of a ship. He set down more ideas for his story, the essence drawn from documents he had accumulated and sifted, from observations made in cafés, from his boredom and his obsessions. He tried to make out a guiding line, some meaning at the heart of this suffering.

4

Wine Tankers and Whaling Ships

———

Oran
28 March 1941

Rumours appear and disappear, they are made and unmade. People attributed motives to inanities, they clung to them, wove conspiracy theories from snippets of some overheard conversation, often in a different language. They said the young researcher living in the sole cabin was a Nazi spy, that only yesterday he had been seen on deck reading a document filled with bizarre annotations – a navigation map or a list of suspects, opinions differed on this last point. A Tunisian man who shared his cabin confided that he typed out reports on a German A.-G. vorm. Seidel & Naumann typewriter. He claimed to be a professor, a specialist in the indigenous tribes of Brazil. He had gone ashore with the French, and people feared he would file his report with the port authorities and the Berlin socialists would be unceremoniously brought ashore. There was a photographer, too, a woman who was always in the company of a girl, a lesbian, people said, and an informer to boot. The passengers were mistrustful, they spied on each other, never missing an opportunity to come up with a theory, to cast aspersions, root out a culprit, denounce a traitor, search out a villain. By 28 March, rumours had spread through even the most rational passengers like a trail of gunpowder, from foredeck to steerage; if not stopped, they threatened to set the whole ship ablaze. For the passengers forced to stay on board, hemmed in by the ship's rail as by invisible barbed wire, the morning was tiresome and interminable. Soldiers patrolled the docks though it did not occur to any of the captives to escape. It was impossible to know when the cargo ship would put out again. Leaning over the railings, people tried to glean what information they could, they shouted questions to the guards who did not answer. 'The British have control of the Moroccan coast,' the ship's cook told the people gathered on the prow, 'No ship is allowed to pass without being inspected. The captain hates the British and he is refusing to allow them aboard, he's even talking about sailing back to Marseilles if he has to.' That night, there came the sound of whispering voices, followed by the screech of pulleys and the bustling of the quartermaster. The lifeboats, covered with thick tarpaulins, and the subject of much speculation from the moment the ship put out, were being shuttled between the *Paul-Lemerle* and the ship docked next to it, the *Sidi-Mabrouk*. The suspect cargo was being brought ashore in Oran. During the night, by the hangars, there were also heated exchanges with the officers of the *P.45*, an old whaling ship decked out to look like a battleship. At dawn on the second day, a sailor was seen boarding the *Paul-Lemerle* and handing Captain Sagols a sealed letter. It was the curiosity of the children aboard that uncovered the secret. Under cover of dusk, they had led an assault on the lifeboats, excitedly and fearfully lifting the tarpaulins, then wriggling inside to find nothing but a tangle of nets. At the bottom of the lifeboats were piles of lead fishing weights. Their eyes shining, the children talked about their find, which some decided were anti-submarine nets fitted with floats. Others spun stories about the theft of gold bullion from the Banque de France, which had been hastily divided into a hundred lots, and was being sent by sea from Algeria and Finistère, they whispered, as far as the Antilles, under the protection of Admiral Robert. It would not be absurd, they said, to imagine that some of the treasure had been hidden aboard this old tub, so that, with peerless French cunning, it could be transported right under the noses of the Germans and the British.

The *Gouverneur-Général-Cambon* pulled out of port, flanked by tugboats. At the Aucour docks near the fish market, Arabs brought ashore merchandise from the ships belonging to the Compagnie des Chargeurs Réunis. Among the ferries, there were ships carrying timber from Africa, a tanker bringing wine from Algeria. André Breton went back up on deck and sardonically surveyed the city, dreary and mundane, a mediocre French provincial city, he said to Victor Serge, filled with colonists pretending to be busy, with women veiled in white and dark-eyed beggars. Alleyways narrow as loopholes, full of traps and blind spots, where the end is invisible, lost somewhere near the vanishing point. He gave a long description of a Berber castle in the mountains, and, facing it, Oran Cathedral with its huge cupola like a bloated, dusty headdress; the deserted shops and the stale air. Angry and bewildered, Breton had managed to cross off barely a third of his shopping list; he counted on buying the remaining items at other stopovers before the big crossing.

Algerian Coast
29 March 1941

After two days of negotiations, the *Capitaine-Paul-Lemerle* pulled out of Oran harbour in the evening, escorted by a symbolic convoy of three ships. On the high sea, they were joined by the *P.45* whaling ship, fitted with three meagre 75-bore guns and manned by veterans of the First World War, armed with machine guns. Lam, who had been in charge of negotiations the previous evening, was on deck, laughing with Etxeberria, a Basque. They were talking in Spanish about the state of the troops and their difficult, limping flight towards Gibraltar. A ragtag mob of elderly men, spurred on by hatred of the British, preparing to do battle with defective weapons, as useless as the rifles they had had for sentry duty back in Madrid, where they were ordered to fire into the air when they saw the 'milkman' – the nickname given to Franco's aeroplanes packed with explosives. The *Capitaine-Paul-Lemerle* had refused to follow the instructions issued the previous day and the day before. And so this motley group of boats was forced to sail along the coast towards the ocean, unable to put into port en route, or to throw anything into the sea – anti-submarine nets or magnetic mines. On board, the passengers understood only too well: having escaped the concentration camps to be deported to Martinique, now, on the open sea, they found they had been transformed into human shields.

Claude Lévi-Strauss had crossed the Atlantic twice on the Ligne des Amériques, indeed some of the crew were old friends, travelling companions who, despite the circumstances, were keen to maintain a certain *standing* with the only seasoned traveller aboard; among the unanticipated considerations – or unearned privileges, depending on one's view – he, Lévi-Strauss, was allocated a bed in one of two cabins reserved for crew members. The young man was divorced – or, more precisely, he was about to be. He had a bushy beard and glasses with thick frames; the combination marked him out and accentuated his strangeness. Some of those who spoke with him felt his air of reserve and crippling shyness masked a certain sternness, others an awkward gaucheness. A staid professor or a bit of an oddball. He looked nothing like an explorer, which was for the best, since this was probably not how he would describe himself, in fact he would not have known how to describe himself ... As a professor, probably, a professor on his way to the United States. He would probably not have described himself as a researcher or a writer, although tucked in his rucksack he had twenty-seven pages of an unfinished novel, *Tristes Tropiques*, he did not know what to do with them. Did he think that this journey would so inspire him that he might finish the novel, or at least get a little further than he had so far? A confused beginning, a rudimentary outline, some scattered notes. He would throw away the plot and the story and keep only the description of a sunset. It had been in February 1934, aboard a cargo ship bound for Santos, that he had attempted to perfectly transcribe every nuance of the skies off the coast of Africa. It was, he remembered, an attempt to fix those evanescent and ever-renewed forms, working from the edges, as with a jigsaw puzzle, jotting down notes, second by second, until he could look no more, bathing in the sensation until it guttered out. This *state of grace*, the phrase kept coming back to him, had melted away, he had managed to complete these pages, but on that voyage he had never again found conditions propitious to writing. He even went so far as to try to artificially recreate the conditions of this apparition, as

46

though it was a secret passage that could only be accessed by standing in a specific place in a library and manipulating a certain book. Every day, he waited and hoped. Thirty sunsets passed, and his novel did not gain a single page. He made copious notes about the indigenous peoples of Brazil, and copied out whole passages from Conrad's *Victory*, praying that perhaps these transcriptions might act like a magical key. Depressed, he prowled the ship's corridors, immersed in imaginings wild as the relentless roll of the waves. He still clung to the idea of this novel, convinced that he was destined to write it, the typewritten pages in his bag were proof. He knew he was capable of a flash of brilliance; hackneyed phrases at least had the merit that they could be boldly, courageously wrested and made one's own, they could be mastered, pounding the keys of the typewriter until eventually accursed reality was forced to give up its treasure and apologise for not being more tractable. The aspect of mankind he could not bear, of master and possessor of nature, was something he learned early on to keep at bay, so that he did not impinge on the surrounding world, on the slow, inexorable course of things, but used it to enrich his vocabulary, to enhance the evocative power of his words, to draw renewed strength from metaphor and symbol. The 1935 crossing had been an epiphany in which he felt he was as much a writer as a scientist, but it had also been an admission of defeat – a subtle form of torture that had lasted a month, and he had been unable to remedy. In the end he had sabotaged his plot, his characters, and every time he tried to revive them, he ended up mangling them, attributing thoughts to them that were not just stupid, but contrived (what matter if the thoughts were stupid so long as they rang true!), such that each time he finished a page, he took his revenge in the only way available to writers – whether good or bad (in this, at least, they are equal) – ripping up the paper, reducing it to confetti, tossing it in the bin not once but twice. What of the plot? Claude loved to talk about the plot, unlike experienced writers who quickly learn that a novel is not simply an idea or a story but a fearsome, complicated machine, one that grows stale with each retelling, meaning that the best advice to give a writer, however confident he is about his tale, is not to talk about it unless it is finished, then add that he can ignore the last part of that sentence, and simply say nothing. It could be

47

formulated as a law similar to causal recurrence in physics: the time a writer spends talking about the idea or plot for a novel in progress is inversely proportional to the likelihood of its completion. But until we came along – and who are we if not some kind of narrator, or at least a small voice, looming above, beside, beneath the water, an omniscient presence that can have no impact on the fate (already played out) of our characters – no one had ever warned Claude of the 'law of the hack'. And so we found him aboard the *Mendoza*, telling the captain what would happen to his characters, what innovations he planned to use in his prose, and the underlying theme that the more attentive readers would recognise when, in a matter of months at most, the manuscript was finished: the virulent critique of a dying world, the thunderous rhythms of a dizzying bolero, a final terrifying cacophony of brass like the portent of some great catastrophe. Even now, aboard the *Paul-Lemerle*, he had not quite abandoned this idea, nor did one have to press him to talk about it with a last vestige of enthusiasm tinged with the frustration of a futile or perhaps unattainable project. The idea for the novel had come from a brief newspaper article about a swindle committed on an island in the Pacific in which a phonograph was used to make the natives believe that their gods were coming back to earth. The characters in the novel were to be political refugees from various countries fleeing the German occupation. They would try to create a civilisation, and tragedy would ensue. In the end, the reader would realise that reality is never to be found in experience. In our search for truth, we create only illusions.

Chafarinas Islands
30 March 1941

Mist on the sea, grey seas in the evening, it could be the Baltic, which I've seen sunnier. The Rif coast. A country made for fighting with fierceness, with love, an elevated way of feeling oneself to be alive.

Melilla, city of no interest, on a bay. Franco set out from here. Further on, the bare heights of the coast are sprinkled with bushes and they have animal-like shapes. Mountain with panther skin.

We are in a convoy of five ships. The one escorting the other four is a comical tub of the 'wartime navy', a filthy trawler covered in rust and armed with a few small cannon. Long wait off the coast not far from Melilla. Signals. The war tub circles around us. Towards evening, in the rain, we pull out again in the opposite direction. It's said that difficulties have arisen in Gibraltar.

The night having fallen I contemplate the lights of the ships sailing parallel to us. Stars, my familiar sky already turned upside down. Taurus draws a perpendicular 'V' below the zenith. The Pleiades clearly visible. They served as my guide on snowy nights when returning from Orenpossad. I pointed them out to Laurette on the road to Air-Bel. Saturn and Jupiter are visible above the crescent moon. These visages of the heavens are totally indefinable. I hope there will be a time when men will have a deeper, more consistently intimate relationship with them. I've not yet seen the nebulae, all I know is that they exist, and I can barely guess at that of Orion. Most men today live without seeing the universes above their heads and which they could see. The gentle sea, ever in movement and moving. One is so full of thoughts that they are no longer thoughts, but rather waves and winds of the spirit. It rains off and on. Neither sad nor fearful, tense, and of your presence.

We pass by small, bare granitic isles, the Chafarinas, Spanish Morocco, where there is a lighthouse, and behind the lighthouse a cottage with an illuminated window.

The Rif Coast
31 March 1941

The sea narrows, a two-lane motorway with no shortcuts and no detours, straight along the arid coast towards the only exit: Gibraltar. The passengers began to dub themselves experts, pointing out the dangers, spotting the warnings, arguing over routes, suggesting manoeuvres and courses. Two hundred and fifty members of a new society, floating, stranded at sea, heading for unknown lands, fleeing a Europe in flames. They looked like citizens of Pompeii, gazing from the deck of the ship at the destruction of their world. A slow-motion tragedy, punctuated by stopovers. Newspapers were passed from hand to hand, taking up to a week to reach the last reader – an old man slumped in a deckchair at the foot of the ladders, reading the 24 March issue of *Sémaphore*, who was proud to see that the *Paul-Lemerle* was listed among the departing ships. The news from Oran would not reach him until 6 April, by which time, who knew, Africa might be far behind them. For the journalists, the businessmen, the officers or simply those who were curious about what was happening in the world, a rudimentary system for broadcasting information had been improvised on the upper deck; there they discussed the latest news, argued over military strategies, supplies and equipment, fuelled by the dispatches that the captain listened to at 6 p.m. which those privileged enough to access the poop deck could hear and relay. The news from Vichy was filtered through the first ear that happened to be on that part of the ship, one prepared not only to meekly accept the news, but to embellish it with an occasional *the world's going to hell in a handcart*, an opportunistic *bloody freemasons*, or a welcome *English bastards* to muddy the waters. What remained of the news once it had passed through the sieve of censorship, a mixture of opinion and folly, made its way down the central companionway, relayed as though through a piece of string connected to two tin cans, glided down the gangways and, by late evening, reached the Spanish mothers who did not understand a word, Yugoslavia had been invaded three times in the space of two days. As a new society, this had only structures, migration and movement. The egalitarianism born of privations and the lack of preparation gave way to a kind of feudalism and later, as though history had been speeded up, to a brutal form of capitalism that took over the ship, lumping passengers into groups and recreating social classes they assumed had been forgotten. The eternal return of the same. On the lower deck, the gangways, in the boiler room, in the hold and on the upper deck, a hierarchy emerged among the passengers, who were only too eager to band together in families and in pairs. All prepared to recreate the same flawed social system on this hunk of rotting wood bound for the New World. The influential financiers quickly annexed an area near the quarters of the officers and the captain. There you would find the art dealer, the diamond merchant, the industrialist, the businessman, the cream of society – in shirtsleeves and braces, sprawled, snoring, and drooling on the canvas deckchairs they used as makeshift beds, but the cream of society nonetheless, with their intricate codes and rituals. They talked about their neighbourhood, about their former lives, the Champs-Élysées, the holidays on the Côte d'Azur, the Grand Hotel in Saint-Jean-Cap-Ferrat: money, as we know, is a great lingua franca, it breaks down borders, and encloses a world turned upside down. And so, when there is nothing to monetise, they monetise that nothing. By the third day of the crossing the ship's cook was running a canteen, a kitchen-cum-delicatessen on wheels where, in plain sight, rations could be diverted, a black market was established, and, for five francs, it was possible to buy fresh bread, for ten to fifteen francs a meat dish, for two francs a grey-brown liquid called coffee. By the fifth day, the commandant's Chinaman, who was not a bad man, but who was not a bad trader either, established a system of full-board that took the place of daily rations. It entailed reducing the rations of the weakest and restoring the privileges of the pot-bellied. Within a week, one could see these fine ladies and gentlemen taking tea in the sun. They played bridge, they discussed business and contracts. Soon a Czech man who was more astute than most pulled out a roulette wheel and styled himself the sole croupier of the Champs-Élysées. For this was the name given to the rich part of the cargo ship: *Les Champs-Élysées*, a little kingdom of first-class passengers with greasy hair who smelled of piss. Montparnasse, la Villette and the place Rosa-Luxemburg brought the filth up from the boiler room, smearing a grubby ring around this makeshift salon Vinteuil, bathing everything in a semblance of equality. The German refugees called them *Wirtschaftsmigranten* – economic migrants – while, to the well-heeled, the political migrants were dangerous Trotskyites, Spartacists, Communists. After Oran, intoxicated by his show of strength, the captain invited members of this counterfeit café society to dine at his table. For one night, in the shade of the terrace, sat a former German banker and his wife, a former Flanders factory owner whose chimney had collapsed under German shelling, killing two people, and an exiled Antwerp diamond merchant said to be worth millions, whose staggering wealth was stored in the vaults of a New York bank; there they discussed peace with Germany, their sense of honour, the lower classes, the decline of the old world and the English, whom they hated more than anything else, more even than the Jews.

*

André Masson and his family had not been able to board the *Capitaine-Paul-Lemerle* on 24 March. Three days later, at the Villa Air-Bel, he received a letter from the Vichy regime: *The Ministry for Foreign Affairs urges the Port Authorities to give safe passage to the West Indies to Monsieur André Masson, artist, at the invitation of the Museum of Modern Art in New York. The Service des œuvres françaises à l'étranger has expressed a keen interest he be allowed to board the next departing ship.* On 31 March, André, Rose and their two children, Diego and Luis, set off on the cargo ship *Carimaré* from Marseilles bound for Fort-de-France.

Nemours
1 April 1941

Passengers began to panic – will we make it past Gibraltar? Booming in the distance came the roar of cannon fire, the return fire and the shelling of a defensive position. The ship turned around, the escort convoy scattered, people eavesdropped on the orders of the officers on the bridge. Down below, the panic of the sailors was mirrored by the apathy of the passengers in steerage. There was talk of the brush between a French ship and a British vessel at the port of Algeciras, the mutual misunderstanding, the warning shot across the bows by one, the retreat of the other. Citing the captain as a direct source, everyone insisted there would be a forced disembarkation before they passed through the straits. In the late morning, the passengers aboard the *Paul-Lemerle* were informed that there would be a stopover in Nemours, an administrative post on the Moroccan border. Once in port, they were told about the incident: four commercial vessels plying the route between Casablanca and Oran had been attacked by a British ship in French waters. Protected by the French naval destroyer *Simoun*, the flotilla had managed to reach safe harbour in Nemours. The night before, as a reprisal, the town had suffered heavy shelling. Rumour had it, there had been ten fatalities. Breton went ashore and spent the afternoon wandering around without finding anything except a military post, a squalid boredom, a stagnant war, an aircraft carrier beached in the desert and officers intoxicated that they had not drowned. A stifling heat in March, and on a street corner by a patch of waste ground, a bookshop and, in the window, *Monna Vanna, Ubu in Chains, A Treatise on Flagellation*. Breton mused in free association – they must have taken Jarry for a specialist in perversions. The presence, here, in this *corner of dead France in a killed Africa*, of Ubu as drawn by Jarry in a bookshop window, the conical cowl, the eyes staring through holes cut into the fabric, looking up or down like an upside-down smile, the rounded costume inscribed with concentric circles drawn with a Sergeant-Major pen. Hand tucked into the pocket of the smock, debonair, about to belch '*merdre*', arm in arm with Mère Ubu. The community of artists at the Villa Air-Bel amused themselves by drawing a set of tarot cards as revised and edited by the surrealists. Gone were the armorial emblems of the Ancien Régime, the ranks and the symbols of court, they were replaced by other values and other demigods. Two red suits and two black suits would raise their standards; the flame symbolised love; the bloody wheel, revolution; the black star, dreams; and the lock, rebirth. Meanwhile the ace, the king, the queen (the knaves had been eliminated) would be replaced by genies, sirens and mages with imagery they would draw from their own pantheon of gods: Baudelaire, the Portuguese Nun, Novalis for the flame, de Sade, a heroine of Stendhal, Lamiel, Pancho Villa and the wheel of the revolution, Lautréamont, Lewis Carrol's Alice, Freud as a star, Hegel, Hélène Smith, Paracelsus for the lock. The joker was none other than Père Ubu, drawn by Jarry himself. In Breton's suitcase there was a set of the Marseilles cards. André drew the lock and Paracelsus' octopus, André Masson took Novalis and the Portuguese Nun, Jacque Hérold did Lamiel and de Sade, Jacqueline Lamba spun the wooden wheel of ancient times, and Baudelaire into the bargain, while Brauner had the difficult task of drawing Hegel and Hélène Smith, Oscar Domínguez drew the black star of dreams and Freud, Wifredo sketched Alice and Lautréamont, and Max Ernst created a card the size of his hand on which shimmered the ace of flames and Pancho Villa.

Breton went into the bookshop, paid ten francs for the endlessly reread copy of *Ubu in Chains* which he might perhaps leaf through aboard the cargo ship, thinking of the captain. Right now, he was engrossed in another book: *The Laws of Chance*.

One of the areas on the boat was known as Belleville. Strolling through it, it seemed obvious that, at the foot of the ladders, one was not far from the heights of the Parc des Buttes-Chaumont, here were the faces one might find at the corner of the rue des Pyrénées or the embankment on the boulevard du Temple. Next to the children's playground, between the storehouse and the collective washrooms, was the area peopled by German immigrants, here they discussed the assassination of Trotsky, the Molotov–Ribbentrop Pact, the death of illusions. Continuing in the same direction, close to the hold and between the kitchen-on-wheels and the stopcocks, was the zone known as la Villette. An open-air dormitory strewn with sheets and blankets scrubbed against washboards with coal tar soap and strung up on ropes between the posts. Here, children made up adventures, as they might in a tent of blankets and pillows, others came to nap, happy to get away from the wind and sun. From here, one could see the little area reserved for Spanish women, a child in each arm, one suckling at a breast.

Her face pressed to the viewfinder of her camera, an Ikarette, she was seen pacing up and down the ship, capturing a face without pausing to stop, surreptitiously catching a moment. Here, amid the thoroughfares created by excited children, beneath the alleyways decked with laundry, on the public squares thronged with military men and the gardens where women sunbathed in their underwear, Germaine Krull recognised a transposed simulacrum of the Paris she had forensically documented with her camera ten years earlier in the company of Eli Lotar. Looking back, she saw a whole section of her life reappear, the birth of the magazine *VU* and commissions from Lucien Vogel – photojournalism beneath the bridges and the cranes, capturing the pulleys, the bolts, the cables and the pistons, the bales of wire and the rickety staircases; the silos and the industrial installations shot in shadow, from below, portraying singular visions caught between the pipework. And, always, the surprise of her kitchen darkroom as she gazed at the baths of developing fluid and watched as there appeared huge steel wheels or the feet of cranes like wading birds with bolted joints. This was

Ironworks by 'Krull-Métal' – the woman-machine she depicted in *Self-Portrait with Ikarette*: face hidden behind the camera, hands barely covered, cigarette smoke eating into the frame, a picture frame hanging from a length of wire. At dawn, while Eli was sleeping, she would explore the seedy areas of Montmartre, wander through Montorgueil while the market was bustling, chat to the street merchants and the porters. She would visit the Seigneurs de la Cloche (Lords of the Street), tramps who lived around the open-air market at Les Halles, wander around Saint-Eustache, down the banks of the Seine, along the quai de Montebello. The pages of *VU* published the work of the Paris school: Brassaï, Cartier-Bresson, Kertész, Bellon; Man Ray was just beginning his experiments with montages and multiple impressions, Walter Benjamin was finishing his *Passagenwerk*, for which, at his request, she provided photographs of the famous iron-and-glass arcades of Paris, the Galerie Vivienne, le Caire, les Panoramas. She had now put on weight, wrapped her hair in a turban, a cigarette dangling from a corner of her mouth, crushing the ash with her whole weight. One had only to move from one gangway to the next to cross all of Europe, to encounter déclassé bourgeois, *decadent* intellectuals, *degenerate* artists – strangers who carried with them the history of a people; a unique gathering forced into a confined space by dint of suffering, by what is called the energy of despair. Germaine Krull was thinking of doing a piece of photojournalism in the style of her friend Jeff Kessel, it could be called *Aboard the Paul-Lemerle*, she would write the captions. For almost ten years, people had known that things would end badly, but how could they imagine that one day they themselves would have to flee like hunted animals? An unbalanced democracy and a rogues' gallery of larger than life characters, a fabulous, compact mass to be captured, a black-and-white microcosm of an era, like one of those paintings of Babel before the fall, a tower weighted down by intricate details. She herself was one of the characters, her friends called her Mad Dog, nothing and no one had ever convinced her to stick to one path, and the very idea of not accepting a call from a stranger terrified her so much that she embraced the vagaries of life, the certainty of danger. Was it possible to live so many lives at once? Did it require plunging, body and soul, into existence, never demanding one's due, losing one's way, planning for nothing except the unexpected, relying on the path less taken as the stimulus, losing one's way again and again until one no longer recognised oneself and only then, perhaps, being reborn? Staking everything to lose everything or win everything. Rejecting compromise and cosy deals, forever remaining the Mad Dog, looking like a hoodlum or a crazed gamine, with a ridiculous accent and a highly personal approach to not being burdened by bores and fools. To be the person no one was expecting. From every possible path, create an ethic, keep a promise. At night, in the hold, after watching the crescent moon weave between the clouds, and stowing the Ikarette in its case, Germaine Krull would make notes in a school exercise book, the name of a woman or a man she had met, a place they had passed, the stuff of future legends in photographic negatives. In the darkroom, create an instant.

People never tired of saying, when in desperate straits, dazed and unthinking, that they had escaped, they had been trapped and had not realised it. For the immigrant prisoners aboard the ship, forced to rub shoulders with each other, there was a certain pleasure in recounting the danger, dramatising and ennobling it, embroidering their own escape, sharing the feeling that they had escaped the worst, that already they were survivors of some greater shipwreck. They knew that this was merely a reprieve, that they could be put ashore anywhere, interrogated, torpedoed, diverted, shipped back to square one. Not 'Who are you?' but 'How did you escape?' – this was how people judged each other aboard the *Paul-Lemerle*. When playing this game, Germaine Krull drew out the story, adapted the effects, replayed the scene, invoking good luck and even astrology if necessary. Sitting on one of the benches that lined the long table by the dining area, next to her Oskar Goldberg, a theologian, Siegfried Pfeffer, a member of the KPD, Alfred and Friedel Kantorowicz, and a young woman from Luxembourg whom Germaine had befriended as they were embarking and protected like a little sister. Pass the time, forget the troubles of the day – this ship that turned around, doubled back on itself, these landscapes that all looked like déjà vu, recrossing the Algerian border in the opposite direction, a manoeuvre, a detour, the end of the journey. For those with a taste for dramatic twists and turns, Germaine's story was a model of the genre – so much so it sounded suspicious – but that did not matter, what mattered, beyond the plot, the surprises, the drama of her story, was the passion, the tone, the spectacle, the sheer entertainment she offered the listener. She would launch in, would invariably begin with a categorical statement like a maxim: 'A person who doesn't know how to gamble cannot lose, and a person who doesn't know how to lose cannot gamble,' and then she would add: 'I spent four years living in Monaco and Monte Carlo, and in all that time I never allowed myself to go into a casino with more than twenty francs on me, I was too much of a gambler, ready to lose a chip as soon as I had one, unable to be reasonable. But on that day, I went in with my last hundred francs, bet the lot on the roulette wheel, on a number that is not even a number and walked away from the table with my salvation. Life is full of surprises ... Like everyone else, I was looking for a visa, at the time I was working for the Monte Carlo casino magazine, and as a stringer for Agence France-Presse. Joris had made it to the United States by then and he'd sworn on the Bible to immigration that he wasn't married. So I couldn't go to the States without betraying him. I was trying to get to London, but that was impossible, then I heard about a Brazilian ambassador to Vichy who admired my work and had copies of all my books, the monographs with Simenon, Mac Orlan, Suarès and Matisse. I wrote to him and he wrote straight back to say the visa was signed and sitting on his desk. He was about to leave for Paris, and then Brazil. I didn't have a passport. A friend went to Vichy to pick it up. But the conditions had changed; now I had to pay in order to get the visa. Five thousand francs was the sum mentioned ... I was living off what Joris could afford to send me, and that wasn't nearly enough. I decided to stake everything on the roulette wheel, I bet my last hundred francs on zero, my favourite. It came up three times in a row. My escape depended on three zeros.' People all but applauded, the pay-off was so surprising. During the time she was staying with Maurice Privat in Monte Carlo, Germaine was obsessed with astrology. She was capable of creating a star chart, played the fortune teller down on the deck, but never dared predict that the crossing would fail.

The Kantorowiczes came next, recounting the incident when their passports were checked by the port authorities, how Alfred's name had appeared on the list, and the name Colonel Riverdi, like a code word, had been a last resort. The pain was still very raw, they would dispatch this story and linger over the strange tale of how they had got their visa. They had been living in Sanary-sur-Mer, but, when war broke out and the situation worsened, they had sought refuge in Marseilles, hiding out in the kitchens of the Villa Valmer. The Emergency Rescue Committee established by exiled German intellectuals took care of their papers and organised their escape. They had managed to get an exit visa and were waiting for a transit visa between New York and Veracruz, but despite letters of support from Hemingway, from the Mexican Consul, Gilberto Bosques, and from their friend Ellen Wilkinson, a junior minister at the Ministry of Home Security under Churchill, the paperwork still languished in an office somewhere. What they needed was a guarantor, a rich American prepared to sponsor them. The ERC set about finding someone. They were told they had been sponsored by Melvyn Douglas, the actor who had just appeared with Greta Garbo in *Ninotchka*. They laughed as they talked about their 'American uncle', a young man with a promising future. A week before they were due to set sail aboard the *Paul-Lemerle*, while they were walking along the quays, they spotted his name on the poster for a movie playing that evening: *Fast Company*. They bought two tickets and spent the screening considering the actor, subjecting him to a sort of assessment and finally deciding, as the credits rolled, that he had sufficient charm, talent and humour to be their sponsor.

Oskar Goldberg and Siegfried Pfeffer had been aboard the abortive sailing of the *Bouline*, a miserable tub flying the Belgian flag which set sail from Marseilles one night, hugging the coast as far as Gibraltar only to be boarded by the maritime police off La Caleta. Twenty-two passengers including ten Polish officers, several stateless persons and Belgian Jews. The Emergency Rescue Committee had paid the twenty thousand francs demanded by the boatman and, five months later, the committee run by Varian Fry would pay for their tickets on the *Paul-Lemerle*.

The young woman from Luxembourg confessed that she was fleeing nothing more serious than boredom, her fiancé lived in Venezuela and she was going to be with him. This was the only ship bound for the Americas, so she had taken it, she would take another when they reached Martinique, and then she would get married. It was banal, she apologised, shamefaced.

The night before the *Paul-Lemerle* sailed, Peggy Guggenheim and Victor Brauner had visited Max Ernst at the Villa Air-Bel, where they bought several of his paintings for the sum of two thousand dollars. To celebrate the sale, Ernst had invited them to dinner on 2 April, at a black-market restaurant near Vieux-Port. When they parted company, Max slipped the key to his room into the pocket of Peggy's coat.

Gibraltar
3 April 1941

Captain Ferdinand Sagols had never imagined playing hide-and-seek with the British along the coast of Morocco, masked by the clownish convoy. Considered a traitor by some, a daring captain and a saviour by his crew, he was either a smuggler or a collaborator in the eyes of his passengers. Nothing about him suggested that he would one day sit down at the table, advance a pawn in this tactical game in the Mediterranean and later on the high seas, avoiding torpedoes, periscopes and pennants. He was a master mariner who had worked on liners in the merchant navy before the war, and only the unexpected re-establishment of commercial routes between France and the Antilles tempted him once again to sail, though there were dangers greater than storms at sea. There was talk of a German cruiser, a cargo ship that was armed and camouflaged and intending to disrupt commercial shipping lanes, to attack ships as they came into harbour, or in the middle of the Atlantic. Ships were blown up by floating mines, others were scuttled by U-boats, like the *City of Benares*, struck by a torpedo, which now lay at the bottom of the ocean with many of its passengers. Privateering was at its height, and the *Paul-Lemerle* and its captain had to reach Fort-de-France before the end of April in order to land the two hundred and fifty passengers. One could not help but wonder whether the risk was too great for such a dilapidated cargo ship. At the helm of this rust bucket, this ageing patched-up freighter no more seaworthy than Captain Haddock's ship *Karaboudjan*, Sagols dreamed of a different destiny. He had grown up in Maureillas, in the Pyrenees, a village trapped between the Lac Saint-Jean and the Spanish border near the Perthus pass. Over time, thanks to a series of opportunities, an exemplary disposition, the makings of a commander, a hard-headed personality and a Republican sense of meritocracy, he gradually climbed the ladder of the Société Générale des Transports Maritimes à Vapeur to become a master mariner. Sagols was not only the first sailor from his village but, following his promotion to captain at the age of thirty-five, he was his family's pride and joy. By chance, he found himself working the transatlantic route, ten years plying the routes between Marseilles, Fort-de-France, Brest, Pointe-à-Pitre, Le Havre, Cayenne. Between crossings, at the café in Rivesaltes where he had lived since getting married, he entertained the locals with tales of the West Indies, talked about the sweltering heat of the Caribbean, the tropical rainstorms, the torrent of rain from any passing cloud that disappears with it, the penal colony of Saint-Laurent-du-Maroni, the fierce Negroes of French Guiana and the Negroes of Martinique, big children living on their island: the shame of France. He never forgot to bring back a crate of rum. He liked the status afforded him by his rank, the natural authority, the deference of his crew, the respect of the passengers. He had come back from war victorious and patriotic, proud to have been among the 'Vengeurs de '70'. After the armistice, he would reconcile himself to Pétain, in time, he would stand on a quay at Toulon and watch the scuttling of the French fleet. A war veteran, after the destruction of the French fleet his visceral hatred of the Boche shifted to a hatred of the British, those liars and diplomats who used orders and counter-orders to impose their authority. The raw pain of Mers-el-Kébir, a wound that for most sailors would never heal, underscored the rationale for a Franco-German alliance at sea. Sagols believed that Pétain was the right man for the job, he would stand up to Hitler and would get France back on its feet by ridding it of the jackasses, the idlers and the pacifists of 1940, the sluggards of the Front Populaire who were beaten before they could fight. Not to mention the scum, the Jews, the cowards, the mongrel degenerates – the majority of his 'cargo' on this particular crossing. The sort of people he had seen at the Camp de Rivesaltes. Deserters and cowards, determined to spread the plague of socialism, bent on creating a hell on earth with their treachery and their depraved miscegenation. German Jews, Polacks, weaklings from Spain and Italy, even Chinamen – a corrupt army that, once across the equator, should be prevented from settling in French territories and encouraged to seek refuge elsewhere. Sagols took the more secret part of his mission very seriously: under the guise of tolerating emigration, the ships were transporting underwater defence materials to the colonies for the besieged French navy. The captain kept two sets of books, as attested by the logbook. In eleven days' sailing, nothing had been noted, despite the fact that he had slowed the journey, decided to make two stops in Algeria and hire a makeshift convoy to escort them from Oran. With a falsified logbook, a suspicious cargo, holds and lifeboats with false bottoms, the radio operator's notebooks censored, the *Paul-Lemerle* advanced wearing a mask. Sagols hated the British so much he was prepared to scuttle his own ship if they tried to board, he had bellowed loudly enough for the passengers to overhear. The list of crew members in the bridge log was also false, names were recorded at the discretion of the officers, just as manoeuvres were recorded at his discretion, while any loading or unloading was redacted before embarkation, there was no mention of the nets and the mines, the goods brought aboard at Oran or those taken ashore at Nemours after the captain's change of tack. In addition to the ship's log and the diary, the captain kept a different account for the authorities, in which he kept a list of suspects, details of altercations and any statements he considered seditious or unpatriotic, filling out the entries with the occasional denunciation. On 1 April, he noted an exchange of cannon fire between a defensive position on the coast and an English vessel in pursuit of a French convoy. He used this incident to explain his decision to turn the ship around and stop at Nemours and, as a precaution, unload the submarine nets there under cover of darkness. On 2 April, he noted the demands of a pedantic writer, a man named Breton, who, claiming to speak on behalf of the passengers, complained about the food. Initially, he threatened that anyone who was unhappy would be put ashore at

Casablanca, then he threatened to close the mobile kitchen and stop selling bread. The passengers instantly bit their tongues and accepted their fate. He promised that at the next stopover, cattle and sheep would be brought aboard to be housed in the barn in the stern, near the communal bathrooms, and very soon they would have more than enough to eat. On their eleventh day at sea, on 3 April, at 8 a.m., the ship entered the straits of Gibraltar. In the distance there were British cruisers, an aircraft carrier, the port of Algeciras. At 11 a.m., in international waters off the coast of Tangiers, the convey celebrated on a choppy sea, the water lapping at the hull like a burst of applause at the successful completion of stage one: they had left Europe, they had reached the ocean.

5

Impure Animals

———

The officers of the watch were transformed into overzealous civil servants who decided who could and could not go ashore at each stopover. Always the same protocol, always the same count, the same people chosen. Casablanca, one fine morning – here we go again! – forty French citizens, the only ones allowed to go ashore, lined up along the ship's rail, one by one reciting surname, first name, profession, and date and place of birth. One officer ticked the name off the list while a colleague checked the photograph on the ID card against the face in front of him. Claude Lévi-Strauss had not rushed to join the roll-call, he had no desire to be at the front of the line – after twelve days at sea, he was exasperated by the shudders of good French citizens, the collective agonies, the shrieks of joy and terror, the choruses of *Ooh* and *Aah*, the way they pawed the ground, stamped their feet – instead, he stood on tiptoe and realised that nothing was moving. Reluctantly, he joined the inspection ten minutes after it had begun and, on his right, on the far side of the ship's rail, he saw a section of the battleship *Jean-Bart*, in dry dock at Maison-Blanche, the keelson half-painted a garish orange. A broad-shouldered man in an off-white linen uniform moved ahead of him, the line advancing to the rhythm of mumbled names and stamped passports. It was then that he heard the name Breton, and the first name André, though he did not immediately connect the two, as though trapped in a time warp. Breton was five metres away, haggling with one of the Arabs on the quay. He was handing over a list, two pages dark with green ink, and a fifty-franc note for the errands, the rest to be paid when it was delivered at the end of the day. So, André Breton was also aboard this rusty tub that had been cast upon the waves, and Lévi-Strauss was surprised, not by the curious coincidence, but by the fact it had taken him so long to notice. While critical of what he considered the infantile tendency to treat the unexpected as a sign of elective affinity, or worse, as the tangible manifestation of magical thinking, to judge an effect by its cause, he could not help but be unsettled by the coincidence. He admired the ground-breaking tendency to introduce things alien to literature, almost by force, without feeling tied to the absurd need for rigorous notation. He was captivated by the fleeting intensity, the insights, and recalled the idea that one had to search elsewhere than in oneself for the echo of one's own obsessions: *A morning paper will always be enough to give me my news of myself*, he had noted down. His cabin berth isolated him; here he shut himself away to read and write, and only rarely wandered about the ship, self-conscious, like a stowaway, and so in the first ten days had met only a white Creole heading back to his island, a Tunisian Jew and two young women his own age. Intimidated, Lévi-Strauss approached the great man and introduced himself, awkward and stammering. Breton had the air of an intellectual from the Enlightenment, which, at first glance, made him seem judgemental and possessed of a natural hauteur, though he instantly set people at ease, being courteous, friendly and curious about everything; he looked at people with a keen attentiveness mingled with a delicate irony. Having been introduced to Breton's wife, Jacqueline Lamba, and to their little daughter Aube, Lévi-Strauss walked with them for a while. This was how Breton determined a good companion, *the street ... the only valid field of experience*; as such, either he casually drifted away, or he took someone's arm, carried on and, asking no questions, listened. As they strolled along together, Lévi-Strauss struggled for the right word, for some anecdote that would hit home, and he stroked his beard as, in his mind, he muddled up his readings of the *Manifesto* and of *Nadja*.

At the entrance to the medina, they stopped and went into a fish restaurant at the end of the Corniche Ain Dib. Lévi-Strauss was careful not to talk about his own essays, about his unfinished play, *The Apotheosis of Augustus*, or the fragment of his novel – he knew only too well what Breton thought of *novelistic fabulations*, between 'the marquess takes tea at five' and 'books that slam like doors'. Over lunch, Lévi-Strauss recounted his war, if it warranted such a term. A war with no fighting, unreal at the time, and absurd when he thinks back. With the nagging impression of participating in a farce, a liaison officer on a supposed front line near Luxembourg relayed the incoherent orders of army rabble who were repeating the instructions of some demented officer. Lévi-Strauss talked about it as though it were a promenade. Poste 193, liaison officer W, second battalion, 164th Régiment d'Infanterie, behind the Maginot line, with no instructions beyond waiting for other recruits. In the end he wandered the Ardennes, strolling through the forest, his mind elsewhere, with no officers, no captain, free as a poacher. *'When the Germans began the offensive, liaison officers from a Scottish battalion showed up, the Black Watch of the Royal Highlanders, and we were evacuated before we had heard a single gunshot, without seeing a battle,'* and, in an effort to add a *bon mot*, he added: *'War as a form of mushroom picking. I could have spent my time creating an herbarium, the countryside was beautiful, the silence was only ever broken by the sound of my footsteps and the wind in the tall oak trees.'* He described the defeat and the walk beneath the blazing sun, searching for his regiment, first in Sarthe, then in Bordeaux, then, after he reached Béziers, being billeted on the plains of Larzac, a wisp of straw dangling like a cigarette from his lips, his boots riddled with holes like a labourer's, ready to cut wheat or pick grapes. This was France, a map marked out by fields, by rivers and estuaries recited in front of a blackboard, by cheeses and départements, by hayricks beneath an open sky and groaning barns where demobbed troops in tattered uniforms spent the summer of their defeat sleeping in meadows under the stars and going down into the villages at dawn, with nothing but the dew to wash themselves. They had played at war and quickly tired of it, they had cast off their uniforms, marched on in shirt sleeves humming 'Le Merle Moqueur'. Breton asked him about his destination – New York, at the invitation of the New School for Social Research, a university founded so that workers could take night classes. His place, his last hope, he owed to professors Robert Lowie, Alfred Métraux, John P. Gillen and Georges Devereux, an ethnologist known for his fieldwork among the Mojave Indians, whom Breton had read. Lévi-Strauss had been offered a grant of five thousand dollars over two years by the Rockefeller Foundation and a thousand dollars to cover his travel expenses. Towards the end of lunch, the conversation turned to the influence of the primitives on avant-garde movements. After his return from South America in April 1939, Lévi-Strauss had worked at the Musée de l'Homme, preparing his thesis on indigenous peoples of the central plateaus of Brazil and cataloguing the artefacts he had brought back with him, tribal basketwork and pottery. He and his colleagues at the museum mocked the regular visitors, the painters and the poets who wittered on without knowing anything about the primitive arts; he saw it as the misappropriation of science by surrealists and cubists, artists starved of inspiration, little more than a form of exoticism. He freely talked about this interest as a fad, though he could not be sure what Breton thought, he vehemently criticised the other crime of the pre-war era, the travellers' tales, the propaganda of alchemists who claimed to turn lead into gold, transforming tedium into excitement, erasing boredom, dressing everything up as an adventure novel. The two of them gleefully lampooned the writings of Paul-Émile Victor, the notebooks of Alain Gerbault. They agreed to carry on the conversation when they returned to the ship.

Left behind on the *Paul-Lemerle*, a *floating concentration camp*, Victor Serge and forty of his comrades welcomed aboard a group of exiles, a league of nations from another ship who had been alerted by post restante and telegram of the arrival of the opponent of Stalinism, the man who had denounced the 'Soviet Thermidor'. *I feel no joy at going. I would a thousand times rather have stayed, if that had been possible: but before liberation of some kind comes its way, the chances are ninety-nine out of a hundred that I shall have perished in some filthy prison. Europe, with its bullet-ridden Russias, its crushed and trampled Germanies, its invaded nations, its gutted France – how one clings to it! We are parting only to return ...* Between the smokestack and the lifeboats on the upper deck, Serge entertained a young

Italian socialist, a Freemason, a French socialist. *We speak of possible perspectives. They are waiting. People are spineless but are beginning to understand.* An army ready to rise up, waiting for orders, longing to do battle. Which was no more than the shadow of itself – all addled by the fall of bourgeois republics, stunned by the pact between the red star and the swastika, flabbergasted by the political assassinations. Serge harangued the crowd, their hearts were no longer in it – yesterday's vanquished, gathered together by a twist of fate – the Republicans from the Workers' Party of Marxist Unification, betrayed in Barcelona, the German Spartacists crushed in Berlin, the Italian anarchists, the French socialists, the pacifists, servicemen, the stateless, the Jews, on the road, herded towards the ports, always moving, gathered on this deck, soon far away. For how long? News had just arrived that Germany and Italy had declared war on Yugoslavia.

Casablanca harbour was protected on one side by a pier known as the *jetée delure*, a barrage spanning fifteen hundred metres, and on the other side by the perpendicular *jetée transversale* stretching from Roches Noires, a rocky outcrop off the coast. In its centre lay the *Jean-Bart*, a massive structure with a brand new 250-metre steel deck and a soaring circular smokestack like a silo, chrome turrets here and there, patched up in places by welders determined to get the job finished, scaffolding clinging to the sides of the ship – imagine such a battleship, gliding out of Saint-Nazaire on the night of 18 June and arriving in Casablanca on the 19th like an escaped prisoner. The *Jean-Bart* had been built in May 1936, in response to the one-upmanship between Germany and Italy, the London Disarmament Conference, the failure of diplomacy, the rising scale of tonnage, from cruiser to aircraft carrier, the planning of a naval battle with serious toys. Even at the planning stage the *Jean-Bart* was oversized. In dry dock, a specially dug trench was to be flooded on 6 March 1940 so that the ship could put out on 1 October. As the Germans advanced, three thousand five hundred labourers worked day and night to finish building the gigantic vessel. Shipbuilders from Brest Arsenal bustled about while the naval architect despaired that this was a race against time he could not possibly win. The boilers were hurriedly installed, together with the engines, the transmissions and several batteries of guns. Finally, on 6 and 7 June, twin propellers with blades as long as trucks were mounted, while underneath a thousand men laboured to dredge the channel so that the *Jean-Bart* would be able to put out from Saint Nazaire between the 18th and the 22nd, during spring tide. When the Germans marched into Rennes, work had to be speeded up; though only half-finished the battleship would have to put out, with the remaining parts loaded onto freighters to follow behind. Then followed a two-day symphony of hammers, the spark of oxy-acetylene torches, men in gleaming helmets clinging to the turrets, six thousand arms moving in sync. The captain, who was determined to put out that night or scuttle the ship, received orders to sail to Casablanca. Fighting broke out along the road to Nantes on the morning of the 18th. The *Jean-Bart*, protected by four block-houses, began to move as battle commenced. During the night, three tugboats had managed to pivot the ship twenty degrees and tow it into the channel. And then, at 4 a.m., still several hundred metres from the sea, and with the German army fast approaching in the darkness, the ship accidentally ran aground. Panic ensued. What had been planned as a precise manoeuvre quickly degenerated into chaos. The engineers took over, leaving the sergeants to crow and the captain to roar. They relocated the tugboats and, after forty-five minutes' work, managed to raise the faltering ship, tow it to the channel and, in the first glimmer of dawn, launch it into the Loire estuary with one last kick up the arse. At 4.30 a.m., the propellers and the Parsons turbines roared into life, and the *Jean-Bart* moved out of the harbour at a speed of twenty knots. Three German Heinkel bombers, flying at an altitude of a thousand metres, attacked the fleeing battleship; at 4.40 a.m. a deafening blast ripped through the air as a one hundred kilogram bomb exploded between the main battery turrets, damaging part of the bulkhead. At 6.30 a.m., the *Jean-Bart* rendezvoused with two destroyers, *Le Hardi* and *Mameluk*, which were to escort her to her destination, and took on fuel and water from the tanker *Tarn*. Now out of reach of German fire, the captain declined an offer from a British destroyer to escort it to England. This was the one triumph of the whole sorry debacle, it made the headlines of every newspaper, the navy was praised for its courage and daring, and much was made of the feats of the crew, who had managed to mount a gyroscopic compass on the open sea. When it arrived in Casablanca on 22 June, space was made in the harbour for the triumphant entry of this last gleaming vestige of the fleet. Here the *Jean-Bart* sat until its exploits were forgotten. It became just one more ship. Attempts were made to finish its construction, but these were quickly abandoned and it was painted yellow ochre.

In the shadow of the *Jean-Bart's* hull, on Delande dock, where huge bales of alfalfa were waiting to be loaded, there was a carnival of animals. Writhing, and bellowing in their harnesses, two bulls, a cow and three sheep were hoisted aboard the *Paul-Lemerle* by crane. The loading of the animals was treated like a sideshow, the Spanish children near the ship's rail watched as a panicked bull flailed and kicked at the empty air as it was winched aboard. Once on deck and released from its harness, the dazed animal lowered its head, twisting it to right and left, as longshoremen and sailors pressed around, one pulling its tail, another grabbing at its horns and laughing. And so it continued until all the cargo had been loaded. The animals were hosed down, the floor of the barn was scattered with straw and the feeders filled with hay, then they were shut up for the long voyage: animals destined for work or for slaughter, the steak on the hoof or the milk churn. A priest read verses from Genesis, as though blessing the ship.

And then they all took to the sea, with *an ocean to cross.*

Coast of Morocco
6 April 1941

As a fine theologian in the rabbinical tradition, Oskar Goldberg launched into a Midrash to dissect this episode from Genesis. No one could say whether it was the pestilential stench of the toilets or the tanks that sparked the argument, but he took the floor after the priest and offered a biblical exegesis on the management of waste and the three divisions of Noah's Ark: refuse and waste water were stored on the lowest of the three decks; humans and clean animals occupied the middle deck, while unclean animals and birds were relegated to the topmost area. In his argument, he made clear that he did not accept a differing interpretation which held that refuse was stored on the topmost deck, from where it was shovelled into the sea through a specially built trapdoor. From his description of it, the Ark was a rectangular box with a sloping roof. There were three decks on the *Paul-Lemerle* – of the seven pairs, there was no mention – but these were quickly divided up into neighbourhoods: la Villette, the place Rosa Luxembourg, Montparnasse, the Champs-Élysées and Belleville. The hold was no longer a refuge but a sweltering sauna where the straw mattresses rotted. The heat on deck was unbearable; every morning, the amateur meteorologists among the passengers worked out the wind direction, gauged the sun's height at noon and, sitting next to the gunwale for shelter, or pressed against one of the lifeboats where, using a tarpaulin or a sheet to protect them from the smells, the stagnant water, the barn and the communal bathrooms, they revelled in their good fortune and defended their kingdom. On the top deck next to the smokestack there was a table, though no one knew why. It was the only table. It overlooked the whole ship and afforded a bird's eye view of the teeming, swarming hive, framed by the waves and the surf. Here, the sun was stronger than elsewhere, the wind gusted up and down, blustered from east to west, irritating even the most patient, unnerving even the most placid. The absence of a bulwark further added to the discomfort and so the only strange animals that ventured here were intellectuals calmed by the mere presence of a table into forgetting their disagreements. The people's university of *Pôvre merle* opened its doors; here people debated everything and nothing, just as at Speaker's Corner in London, where any humble subject of the Crown equipped with a chair or a crate has the right to hold forth, to harangue, to talk about his recipe for scones or the ideal structure of government to anyone who chooses to listen. Here, at the table by the smokestack, there were talks about the Fourth International, the meaning of the novel, the art of developing photographic film, George Darien's novel *Le Voleur* and the poetry of Swift, the traditional body painting of Kadiweu women, the works of Picasso or the fascist treason of Dalí, in front of a small group of people of various nationalities who rose to the art of conversation, of discussion, of debate and dissent. Here, a person could put the world to rights, reinvent it, even dispute its existence or its form on condition that the argumentation and the skill of the speaker could offer a listener a moment of oblivion, a brotherhood of discourse, a gay science. All this studded with readings from novels, fragments of remembered poems, weaving an exquisite corpse of mingled memories. The meetings were convened at dusk, after dinner, as Montparnasse was lighting up. In turn, the artists, writers, actors and film directors, politicians and scientists sitting around a single table would speak, raising their voices to drown out the wind whistling in the rigging, the slapping of waves against the hull and the clamour drifting up from the lower decks. Sitting cross-legged on the deck, leaning against the smokestack or standing in the lifeboats, people listened to an episode from the Russian revolution, the portrait of a police chief in São Paulo, a tale of exile in Guernsey, the sacking of the Café Maldoror, the burning of the Reichstag. As the blue hour took hold, the trapezium of Orion appeared above a horizon of limp dunes and the sea merged into sand, the heat of the day began to dissipate, a gentle breeze swept along the deck, the evening could begin. André Breton offered an account of Marigny de Grilleau's treatise *The Laws of Chance*, whose subtitle promised to teach the assembled company to *Win scientifically – at Roulette or Trente-et-Quarante*. Breton said that he had bought it – by chance, naturally – in a bookshop on the place de la Vieille-Charité, and that the book had been published in 1926 by Moullot, a Marseilles publisher on the avenue du Prado. It bore a striking title and the promise of a powerful potion – the scientific jargon guaranteed as much. 'What is entailed is not less than mastering the rhythms and periodicity of the inevitable, for know this, my brothers, there is no such thing as chance! This is the great news! Everything is rhythm and periodicity!' Having read aloud the introduction, where there was talk of *units of profit*, *compensatory gains* and *convergent disparities*, Breton raised his voice and promised the dissolute an end to the hegemony of banks, a rebellion of gamblers, a fortune, my friends, a vast fortune! And, for a ship divided not only by Paris neighbourhoods but also by card games – bridge, belote, rami, tarot – the conference of 6 April was a subject dear to many people. No one understood a word of Grilleau's method, but there was much laughter. All they remember was that, in order to circumvent chance, it was important to keep a *personal notebook*. In a grave tone, the orator insisted: 'The notebook is everything, the gaming table is nothing; the tables do not matter since you have not been able to note down the numbers of every table.' Priceless.

After the stopover in Casablanca, Lévi-Strauss was introduced to the former guests of the Villa Air-Bel: Wifredo Lam, Helena Holzer, Victor Serge and his son Vlady. He proved a welcome novelty in a group where harmony was beginning to crumble. One had only to meet each of them to feel the weariness and the frustration, and sense in their categorical opinions on such-and-such a subject a hostility about to break out into open confrontation. Victor Serge was no longer prepared to take lessons in literature from Breton. Those things that had seemed bearable at the Château – his arm-chair revolutionary air, his bourgeois acts of sedition, his little games – seemed vain here on the ship, sometimes grotesque, often embarrassingly pedantic. Serge spent his time writing in his note-books, or trying to finish a novel. Breton was uncompromising, and whether in the Villa Air-Bel or here at the impromptu conferences on the upper deck, he was voluble on the subject of the novel: it was vital to destroy the counter-revolution of realism, the pathetic reactionary mediocrity eating away at literature, all the grotesque, dispassionate fabrications dressed up as truth; such things were symptomatic of a greater evil: the sense of seriousness. Breton cited examples of this *diseased* literature chosen at random; one would have had to be an idiot not to notice his attacks on Serge's work, which he considered inconsequential. These aggravations further added to Serge's nostalgia at being exiled and being separated from Laurette. In Casablanca, he had had a letter, which he read and reread, angry at his decision, at the love that had been ripped away. He could be seen pacing up and down, alone, melancholy, and soon he drifted away from Montparnasse and its café activism and trailed his dour mood on the foredeck at la Villette, joining in the spontaneous discussions between banished Germans, pro-Republican Spaniards and Basques, anti-communist Russians, Poles – in a sense he was moving from the Sorbonne of the skies to the Comintern of the seas, preoccupied by different controversies:

here, people argued bitterly over the invasion of Yugoslavia and the Molotov–Ribbentrop Pact. Sometimes, Serge would loiter at the place Rosa Luxembourg, watching without getting drawn into discussions while fleeing as members of the KPD hurled insults at each other or voted by a show of hands on motions of censure, condemnations in absentia. He listened to Kantorowicz, austere, implacable, presiding over the parliamentary sessions of stateless Germans. His son, Vlady, was bored to death, he had already tired of these old men, at the tender age of twenty, he carried his youth like a burden, and spent his time sketching. Breton had made fun of him, 'Nonsensical doodles,' he had announced having looked over the boy's shoulder. Background music. Vlady had threatened to smash his face, but his father had managed to calm him.

For his part, Breton could no longer hide his misery, he worried about the crossing, he loathed the conditions and was constantly complaining. He had stopped writing. From time to time he would argue with Jacqueline and she would stalk off, only to come back and stare at the sea and the stars with Aube. Breton was fascinated by the tales of Lévi-Strauss' expeditions and urged him to recount them to his companions. Lévi-Strauss was keenly aware of the mordant irony of Breton, who made no attempt to mask the boredom and the disappointments of the crossing, but accepted the task with good grace, used every ruse and wile, reeled off lists of places and studded his accounts with Hispanic and indigenous tones. He talked about the hierarchical social structure of the Bororo, which, to an ethnologist, was a prize for a king – Breton liked the expression – in that their complex social structure was directly encoded in the layout of their villages. A little like the structure of this rusty tub, Lévi-Strauss added sardonically. The Bororo live in circular villages – like a cartwheel, with the family huts set around the rim, the paths as spokes, in the centre a much larger hut, the men's house, an all-male club where single men sleep and married men work. He explained that Bororo society is matri-archal, the family huts belong to the women and, as a result, the men live with them. Their only place is the central club. Apart from this surprising layout, each hut or group of huts belongs to a par-ticular clan and the village is divided into two halves; a man who comes from one half can only marry a woman from the other, and

73

vice versa, such that a man born in one half grows up in his mother's hut, but, when he marries, he crosses this border and goes to live on the other side, in the hut belonging to his wife.

Lévi-Strauss sometimes ventured to describe his concept of the novel – perhaps he said 'novel', perhaps he did not use the word – one that would replace a linear journey with an internal geography, replace expression with the spontaneous drift of recollection, create a patchwork prose made up of interwoven memories, plagiarise itself, the willing victim of collage and of its own documentation. The conversation became more intense, though Lévi-Strauss did not quite know what Breton thought – and, when they parted company at the end of the evening, Lévi-Strauss promised to set his thoughts down on paper. There are subjects that can only be expressed in writing – and Breton agreed to respond.

The blue-black tinge of the ocean, the ultramarine sky, all cloaked in the thick mantle of a starry night. Half-dozing in his deckchair, wrapped up in his grey coat, Victor Serge was rereading the letter from Laurette. He could be seen toying with the slim envelope, sliding a fingernail into the slit, moving it over and back. He was thinking about their walk together along the banks of the Rhône, near the necropolis of Alyscamps, one breezy summer evening. As they strolled past the crumbling Roman walls, they entertained themselves by inventing new names for each other. What Serge most remembered was how much they had laughed. A frozen moment, a fragment wrested from the past and offered to the present. He had only to plunge into it to see Laurette's yellow dress running like a watercolour, her hand on her waist draped with a fold of fabric. The mistral whistling beneath the arches of the bridge at Trinquetaille, when the river grows still and the wind darts and turns on the surface of the water, and the ripples formed by a gust a moment earlier collide with those now being drawn upon the surface by the squall. The letter brought to Serge by Monsieur André Breton had reached the post office in Casablanca, by one of the Aéropostale planes at Camp Cazes. He whispered the first lines to himself:

My beloved Victor, I only received your letters from Oran today. I have just read them all one after another, I was so hungry to hear from you. Everything you say is so beautiful that I feel terribly overcome. I will never understand the miracle that made you love me. When I think that you might not have existed in my life, I am terrified, it is as though I came into the world blind and deaf. I live for you and I will try to be better to be worthy of you. The word is ugly and sounds a little stupid to my ear, I can find no other to express this feeling of 'undeserving' that I feel in spite of everything in the face of your love which is so great, so beautiful, so profound, this love that is in your image, which is simply yourself. It is curious, ever since I lost sight of you, the other day, on the harbour, I have been living in a sort of cloud. I am weightless, I float and, until now, I have found it impossible to take form, to focus on something. This is why I have not written a word, though not a moment has passed when I have not been thinking of you. Your letters bring something of your presence and make it possible for me to regain my self-control, to see more clearly within myself.

Off the coast of the Sahara, Rio de Oro
7 April 1941

Like an eager student who, having sweated blood and salt, has finally managed to wrest an essay from a sheet of blank paper and rushes to get it to his tutor, by mid-afternoon Lévi-Strauss had delivered his note to Breton. Having woken early and spent the day holed up in his cabin, he jotted down random ideas in his notebook, desperate to dazzle, outlining the supposed framework for a thesis on the meaning of a work of art and the place of the document. The single thing that is certain about this journey, as his mind prepared to parry blows or pre-empt contradictions, is that he wrote it in a single sitting, crossed out two words, and added a title in block capitals:

A COMMENTARY ON THE RELATION
BETWEEN WORKS OF ART
AND DOCUMENTS,
WRITTEN AND DELIVERED TO ANDRÉ BRETON
ON BOARD THE
CAPITAINE PAUL-LEMERLE

In the Manifesto of Surrealism A.B. defined artistic creation in terms of the absolutely spontaneous activity of the mind; such activity may well result from systematic training and the methodical application of a certain number of prescripts; nevertheless the work of art is defined – and defined exclusively – by its total liberty. It seems that on this point, A.B. has modified his position appreciably (in La Situation surréaliste de l'objet*). However, the relation that, according to him, exists between the work of art and the document is not perfectly clear. If it is obvious that every work of art is a document, does this imply, as suggested by a radical interpretation of his thesis, that every document is therefore a work of art? Starting from the position of the Manifesto, three interpretations are, in truth, possible:*

1) The artwork's aesthetic value depends exclusively on the degree of its spontaneity: the most valuable work (as a work of art) is defined by the absolute liberty of its production. As everyone, once suitably trained, is capable of attaining this complete liberty of expression, poetic production is open to all. The work's documentary value merges with its aesthetic value; the best document (as judged by its degree of creative spontaneity) is also the best poem. In principle, if not in fact, the best poem can not only be understood, but produced by anybody. One could then conceive of a humanity in which everyone, being trained in a sort of cathartic method, would be a poet.

Such an interpretation would abolish all the ascriptive privileges implied until now by the term talent. And if this interpretation does not deny the role of work and effort in artistic creation, it relegates them, at the very least, to the stage prior to creation proper – that of the difficult search for and application of the methods required to sustain free thought.

2) One can maintain the preceding interpretation but nevertheless note, a posteriori, that if all the works obtained from a large number of individuals are equivalent from a documentary point of view (that is, they all result from equally authentic and spontaneous mental activity), they are not at all equivalent from an artistic point of view, as some of them give pleasure, whereas others do not. As long as the work of art is defined as a document (that is, as any product of the mind's activity), one can admit the distinction without attempting to explain it (and without having the dialectics to do so). One will simply note that some individuals are poets and others are not, despite the fact that the conditions underlying their productions are exactly the same. Every work of art will still be a document, but there is room to distinguish between those that are also works of art and those that are just documents. As both are still defined as products of the mind, the distinction, being established only a posteriori, will have to be considered a primitive given, which, by definition, escapes all interpretation. The specificity of the work of art will be recognised without being able to be explained. It will become a 'mystery'.

3) Finally, the third interpretation, while still maintaining the funda- mental principle of the irreducibly irrational and spontaneous character of artistic creation, distinguishes between the document, the raw product of mental activity, and the work of art, which always involves an element of secondary elaboration. It is obvious, however, that such elaboration cannot be the work of rational and critical thought; the very possibility must be radically excluded. But it can be supposed that, under certain conditions and among certain people, spontaneous irrational thought may well become conscious of itself and become truly reflective – it being understood that such reflection is carried out in accordance with its own norms, and that these norms are as impermeable to rational analysis as the matter to which they are applied. This 'irrational intellection' leads to a certain elaboration of the raw material as expressed in the choices, omissions, and arrangement, them- selves a function of mandatory structures. If every work of art remains a document, as a work of art it transcends the documentary level, not just in terms of the quality of its raw expressiveness, but in terms of the value of its secondary elaboration. The latter, moreover, is 'secondary' only in relation to the mind's basic automatic functioning; relative to rational, critical thought, it presents the same irreducible, primitive character as the automatisms themselves.

The first interpretation does not accord with the facts; the second removes the problem of artistic creation from theoretical analysis. The third alone seems capable of avoiding a certain confusion (from which surrealism does not always appear to have escaped) between what is or is not, or is more or less, aesthetically valuable. All documents are not necessarily works of art, and all that constitutes a break may be equally valuable to the psychologist or militant, but not to the poet, even if the poet is also a militant. The work of someone mentally deficient has a documentary interest equal to the work of Lautréamont; it may even have greater polemical value. But the one is a work of art and the other is not, and there must be the dialectical means to account for their difference, just as one must also be able to account for the possibility that Picasso is a greater painter than Braque, that Apollinaire is a great poet and Roussel is not, or that Salvador Dalí is a great painter but an appalling writer. Judgements of this type, though they may differ from or

77

be contrary to my own, and the judgements given here are only examples, constitute the absolutely necessary conclusion to the dialectic between the poet and the theorist.

Since we have recognised that the fundamental conditions of the production of the document and the work of art are identical, these essential distinctions can only be acquired by displacing the analysis from the production to the product, and from the artist to his or her work.

6

An Ox on the Deck

―――

Every morning now a brief bulletin indicating the ship's position was posted by the central companionway. The *Paul-Lemerle* followed the shoreline, tracing the route of the Atlas Mountains. If anyone were looking for a new world, they would put ashore here, lost in a mirage, convinced they had set foot on Mars. Those leaning on the port rail were disheartened by the unchanging landscape, weathered and ochre, a stage set or painted world operated from behind the scenes; on the starboard side, where the false hope of the forbidden ocean stretched away, passengers gripped the rail, swaying, not daring to take the plunge. On the middle deck, people barracked the officers, threatening to mutiny at the rumours that they were to be put ashore at the camp at Dakar. They quickly quietened down, imprisoned as they were on this vessel, enveloped by a sky of admiral blue, a dark vault punctured by stars at midnight. The children goaded the cattle, poking sticks through cracks in the door of the barn. The more daring climbed onto the roof that threatened to collapse and, like spectators at a bullring, reached between two rickety planks to stroke the bull's horns and harry the animals, who could only bellow in frustrated rage. Despite these recent additions to the cargo, the food on board had not changed, and in fact meat had vanished from the menu, so what was ladled into the mess tins was only vegetables. Only after meeting with a special delegation representing a majority of the passengers did the captain and his crew agree to slaughter one of the cattle.

The execution took place at dawn. People watched, eager and impatient, as they might a general strike. The ship's cook stunned the animal, slit it from throat to tail, then strung it up, the head half-hanging off from the deep wound left by an uncommonly long knife, suspended from a makeshift gallows of ropes and pulleys between the toilets and the washrooms. The assembled children screamed themselves hoarse, darted forward to slap the dead animal and then ducked back into the crowd, proud and terrified, they dipped fingers in the palette of blood-red that dripped onto the deck and, with a disgusted pout, wiped them clean. It was like a village fair, the great game of life and death played out in a tiny arena. The hulking kitchen boy, whose head seemed too small for his body, pushed through the crowd to the cheers of the children, picked up the basin under the bloody head and, as the highlight of the spectacle, drank great gulps of the hot blood. He wiped his face with the back of his hand which he smeared on his dirty apron. Standing in a semicircle behind the bales of hay, the children in the front row and their parents applauded the butcher as they might a circus strong man in leopard skin effortlessly lifting a pair of huge dumb-bells. From the ship's rail to the foredeck to the bridge, people ecstatically watched the animal bleed out.

Villa Cisneros
9 April 1941

Sixteenth day at sea. Like a victim dangling from a gibbet, body rotting, entrails spilling out, the cow hung there, day and night, until it had been cut up by hand. Hanging in a cramped space between the two mouldering wooden walls of the toilets and the showers, saturated and impregnated by the smell, like wine in a cask, the beast seemed to move, shimmering with the blowflies that feasted on its entrails, the wasps that darted around the carcass, drunk on putrid flesh. The stench quickly made life unbearable for the passengers on deck; those same people who, the day before, had pleaded for this sacrifice were now protesting and demanding that the carcass be tossed overboard. Standing at the foot of the ladder, Breton contemplated the *grotesque meat*, a nautical variation of a *slaughtered ox*. Was he thinking of the story of the meat delivered to Soutine's studio on the rue du Saint-Gothard? It was said that he greeted it with the stifled cry of a child and the joyful smile of a butcher slitting the throat of a goose and bleeding it. Or was he trying to mentally recompose a painting in the Louvre, Rembrandt's *Slaughtered Ox* – a butchered still life – like a bed frame hung upside down, legs in the air, broken bones painted in thick impasto – evisceration in a palette of ochre and crimson – and, peering around the door, the head of a servant, a face ripped from blackest night. Amid the tangle of ladders and cranes, he stared at the slaughtered cow, which dangled helplessly, framed by a blue as vivid as the pigments on the chiselled geometric tiles set in circular mosaics known as *zellige*. He stood there, lost in an association of ideas and distant echoes. He thought for a moment, then wrote in his notebook:

A slaughtered ox, still hanging from the night before, the pennants in the stern of the ship, the rising run.

Off the coast of Cape Verde
10 April 1941

He handed over a thick envelope and went off to bed. It was a response to the note, a single sheet folded in two; a few underlined words stood out in the dense, hurried handwriting. Lévi-Strauss rushed back to his cabin, lay on his berth and read it straight through. He reread it, paused for a moment, thought. In the middle of the war, aboard one of the few ships sailing for the Americas, he had begun an epistolary correspondence, hand-delivered letters about the relationship between aesthetic beauty and absolute originality. It occurred to him that only danger can offer such joyous reversals.

RESPONSE BY ANDRÉ BRETON
TO THE HANDWRITTEN NOTE
OF 7 APRIL 1941

The fundamental contradiction that you are pointing to has not escaped my attention: it remains despite my efforts, and those of several others, to reduce it (but this doesn't really worry me because I realise that it contains the secret to that forward movement on which surrealism's survival depends). Yes, naturally, my positions have varied considerably since the first manifesto. One should understand that in such programmatic texts, which do not tolerate the expression of any doubt or reservation, and whose essentially aggressive character excludes all nuance, my thought tends to take on an extremely brutal, that is, simplistic character foreign to its real nature.

The contradiction that you find so striking is the same one, I believe, that Caillois reacted so strongly to (I told you about this). I have tried to respond in a text entitled 'La Beauté sera convulsive' (Minotaure, no. 5) and reprinted at the beginning of L'Amour fou. *Indeed, I find myself pulled in two very different directions – and after all, why not? For I am not alone in this respect. The first leads me to search for the pleasure the work of art gives (the word 'pleasure', which you used, is the only really appropriate word, for when I consider my own reactions, they appear to me as para-erotic). The second, which may or may not manifest itself independently of the first, leads me to interpret the work of art as a function of the general need for knowledge. These two impulses, which I am distinguishing on paper, cannot always be easily separated (they tend, for example, to merge in many a passage of* Une Saison en enfer).

It goes without saying that, if every work of art can be considered from a documentary perspective, the converse is by no means true.

On examining your three interpretations one after the other, I have no difficulty in telling you that I feel close only to the last one. A few words, however, regarding the first two:

1) *I am not certain that a work's aesthetic value depends on its degree of spontaneity. I was much more concerned with its authenticity than its beauty and the definition of 1924 testifies to this: 'A dictate of thought ... beyond any aesthetic or moral preoccupation.' It cannot have escaped your notice that, had I omitted this last part of the sentence, I would have deprived the authors of automatic texts of a part of their liberty. It was imperative that, from the beginning, they be sheltered from all*

such judgements, if one hoped to prevent them from being subjected to any a priori constraint, and acting accordingly. This, unfortunately, has not always been the case (in my letter to Rolland de Reneville, published in Point du jour, I deplored the minimal alterations required to turn an automatic text into a poem – but it is easy to proclaim one's concerns while abstracting them from the work under consideration).

2) I am not so sure as you that large qualitative differences exist between the various texts obtained by entirely spontaneous means. It has always appeared to me that the main reason why so many of these texts are so mediocre is that many people find it impossible to place themselves in the conditions necessary for the experience. They are satisfied with a rambling, disconnected discourse which, with its absurdities and sudden shifts in subject matter, gives them the illusion of success; but the signs are easily detected which suggest that they haven't really 'gotten their feet wet', and that their supposed authenticity is a bit of a sham. If I say that I am not so sure as you, it is largely because I do not understand how the self (which is common to all) is distributed among different individuals (whether equally or, if unequally, to what degree?). Only a systematic investigation, and one that provisionally leaves artists aside, can teach us anything about this matter. But I am hardly interested in establishing a hierarchy of surrealist works (contrary to Aragon who once said: 'If you write dreadful rubbish in an authentically surrealistic manner, it is still rubbish') – nor, as I have made clear, a hierarchy of romantic or symbolist works. It is not just that my classification of the latter would be fundamentally different from those now current; my major reason for objecting to these classifications is that they cause us to lose sight of these movements' profound, historical significance.

3) Does the work of art always require secondary elaboration? Yes, undoubtedly, but only in the very broad sense you give it when speaking of 'irrational intellection' – though one wonders at what level of consciousness this elaboration occurs? We, at any rate, would still be in the pre-conscious. Shouldn't the productions of Hélène Smith, when in a trance state, be considered works of art? And if someone demonstrated that certain of Rimbaud's poems were simply day dreams, would you enjoy them less? Or would you relegate them to the drawer labelled 'documents'? I still find the distinction arbitrary. And it becomes positively specious in my eyes when you oppose the poet Apollinaire to the 'non-poet' Roussel, or the painter Dalí to the writer Dalí. Are you sure

that the first of these judgements is not too traditional, that it is not indebted to an antiquated conception of poetry? I do not consider Dalí a great 'painter', for the excellent reason that his technique is manifestly regressive. With Dalí, it is truly the man that interests me, and his poetic interpretation of the world. Again, I cannot associate myself with your conclusion (but you already knew this). I have other, more pressing reasons for not accepting it. These reasons, I insist, are of a practical nature (adhesion to the mater. histor.). If a loosening of psychological responsibility is necessary to obtain the initial state on which everything depends, so be it, but afterwards, responsibility, both psychological and moral. The progressive identification of the conscious 'me' with the totality of its concretions (this is badly put), understood as the theatre within which the self is called on to produce and reproduce itself. A tendency to synthesise the pleasure principle with the reality principle (I must be excused for still remaining at the limits of my thinking on this matter); the agreement at any price between the art work and the extra-artistic behaviour. Anti-valeryism.

On the open sea
11 April 1941

They called him doctor, or *maître*, or simply Monsieur Smadja, with the deference accorded to those innately blessed with the qualities of ease and power. The captain was even seen greeting him with a cry of *Smadja*, and a clap on the back. Some spoke of him as a man on the run, others of a man making a business trip. Some went so far as to imagine he was on an active mission, and the very ambiguity surrounding his circumstances had people dubbing him a double or even a triple agent, though without knowing for which power – an intermediary for the Tunisian political party Neo Destour, an intelligence agent, an informant in the pay of the Germans, a spy keeping watch over passengers and cargo for Pétain, or an ally of de Gaulle surreptitiously working for the British. He moved in shady circles like a chameleon, taking tea with the industrialists, dressing in the latest fashion, he was a coveted bridge partner, friendly and polite yet mischievous, a ladies' man, a cigar aficionado, a regular evening visitor to Montparnasse where he regaled the assembled company with his keen wit; he was respected by the surrealists, a confidant of the taciturn Victor Serge, he was equally likely to be seen chatting in the officers' mess at dawn, staring out to sea with the captain, strolling along the quays of Oran or Casablanca, shaking hands with a café owner, flattering an admiral. Henri Smadja as we shall call him, though his name appeared on no register and cannot be known for certain, was a man whom everyone mistrusted yet who was a friend to everyone. A living paradox and a character from a novel. Although no one knew quite how, a place had been waiting for him in one of the two available cabins, he had turned the upper berth into a study-cum-bedroom, next to a young scientist and a demobbed white Creole heading home. His suitcase, briefcase or attaché case lay open on the bed, a pillow propped up in one corner, books lined up along the porthole and his notes, contracts and certificates spread out over the rough blanket. He was enigmatic, adapting to every discussion, subtly changing his own story, he seemed incapable of giving an uninterrupted account of his journey. Everything was revealed in snatches, a trivial anecdote here, a minor indiscretion there, and all the while he was asking you about your plans. He did not admit to anything, did not respond to questions, but never caused offence, he simply steered the conversation elsewhere, swiftly, with a digression so subtle that his interlocutor forgot the question they had asked. He was neither a liar nor a hypocrite, he was something much greater, he was Smadja. He was a little Paul Batala, the character played by Jules Berry in *The Crime of Monsieur Lange*, cunning, wily, the sort of man whose vices one would overlook because he deigned to spend time with you. A Jew from Tunisia, he had been a doctor, a wealthy landowner, an olive grower. He had qualified as a lawyer and, disdaining boredom and idleness, had launched himself into politics in a manner favoured by many men of few convictions, he had founded a newspaper and appointed himself defender of the freedom of the press and of opinion. *La Presse de Tunisie* was pro-colonial and against the Front Populaire. But for a man who wishes to win at the ballot box, a newspaper is not enough, you need a football team. Football taught Camus about morality and Smadja about populism. This was why he became president of Union Sportive Tunisienne, the oldest football club in the country, a multi-denominational team which, during his stewardship, won three championship titles and five national cups. He became a member of the Grand Council of Tunisia. After the abolition of the Crémieux decree in late 1940, he was forced to close La Presse de Tunisie and resign as president of Union Sportive Tunisienne. He was leaving only to return, and so he claimed he would be sorting out his business affairs in New York in the coming weeks. Nonetheless, the other passengers could not help but wonder about the cunning of this man who moved about the ship without revealing his credentials, went ashore despite having no passport, came and went from the captain's cabin, effortlessly shifted from one language to another, from the Arabic of the dock workers to the Catalan of refugees. To those who credited him with great power, Smadja was a spy. To others he was simply a shark, an unscrupulous travelling salesman. Lévi-Strauss liked him but did not trust him. Victor Serge thought likewise. Both had experienced a similar scene, a matter of paintings and a suitcase, though they differed as to the name of the artist. Smadja had first brought Serge to his cabin and, dropping his voice to a confidential whisper, said: 'You're about to see something marvellous, I promise you!' From beneath a pile of shirts in his suitcase, he took a small painting which he had bought second-hand in Algiers. It was genuine, he insisted, a masterpiece he had acquired for five hundred francs ... Serge recognised it as a portrait of Berthe Morisot, *a recumbent woman dressed in warm blues: it's a Manet ... dated 1873.* Then, even as he was boasting about selling the painting for ten times, a hundred, even a thousand times the price he had paid, he pleaded poverty and claimed to be saving culture: *Five hundred francs, five thousand, or five million, I don't give a damn, but to buy, to save a painting, to take joy in this, to save a moment of its soul at the moment when the great ship 'Civilisation' risks sinking straight to the bottom with all its Sistines and its Curie laboratories is good, Doctor, is splendid!* While they agreed about the identity of the model, Lévi-Strauss was convinced that it was a Degas. They went on to discuss Manet's *Olympia*, the artist to be seen in the painting, the electrified expression of the black cat on the bed. They did not discuss Soutine or Rembrandt.

7

Field Prawns and Flying Fish

———

On the open sea
12 April 1941

They rode out a storm, this was a warning. The ship was heavy and antiquated, it pitched and rolled, the waves crashed over it, cleaning out the barn and washing the deck. Three reckless boys defied the ocean, clinging to the ropes, a woman who some claimed was mad spent the storm sleeping in her deckchair and was found in the early hours, soaked to the skin. Some said they had heard over the radio that a British cargo ship, the *Saint-Helena*, had been sunk off the coast of Freetown, torpedoed by a German U-boat. The bluish water gushed into the hold; a dull thud seemed to be coming from the propeller blades. The officers laughed at the general panic; what the passengers saw as an inundation, they spoke of as a drop in the bucket, nothing more. Once in the tropics, one sailor warned, once caught up in the doldrums, in the unsettling equatorial calms where the sky is streaked with bizarre clouds and water becomes sluggish as oil, *an enclosed space distinct from the open sea*, they would lose all sense of time. A decompression chamber from which all air has been forced, a place where the sins of one world could be expiated, and the impetus of another sucked in. The wind would steadily grow stronger, whipping the rough sea into fearsome waves and yawning dips, vicious surges – the hurricane season was over, and the crossing would be smooth as long as the sea was afforded the respect due to it. The sailor reeled off a list of words that were never to be used on board, at least by the crew, and ancient traditions dating back to the caravels. The use of the word ropes was forbidden, instead they were called shrouds, lines, wires or stays – the word rope was used only when hanging mutineers, and even then was called the hanged man's rope. He explained the rituals and the customs, the legends of phantom seamen or of vanished sailing ships, of the Roaring Forties and the Furious Fifties. Easter was coming, it was Good Friday, and on Sunday the bells would toll and the rabbits gambol. 'Oh, Good God, not rabbits! If any animal is cursed it's the rabbit, it is the bane of every sailor. We never mention it, and if we do we call it by another name, the long-eared animal, the hare's cousin, the racing cyclist, the *zébro*, the *pollop*, even the field prawn. To us, the rabbit is like a black cat, it's worse than having a priest or a woman aboard. It dates back to the days of ships when cargo was lashed down with jute rope, them little bastards would gnaw away, the cargo would come loose and rattle around the hold, destabilising the ship so much it sometimes sank. On the old wooden boats, they would eat away at the oakum caulking between the planks ... So, you can forget about Easter at sea ... But we'll have our own fun on Sunday, it'll be like a carnival on Sunday, you'll cross the line!' For those who had never crossed the Atlantic, he explained what it meant to cross the line, he talked about the Feast of Neptune. 'It's like a carnival, you'll see, even the captain joins in, we all dress up, we dance and sing until nightfall.' Those passengers initiated on previous voyages recounted the curious madness, the dances of Queen Amphitrite, the songs of King Neptune, the antics of the judge and the bishop of the line, the phoney astronomer and the hordes of noble savages, the baptism in the pool or the anointing with the fire hose, the treasure hunt and the tug of war, the embarrassing ordeals and, after dark, the music hall turns, the songs, the sketches, the shaggy dog stories and the skits. War or no war, this would be fun, they thought, after all dancing in the fire is the ultimate defiance of misfortune. Down in the hold, they organised the festivities, the parades and the scenes from operettas, divided up the tasks, building a pool using tarpaulins, constructing the judge's bench, making paper crowns and cardboard tridents, cooking up papier-mâché to fashion the huge sceptres.

They re-emerged at noon.

First flying fish. They leap out of the waves and fly over them with a long wavy movement, zigzagging just like birds. Probably hunting or being hunted.

Yesterday was winter, tomorrow will be summer.

The Doldrums
13 April 1941

The time was set in the wheelhouse. The operator calculated their position and, confident of his prediction, announced that the *Paul-Lemerle* would cross the Tropic of Cancer at about 5 p.m. The officers of the watch set about organising the afternoon's festivities. A crowd had gathered to listen to their instructions, the Poles interpreted for the Germans, who translated for the French, who had already understood and were translating for the Spaniards, and though this game of Chinese whispers was muddled and confused, to the sailors' astonishment, the instructions were observed to the letter. Within the space of a single morning, half the cargo ship had been transformed to look like a theatre, with the stage positioned in the prow, the makeshift pool was being filled with seawater, the clatter of the pumps adding to the general commotion. Overwhelmed by the sun and the humidity, Anna Seghers watched the women bustling on the deck. The Spanish women had refused to participate, unanimously declaring that they would not sing a note until the men they had been forced to leave back at the harbour were returned to them, or even that they would never sing again. The barrels, the children and the dogs were relegated to the bow of the ship, as one might clear the living room on the night before Christmas so that children do not see the presents being brought in. The Spanish women agreed to look after the unruly brood. The audience booed the arrival of Neptune and Amphitrite, the cherubim trooped in to the crack of fireworks. After lunch, the festivities picked up pace, the celebration was to be impressive, the big top was raised and a hulking man from

Marseilles, enlisted to act as ringmaster, reviewed the acts one by one. High above, hanging from a turret, a man who quickly earned the nickname the Flying Czech was whirling in the air, attached to one of the harnesses for the cattle. He lowered himself by means of a pulley, which he managed to handle without gloves, then set himself whirling, spreading the tarpaulin like wings on either side: *zzzziiiiiiiiipppppppppp*, came the shrill sound of the wires. The sky grew pale and, in an instant, it clouded over, heavy raindrops spattered the deck and soaked the bridge only to instantly evaporate on the planks and in the air. Rainwater diluted the seawater; people shook their clothes dry. Below, teenagers in swimming trunks were splashing each other in the pool. Every part of the ship was busy preparing for the ceremony. Near the hatches, in the costume department, the finishing touches were being made to the judge's robes, a red scarf trimmed with buttons from a blue blazer, while others worked on Neptune's robe and baggy breeches. Over by the hold, phalanxes of sculptors and carpenters were working busily, Wifredo Lam was sandpapering a piece of timber, building a small puppet theatre. Further back, in steerage, the workshop making wigs was in turmoil, they had run out of hemp to make Neptune's whiskers, and the resulting beard made him look like Santa Claus, or rather – with his paper crown set on his head – like the character of St Nicolas in Alsace.

A treasure hunt was launched. The only treasure that mattered aboard ship was not silver, gold or jewellery, but packs of cigarettes and tins of sardines, which had been hidden all over the ship, like Easter eggs. People raced in all directions, scouring the hold, running their fingers under the gunwale, and, on the topmost deck, between the struts of the lifeboats. The winners paraded about with cigarettes dangling from their lips, or dipping two fingers in the oil, gorging themselves on sardines. The bell tolled and a sailor shouted that they had just crossed the line, as though it were the finish line of the boat race on the Thames. The children were let loose and the ceremony began. Stepping from the gangway, Neptune advanced, triumphant, regal, on the arm of Amphitrite, dressed in a white dressing gown, followed by a parade of screaming children, while the tolling bell marked time. The landlubbers among the passengers waited by the makeshift pool to be 'baptised', flanked by the judge and the bishop, who were to weigh their merits. Nymphs and satyrs scrambled down the ladders to the deck. Sailors hunted down the wayward souls and marched them to the front of the ship: the judgement of one's soul was no laughing matter. The ceremony began. The hulking man from Marseilles solemnly called for silence, growling in a deep bass tone that echoed around the arena: 'Ladies and gentlemen!' Then he reminded the assembled company of the rules – all ranks and titles were hereby abolished in this carnival, sailors and passengers gathered together in the teeming crowd, like the court of Olympus. In order to cross the line, tribute had to be paid to the god of the sea, and the newcomers had to be baptised – plunged into the pool of water. One by one, they were called to the bar, one by one they were plunged into the water, one by one they were deemed worthy. Even the bald Viennese lawyer was tossed into the pool. Soon the drenched outnumbered the dry, and when there was no one left to baptise, they grabbed the captain, dressed in full regalia, and gently, respectfully, dunked him under the water. Perhaps Lévi-Strauss was intrigued by this unusual syncretism which brought together the gods of Mount Olympus, the clergy of the Christian God and the temporal powers of captain and judge. Perhaps he was even reminded of Arnold van Gennep's *Rites of Passage*, which he had taught to students in São Paulo in 1935 as part of a module on elementary aspects of social and religious life. Perhaps he had even leaned over to Serge, or to Breton, and offered a running commentary, explaining how, in the ancient world, city gates, milestones and boundaries were considered sacred, and to cross them entailed a series of precautions. Just as here, it was a passage from one world to another. Perhaps he told the story of the king of Sparta who, as he was setting out for war, stopped at the city boundary in order to make sacrifice. Only then was he prepared to enter the intervening space where battle could take place. With this leitmotif, this image of crossing a threshold, he would perhaps have concluded with some words about the notion of the intangible, a concept common among civilisations, among cultures, through the centuries, and one that made it possible to compare rituals which, at first glance, seemed to have little in common, like marriage ceremonies, baptism, circumcision, purification rituals, totemic cultures, shamanic initiations, fertility rites and this festival of Neptune.

As night fell, the passengers put on clean clothes, they combed the hair of the boys, tied the girls' hair up in ribbons, dressed in their Sunday best for the première, for the one-and-only performance of the bridge theatre. The stage was lit by a spotlight, a single dazzling bulb. Curt Courant, who had worked as cinematographer with Fritz Lang, with Tourneur and Renoir, no less, acted as lighting technician, using a confusing battery of gadgets – for a follow spot, he used a side light, a powerful beam that cast shadows on the taut canvas, giving the illusion of a burlesque theatre. Crouching on the deck, the audience witnessed a series of improvised sketches in various languages, Bulgarian, English, Russian, a monologue in French intelligible only for its fury, a Russian choir sang the 'Volga Boat Song', three sea shanties, a Spanish girl recited a poem, two Serbs – a doctor and a diplomat in ordinary life – parodied life aboard the *Paul-Lemerle*, mimicking the bullying and the orders in a pidgin French composed of onomatopoeias, and amid the howls of laughter, came the imperatives: 'PAYPERS PLEEZE! ZE-VIZA AND ZE SAFE CONDUK!' Or 'ZOUPE'S UP!' A couple of Marx Brothers, the stars of the evening, were greeted with wild applause in the finale. A Polish man ended the performance with a melody played on the accordion, a lament that stretched away into the distance.

8

Anna's Jars

___

On the open sea
14 April 1941

In that moment, what do you take with you? When, overnight, you are forced to pack a bag and leave behind a world to which you cannot hope to return? What is the most precious object, the one for which you would run back despite the dangers, or pay the thief to buy back his haul? Would you realise that the moment was irrevocable? Would you instantly know what it should be, this thing? This was the question that obsessed Anna Seghers; what was at stake in the heat of the moment, she would explain, beyond the common notion of ownership, is some shard of truth from which you cannot hide. Though the idea was nebulous, it was crucial. A typewriter, a deed of ownership, a painting, a piece of jewellery, a photograph, a watch, a letter, an egg cup – the object to be saved did not matter. If you were being forced into exile and could choose only one, which would it be? She imagined that the list of two hundred and fifty objects of the two hundred and fifty passengers aboard would be an anthology of stories, and retracing the path of each would be an epic.

She remembered the morning of 10 June 1940, the empty streets of Bellevue, the mist hanging over the Seine, the crackle of the news bulletins on the radio: Italy had joined the war, more refugees were taking to the roads. Her husband, Rodi, had been arrested in April and held at Roland Garros stadium before being deported to the camp at Vernet-d'Ariège, in the Pyrenees. At about eleven o'clock that morning, Jeanne Stern, who had just come back from the editorial offices of *L'Ordre*, told her: 'Anna, the German army has broken through the last lines of defence. Within days, they will be marching through Paris. You have to leave right now, take the children and try to get across the Loire to safety.' That very afternoon, Anna, Ruth and Pierre set off on foot, carrying their backpacks, heading for Orléans. In their luggage, enough clothes for ten days, a gas mask and a blanket. Pierre had brought his pocket telescope, a red silk cushion cover embroidered with a yellow and orange dragon, and a copy of Selma Lagerlöf's *The Wonderful Adventures of Nils*; Ruth had brought a rag doll she chewed so often that it was threadbare; Anna had packed her notebooks and a handful of books, Homer's *Iliad* and *Odyssey* in a German translation by Johann Heinrich Voss, *Lord Jim* and *Typhoon* by Joseph Conrad. Only when they were already some distance away did she realise – as little Pierre, in short trousers, guided them along the country roads, Michelin map in hand – that she had left the manuscript for *The Seventh Cross* in her desk drawer. As a precaution, she had already sent a copy to Franz Carl Weiskopf in New York, begging him to find a publisher, another to Wieland Herzfelde, and a third had been entrusted to Rodi's friend, Fernand Delmas, so that he could translate a ten-page excerpt. The last copy she had hidden in the apartment of Bruno Frei, who had been sent to Vernet internment camp. Rather than reassuring her, these copies of her novel became the reason for her concern. What if they all disappeared, she thought, would the book be lost for ever? She worried, though she did not say anything; after a day spent walking, her home back in Meudon seemed so far away. Anna had always thought of this novel dedicated to anti-fascists – like the many people being persecuted in her own country – as a book of exile, an allegory penned with anger and nostalgia. Anger, as she gathered first-hand accounts of persecution from among the community of exiles, heard the relentless barbarism, the dull, constant terror. One of these accounts had provided her with the central plot and the title for the novel. According to the story, the commandant of a concentration camp had had recaptured prisoners lashed to crosses. From the account of those crucified as an example to others, she wove the story of the escape of seven German political prisoners interned in an extermination camp in the Rhineland. One, a circus acrobat, seeks refuge on a rooftop and is gunned down in a hail of bullets; another, an elderly farmer, collapses from exhaustion and emotion when he once again sees his hilltop village; a third, a timid middle-class citizen, surrenders to the Gestapo; in the novel, only one fugitive manages to escape and cross the Dutch border, only one cross remains empty; this is the seventh cross, *Das Siebte Kreuz* – hope.

After days spent travelling, having run out of food and been overtaken by the Wehrmacht offensive, Anna Seghers gazed around, bewildered, at the hundreds of motionless vehicles, the tanks abandoned in the fields, the bicycles weighed down like hay carts, and decided that she and her children should go back to Paris. They hitched a ride back in a trailer towed by a military truck. Anna read the last chapter of the *Odyssey* to her children, when Penelope shows Odysseus the bed carved into a living olive tree. The sun was shining, the wind ruffled their hair, they lay between the sacks in the juddering flat bed of the truck, they savoured the taste of adventure. They entered Paris by the porte d'Italie, drove down the deserted avenue des Gobelins and eventually ended up in a hotel near the Odéon, a tiny room on the rue Saint-Sulpice. Anna Seghers knew that the Gestapo had a warrant out for her, but under her pen name – so she had a head start. To her neighbours in Meudon, they had been Netty and László Radványi, a Hungarian couple who called each other *Netty* and *Tschibi*. Anna quickly sent Pierre to get the manuscript she had given to Bruno Frei. He came back shamefaced and told her that the building had been destroyed by the first German bomb to fall on Paris. There was talk of apartments being looted, whole buildings being requisitioned. Someone urgently needed to get back to their house in Bellevue, to fetch some winter clothes and the original manuscript of *The Seventh Cross*. Else, a Polish friend, went with Pierre. They came back with a suitcase full of sweaters, trousers and blankets, but no manuscript. A neighbour, a former factory owner from Sèvres, had explained that the Gestapo had been to the house. Else was terrified at the thought they were being followed, that she might be arrested, and she decided to burn the manuscript in the kitchen stove 'so it didn't fall into the hands of the Nazis,' she said, apologetically. Anna wept as she listened. You can only rely on yourself, she thought, furious that she had not remembered to take a copy when there was still time, for not going back to Meudon herself. The only other copy in France was one she had given to Delmas to translate. Secretly, she hoped that he had already crossed the line. Fortunately, Delmas's copy was still in Vésinet. They stayed there for three days, playing cards and planning their escape. Anna vowed never again to be parted from the manuscript. She decided they would go to a little village in the Pyrenees near Camp Vernet, free her husband Rodi, and get the hell out of this damn country. She stuffed the manuscript into the bottom of a bag which she put at the bottom of her suitcase, believing this would ward off evil and save it from the flames. Getting to Le Vernet was a difficult endeavour, they tramped through fields and followed a woodcutter's trail to get to Moulins, then, recklessly, they caught the train to Vichy via Saint-Germain-des-Fosses, Limoges, Agen and Toulouse. They alighted at the gare de Pamiers, a few kilometres from Vernet. Anna was granted permission to visit Rodi. The camp was teeming with wave after wave of immigrants, Spanish Republicans, veterans of the International Brigades, anti-fascists, *undesirable aliens* fleeing Spain and Germany, trapped in the foothills of the Pyrenees. Among Rodi's companions were the writer Friedrich Wolf, Max Friedemann and of course Bruno Frei, who discovered from Anna's lips that his apartment, his books, his letters had all been destroyed.

The family moved into 4, rue du Portail Rouge, known as the house of 'Madame Jeanne', their host a fortune teller from Pamiers. With the children now going to the village school, Anna went back to her old ways, she would sit in the village café with a coffee and a glass of water and hours of peace and quiet. She devoured books two at a time, and gradually forced herself to write again to deal with the endless nights. Noises never bothered her and conversations did so only if she was the subject. She borrowed the multiple volumes of *La Comédie Humaine* from the library and spent hours dissecting the narrative framework, obsessed with Balzac's ability to isolate an event, place it in the centre of a novel and scatter his characters around it. She also immersed herself in the language, copying out long passages from *La Maison Nucingen* or from *La Fille aux yeux d'or (The Girl with Golden Eyes). Ah! once for all, this drama is neither a fiction nor a romance! All is true, – so true, that every one can discern the elements of the tragedy in his own house, perhaps in his own heart.* And now she was toying with the idea for a novel – just as she had used allegory to convey the brutality of the Nazi persecution, now she worked tirelessly, compiling notes and newspaper clippings for a novel about the flight, this exodus. She would trace the paths of an enforced exile from one country to another, caught in a moment as in a mousetrap. The search warrants, the lost manuscripts rediscovered, the paintings hidden or stolen, the libraries abandoned and burnt, the loathsome demarcation lines, the borders. *'Acculer': to be driven back to a place or a situation from which retreat is impossible. The involuntary backward motion of a ship propelled by the wind, the tide.* She noted the definition of a French verb whose various meanings seemed to best reflect the feeling of helplessness they all felt, a term redolent of hunting and of ships. German, she thought, allowed the writer much more flexibility, for it offers a glorious complexity to those who can master the language, a treasure trove of words that give flesh to nebulous impressions without approximation or circumlocution; she kept a list of long portmanteau words that circumscribe the inexpressible by appending one word to another to form a whole. As she explained to the café owner, there was a German word to describe the irrepressible autumnal pleasure of kicking over a pile of fallen leaves, *Herbstlaubrittvergnügen* – a combination of four words: autumn-leaves-kick-pleasure. There is a word for everything, she thought, as she searched for a faithful description of the absurd situation of the exiles fleeing Germany one day, welcomed in France the next, imprisoned first and foremost because they were German, the enemy within, then threatened with the camps, pursued and hunted down because they opposed a regime now allied to Germany. An untranslated portmanteau word: exile-welcome-enemy-prison-transit-flight.

Transit is permission given to pass through a country, providing it has been ascertained that one has no intention of staying. In December, after much bureaucratic wrangling, Anna Seghers received a Mexican visa and an exit visa 'to travel to the United States and Mexico, via

97

Marseilles'. On Christmas Day, László Radványi was transferred to Milles, a camp for foreigners who had been promised a visa, near Aix-en-Provence. In Marseilles, at the Mexican Consulate, Gilberto Bosques stamped her passport – issued in her real name, stating that she was Anna Seghers, writer. Her notes became more detailed: *to be driven back to port* – in the hotels in Belsunce, the restaurants in Noailles, Le Brûleur de loups at le Ventoux, waiting for a visa, for a ship, for some means of escape; *driven back to port, driven to suicide.* It was here that she learned of the death of Walter Benjamin, of Ernst Weiss, the story of their manuscripts, lost, found, saved. This, surely, was the thing to which she had to bear witness. A novel like the way of the cross, a series of pilgrimages to embassies and consulates, the endless waiting, like purgatory, in corridors or in shipping company offices. She finally put it all into a single word, *Transit*, written at the top of a loose sheet of paper. *Those fleeing all the real and imagined dangers of this world.* She began to write in the present tense, Marseilles would be the blind alley where her narratives would intersect. The story that she had decided she wanted to write could be heard in waiting rooms, in seedy cafés, in the offices of refugee associations. Feverishly, she filled a diary, convinced that she could draw on it for the material for *Transit* – that, once the plot was fleshed out, she would need only to check the timelines and the pronouns, change the names of the characters and the streets – the rue Weiss, a tiny alley on which the Hôtel Aumage was located, would become the rue Weidel. Whole sections of their journey would provide the basis for this novel of exile, which she dared to hope would have a happy ending. Two days before sailing on the *Paul-Lemerle*, the family had dinner with Kantorowicz and his wife Friedel in a pizza restaurant on the harbour – *Pizza is really a remarkable baked item. It's round and colourful like an open-face fruit pie. But bite into it and you get a mouthful of pepper. Looking at the thing more closely, you realise that those are not cherries and raisins on top, but peppers and olives. You get used to it. But unfortunately they now require bread coupons for pizza, too.*

Twenty-first day at sea. Anna was still working on the first draft of the novel. Next to her, Ruth was sleeping, Pierre was reading a Tintin book. To make him laugh, she read aloud the caption: 'Who is afraid of nothing, absolutely? Tintin! And who follows him everywhere, absolutely everywhere? Snowy!' Sitting in her deck-chair, she immersed herself in her notebook, *isolating herself alone with the ocean. [...] Poorly dressed, her hair unkempt under a carelessly tied grey kerchief, she would talk to herself, her gaze mad, her face tormented by distortions [...] She would sometimes take a thick school notebook from her clothing and write with her pencil, moving her lips all the while.* Of all the materials in the world, she noted, paper seems particularly difficult to burn or destroy. She leaned towards Pierre:

'The hero of my novel, the main character, should he stay in France at the end or should he leave?'

'He should stay!' her son replied without a moment's hesitation.

Anna agreed with him. She wrote the opening of her novel. The *Montréal*, a cargo ship that sailed from Marseilles, sank between Dakar and Martinique. The narrator is talking to you, the reader, he is sitting on the terrace of a harbour café, he suggests you take a seat, invites you to share dinner, a glass of rosé and a slice of pizza, and because you are bored, he suggests you listen to his story.

You know yourself what these fleeting acquaintances you make in train stations, consulate waiting rooms, or the visa department of the prefecture are like. The superficial rustle of a few words, like paper money hastily exchanged. Except that sometimes you're struck by a single exclamation, a word, who knows, a face. It goes right through you, quickly, fleetingly. You look up, you listen, and already you're involved in something. I'd like to tell someone the whole story from beginning to end. If only I weren't afraid it was boring. Aren't you thoroughly fed up with such thrilling stories? Aren't you sick of all these suspenseful tales about people surviving mortal danger by a hair, about breathtaking escapes? Me, I'm sick and tired of them. If something still thrills me today, then maybe it's an old worker's yarn about how many feet of wire he's drawn in the course of his long life and what tools he used, or the glow of the lamplight by which a few children are doing their homework.

On the open sea
15 April 1941

Twenty-second day at sea. Between the serried ranks of deckchairs, the chess players and the bridge players have set up tables, or rather upturned crates. Serious, silent ladies and gentlemen, who can be heard speaking the same silent language, the language of games. Not one part of the ship is more diverse, more cosmopolitan; one might see a Dutchman on his way to Java playing a bankrupt Belgian industrialist who dreams of rubber plantations in Amazonia; witness a game between Monsieur Harcourt, a wealthy factory owner from Lille going to rejoin his wife and his money in New York – both are already there – and the undisputed champion aboard the ship, a Czech, a former Škoda engineer, a gun manufacturer, fleeing to the Americas, since even that is better than working for the Germans, one might hear him say, this curious gunner who has no taste for war, despite or perhaps because of his profession, it is impossible to tell. Among those who competed in the numerous chess tournaments organised during the crossing, Anna Seghers' son, Pierre Radványi, was an excellent player. That morning, at the tender age of fifteen, he had challenged another regular, Dyno Löwenstein. Both were sons of German emigrants, both had been reluctant to leave; between moves they talked eagerly about their home towns. Dyno about Toulouse, Pierre about Meudon-Bellevue. About the late Sunday afternoons with the Radványi family when friends came to visit and the writer Egon Erwin Kisch recounted his extraordinary tales, about the way he acted out the scenes in front of the fire. There was also Otto Katz, another Czech writer who had taken Pierre and his sister Ruth to the Théâtre des Champs-Élysées to see *Snow White*, the first major colour feature film by Walt Disney. On another occasion, he said, Herr Katz had taken him to dinner with the black American singer Paul Robeson and his son, a boy of about the same age. Pierre, whom his mother called Peter, was a bright, resourceful and charming young man. He attended all the impromptu conferences of the upper deck, where he sat cross-legged. The most recent had been a presentation about the research of Ivan Pavlov. It was Pierre who brought the latest updates from the front to the hold, having gleaned from the radio operator the bombing of Belfast by the Luftwaffe, German troops occupying Sarajevo, the allied forces' attack on Mount Olympus, or the sinking of the cargo ship, the SS *Aurillac* off the coast of Portugal, torpedoed by an Italian submarine, and the *Ville-de-Liège* torpedoed off the coast of Iceland by a U-52.

9

A Pod of Porpoises

———

Open sea
16 April 1941

The heat was such that the passengers spent the whole day dazed, drained and exhausted, scrabbling from the hold and seeking refuge beneath tarpaulins so as not to burn as they waited for night to draw in, lying beneath a makeshift tent, suffering a sort of reverse hibernation, an indeterminate sleep that was the only cure for this listlessness. At dusk, another day began, everyone gathered on deck as on a village square on a summer evening, a little woozy, and wrung out from doing nothing. The captain's Chinese cabin boy served cocktails and hors d'oeuvres, people chatted about overcrowding and their brush with death, the fear of being ship-wrecked and the absurdity of this interminable drift, brief tales that sparked and faded in the space of an evening. Towards mid-night, those who had coupled up for the night took shelter in the lifeboats, beneath the thick tarpaulins, writhed and sweated a lot, fucked a little, stinking but happy!

> *What enormous inferno are we approaching? The very air fills with heat, a uniformly grey sea, overcast weather. Dissolvent calm, then slight nervous excitement. 'The equatorial atmosphere,' Lévi-Strauss says.*
> *Once evening comes we feel better. We gather – the forty militants,*

escapees from various concentration camps sponsored by the IRA, which is paying for their voyage – in Montparnasse, that is, on the superstructure that encircles the upper part of the smokestack and supports the lifeboats. (Couples sometimes hide in these boats at night to make love.) The vents bother us. No guardrails, we see the lapping of the sea, no obstacle between it and us. The paleness of the tense faces stands out in the cool darkness, and one realises that a vaporous and penetrating light reaches us from constellations rent by the clouds. I speak of another long voyage I once took, twenty days on the North Sea and the Baltic at the end of the other war, at the birth of revolutions, at the birth of our victory in Russia. Indeed, a voyage symmetrical to the one we are now on: we were climbing and we are descending history's slope. And we will climb again! I paint a portrait of Ilyich [Lenin], his simplicity, his basic, average-man personality, his lack of affectation and ambition, his disdain for effect; of Leon Trotsky, by contrast, sparkling with sarcasm and intellectual ardour, clearly superior to those around him in his splendour, his elegance, and his pride. I say that we are defeated only in the sense of fighters in a great army that has time on its side; that we mustn't let ourselves feel defeated but maintain victory in our souls; that we have an unforeseeable future in our hands, and that we have proved our capacity to face up to everything, to undergo everything, and to accomplish everything.

Open sea
17 April 1941

In his diary, Serge addressed himself to Laurette, describing the crossing to her stage by stage and sometimes, in the course of some reflection, some anecdote, he abandoned the partisan *we*, the *I* of memoir, and gradually drifted towards a delicate *you*, he wrote *your courage, your love, your eyes*, dreamed that she was looking up at the same sky, pictured her, hoped she was on her way, called her Laura. Being stateless, a revolutionary with no passport, he feared yet another journey, to seek asylum in Mexico, where political opponents were assassinated by killers who travelled halfway around the world to track them down, where there were moles, sleepers, fake intellectuals, ready to bury an ice pick in your back. Keeping a diary is a funereal business, he thought. All his comrades aboard the ship were heading to Mexico. They had been forbidden from entering US territory with anything other than a transit visa, so Santo Domingo and the peninsula offered the only salvation. People spoke of it as an arid land, they feared the heat, they knew little else, Slavs relocated to the Tropic of Cancer, or Germans from the Baltic cast adrift in Central America. On the bridge, Jacques Davidoff, a handsome man of about twenty, chatted to Serge in Russian. He had spotted him on deck earlier, smoking an English cigarette, he had watched him wander around, had climbed the ladder. He went over to Serge, hunkered down, as though to sit, and asked if he could have his cigarette end. He smoked the stub until it burned his fingers. They began to chat, two Russian exiles on a ship with a novel in them – Serge, the son of exiles living in Belgium, a hero of the October revolution, a vocal opponent of Stalinism, a stateless person; Jacques, a Jew from Grodno, who had fled the pogroms with his parents at the age of eight and ended up in Paris. Now, both were heading to Mexico. Jacques was travelling with his parents, Grisha and Manya, his brother Leo and Leo's wife Ruti. In Mexico, they were to join his uncle, Alberto Kosowski, an unlikely relative, forgotten by all. But it was thanks to this black sheep now living in Central America that they had been saved: 'When you're not an artist or an academic or a militant, the only way to get a visa is through family. Alberto is one of my mother Manya's brothers. When I was a boy, my mother never mentioned him, he had a terrible reputation. People said he cared only for women, gambling and boxing ... My grandfather Oscar was a devout man, a prominent member of the Jewish community in Grodno. People said that, after one of many lewd escapades, he decided to send my uncle as far away as possible, to the far side of the Atlantic, to a land of debauchery. In a sense, he banished him. Not that he put it like that, no, he claimed it was voluntary, a choice. With the money for his ticket in his pocket, he left Grodno without ever looking back. By the time my mother got a letter from her brother two years later, he had moved to Mexico, and was married. In the envelope, there was a photograph of the family with a newborn baby. Even so, it's funny to think that our banished uncle is the person coming to our rescue.' Serge laughed. 'It's been five years now since I left Russia. Over there, in the deckchair, that's my son Vlady, he is about your age. I'll introduce you.'

As night fell, at the People's University of Montparnasse on the top deck of the ship, a young German gave a lecture about pre-history. André Breton proposed to end the session with an oral variation of Exquisite Corpse, a game in which answers are given to questions that have not yet been posed. To a question he had not yet been asked, Victor Serge gave the promising response: 'A defeat we transform into a shining victory.' Only afterwards was he told the question: 'What is historical materialism?'

As the crossing continued, so the *Paul-Lemerle* evolved, some-times it was a liner, sometimes a barge, a convoy, a canteen, a dormitory, sometimes sheer chaos, sometimes a barn or a toilet. For two days, people had been sleeping under the stars, happy to gaze up at a sky illuminated by other stars. The straw mattresses had been folded, hauled up and laid out on the deck so that, at dawn, it was necessary to pick a path between the bunks, and it required a delicate feat of acrobatics for those who loved to smell the sea air in the morning. From time to time, a rainstorm burst over the passengers, torrents of water sluicing the old tub, at which point they beat a hasty retreat and sheltered under tarpaulins that groaned beneath pools of water about to burst. The heavens took care of scrubbing down the deck while people sheltered in the tarpaulin tents. Sometimes, though rarely, the rain continued to fall. In an instant, the cloudless, starry sky grew dark and over-cast, light streamed from a distant spotlight as a storm rolled in, the still sea rose in lofty waves, breaking over the deck where it merged with the torrential rain. For a fleeting moment it seemed, like everything on this crossing, sea and sky would collide, crush-ing the slender steel vessel on the surface beneath their combined weight. The downpour lasted so long that it blocked the overflow pipes, flooded the bridge and drenched the mattresses set between the smokestacks and the turrets. Serge and Vlady dozed happily, oblivious to the hammering and amused by the panic on the upper deck, here a child bailing out water with his shoe, there a dodder-ing old merchant, shivering and holding his mattress over his head. An officer appeared and ordered the restless sleepers to be quiet: 'Come on, now! You'll wake the captain!' To the disapproval of a fellow passenger worried about upsetting the crew, Serge quickly retorted: 'Maybe the captain should come check on his passengers!'

ADVERTISEMENT PUBLISHED ON 18 APRIL 1941
IN THE *COURRIER DES ANTILLES*
FORT-DE-FRANCE

A MAJOR EVENT IN **MARTINICAN** INTELLECTUAL LIFE
Absence of any real culture
Mercenary attitude to mind and consciousness
Creative inferiority

THESE ARE
THE CHARACTERISTICS OF ANTILLAIS SOCIETY
THE QUARTERLY REVIEW
'TROPIQUES'
EDITOR: AIMÉ CÉSAIRE

proposes to fight against:
1) intellectual pauperism
2) Contempt for the colours of life
3) Artistic parasitism

In summary: articles concerning philosophy, literature, music, poetry.
This tastefully edited magazine *is now on sale in the CLARAC bookshop.*
Price 12 francs.

The Caribbean Sea
18 April 1941

A pod of porpoises appeared, soared and dived beneath the ship leaving behind a vortex at the surface. The crossing had taken almost a month, and the bulletin posted today announced that the ship would reach land on the morning of 20 April. The prevailing mood was frustration and seething excitement; distance triumphed over everything else, so frustration prevailed. Besides, no one on board had a clear image of this fantasy island, this sliver of France that some pictured as a Gauguin painting, others as the penal colony in French Guiana, and still others as a free country, almost America, but which most of the passengers saw simply as a temporary refuge, a little comfort, a hotel room, a bath. A landing stage before the mainland, a stopover they would just pass through before drifting south or heading north to Florida, and eventually Ellis Island. The passengers' anxieties and concerns related to their nationalities, and their political affiliations. Only the day before, Toribio Etxeberria and Juan de los Toyos, two Basque men who seemed like twins, had been worrying aloud: 'When all's said and done, at least we're safe at sea. Maybe not from submarines or shipwreck, but from everything else.'

The offshore wind felt warmed and tainted with something cruel, unhealthy and decidedly French. If the truth be known, the rampant suspicion on board, the hunt for spies, was rooted more in reality than paranoia or hallucinations. It was an entirely plausible scenario; people wisely said little about their ancestry. Toribio and Juan had been born at the end of the previous century, one in 1887, the other in 1890, and so were survivors of the selection process in Marseilles. They had joined in every struggle, and had in fact lost them all. But they were convinced that the battle would carry on when they reached the other continent. Both were founding members of the Partido Socialista Obrero Español, built on the model of the working men's cooperatives of Alfa or Vizcaya. An old man now, more disillusioned than his travelling companion, Toribio railed against the festivities on board, he had expected a more cramped cage, a blind alley, a floating prison for undesirables. He was crumbling beneath the weight of doubts and fears, of a mistrust that, while entirely rational, had turned to despondency, as though, now that his goal was in sight, exile could lead only to the slaughterhouse. On the brink of the abyss, truth took on the guise of lies, while lies delighted in masquerading as truth. Birds could be heard fluttering between the rigging, and soon there would be cries of *Land, Land Ho!* from whoever first sighted it, leaning over the gunwale in the bow. 'It will be just like France, we will probably be in a camp, Martinique is just another part of Vichy, maybe better, maybe worse, but worse is a safe bet. To live the life we lived, you have to learn to deal with treachery. You'll see, you'll see ... they're all cowards. At the Rivesaltes camp, the stop just after the Pyrenees, we were lucky to get out alive!' With a dull stare, he cleaned the grubby lenses of his glasses on his shirt tail as he contemplated treachery.

The passengers hastily gathered together their belongings, cleaned their best suit, their dress or shirt in the laundry, scrubbed at the collars and the dark stains under the armpits, shaved in a basin with a shard of mirror, put their affairs in order, prepared their papers, counted and recounted their savings. A desk had been set up on the upper deck where duty officers returned the passengers' passports. Here was an opportunity to hear the sonorous map of names, over there, the thirty-five refugees from the International Relief Association, Kuno Brandel, Hans Titell, Carl Heidenreich, the Krizhaber family, Alice Fried, H. Czeczwieczka, E. Bersch, K. Braeuning, Mr and Mrs Orsech, the Osner family, I. Reiter, H. Langerhans, M. Flake, B. Barth, J. Weber, Mr and Mrs Pfeffer, Capari, F. Bruhns, F. Caro. People gathered together in groups according to the networks, the American Relief Committee, the Zionist or Spanish associations – over there, a couple of German merchants, personal friends of Albert Einstein; three paces away, a Viennese urologist, born in 1850, regaled the younger passengers with his service record in 1914, while his wife, a queen, sat regally in her deckchair. There, a Catholic banker from Austria insisted he was under the protection of the Vatican, he planned to emigrate to Brazil. To hell with grime and poverty, they would take out the carefully folded suits from the bottom of their trunks.

There were young and pretty women on board; flirtations had begun and sympathies had ripened. For them to appear in a favourable light before the final separation was more than mere coquettishness: it was an account to be settled, a debt to be honoured, a proof they felt they were owed of the fact that they were not fundamentally unworthy of the attentions bestowed on them. With a touching delicacy of feeling, they had taken these attentions only, as it were, on credit. So there was not only an element of farce, but a slight hint of pathos in the cry which arose from every pair of lungs. Instead of the call 'Land! Land!' as in traditional sea stories, 'A bath, at last, a bath tomorrow!' could be heard on every side, while at the same time people embarked on a feverish inventory of the last piece of soap, the unstained towel or the clean blouse which had been carefully preserved for this great occasion.

Part Two

—

Snakes and Ladders

the night ablaze the night unbound the dream compelled
the fire that from water restores to us
the horizon outrageous sure enough
a child will half-open the door.

Aimé Césaire, 'In Truth', *Ferraments*

Continue to advance in the only valid way possible: through the flames.

André Breton, *Martinique, Snake Charmer*

10

In the Lion's Mouth

———

Off the Antilles
20 April 1941

By 5.30 a.m. the sun was pounding on the deck, a sweltering oppressive heat that seared the tarpaulin, turning the shelter into a furnace – and so, with the sun barely above the horizon, the passengers woke up and roamed the deck like ghosts, their faces pale, their eyes peering into the distance, scanning for the island. In the bow of the cargo ship stood a trio people imagined were joking together in the gloaming. Like those travellers who, long after their departure, stare at a fixed point on the open sea, calculating how far they have sailed, they were waiting, searching for the coastline in the distance. From behind, they heard the sound of footsteps, the captain was approaching, a cigarette dangled from the corner of his lips, the smoke was instantly whipped away by the breeze, he looked happy, contented: 'Martinique, the pearl of the Antilles ... and the shame of France.' It was like the slogan appended at the bottom of a naval chart. The three men looked at him and said nothing. Just before seven o'clock, the island appeared, an olive-drab streak compressed by the horizon. Gradually it swelled to become a rock, gaining in size as the ship drew closer, imprinting lush lines against a backdrop resembling a gulf, a coast painted the whole width of the boat, line by line, like a cross section. Mount Pelée rose over Saint-Pierre like a hot air balloon hovering in the sky, ringed by a corolla of low clouds, a tutu around the hips of a hippopotamus. At the foot of the mountain, still some distance from the coast, the *Capitaine-Paul-Lemerle* tacked and followed the shoreline. There was an echoing chorus of animal noises. Pressed against the rail, the passengers shifted the weight from one side to another; they could see long swathes of jungle, then arches carved into the landscape, finally, as they neared the village of Carbet, whose name they did not know, they spotted fishing boats at sea. Until noon, they gazed in wonder at this scene as at the Christmas window of a department store, from time to time the ship slowed and seemed about to stop, *a village shaded by coconut palms, a cataract spilling water onto black sand where the light flickers with little 'gommiers' with quadrangular sails.* Towards midday, they caught a glimpse of Fort-de-France, a city set on the vast sweep of a bay that evoked a Swiss lake. It was not so much a fort as a bastion from another century, half-hidden by the warships gathered in the harbour next to a simple timber pier. The ship sailed on towards the south, between the twin shores of the bay. It was then the passengers realised they would not be disembarking.

The clean-up began. Sailors wearing protective scarves surveyed the now empty hold in a cloud of dust that swirled in the sunlight; others sluiced and scrubbed down the deck yellow with the children's urine. To escape the sun, the passengers all gathered under the tarpaulins, the children and the elderly in deckchairs, the others perched on folded mattresses, on trunks and suitcases stacked against the coal bunkers, all of them literally seething. This had little to do with the sun at its height or the terrible ordeal, but the fact that the wait was still not over. They stood in groups near the gangway. Two hours later, a gunboat appeared with a whole convoy in its wake; from the helmets and the uniforms it was clearly a battalion from the Sûreté. Just when people were beginning to lose hope, or contemplating jumping overboard and swimming to the distant shore, the authorities came on board. There was a confused, diffuse murmur, a sound that spread through the crowd. The soldiers surrounded the passengers and formed a line outside the door to the captain's cabin.

Lieutenant Castaing of the Sûreté Générale was having a conversation with Captain Sagols.

Regulations required that passengers be interviewed prior to being allowed to disembark. Interviews that dragged on for hours, peppered by insults and sniggers that quickly justified their worst fears about the colonial troops – *army rabble in the grip of some form of collective mental derangement*. He shouted, they threatened. In the late afternoon, Lam, whose French was poor, was interrogated. Despite his attempts to make himself understood, they initially ignored his valid visa. Eventually, they stamped the document and all he heard, all he remembered, was the name of Camp Balata and the fee payable as a security deposit. They mocked Breton and took away his safe-conduct pass: *Writer. Supposedly invited to give conferences and publish books about art. A lot of use he'll be in America. Permission to go ashore, but discreet surveillance.* Next came the turn of Lévi-Strauss. Commended by the captain, he managed to avoid the quarantine area of the transit camp, but not the lieutenant's insults: *No, you're not a Frenchman, you are a Jew and as far as we're concerned French Jews are worse than foreign Jews.*

Castaing's troops had sole and complete power, but, stupefied by the tropical sun, and entrusted with the mission of importing the national revolution and protecting the gold transported from the Banque de France, they used this power to vent their anger and pathetic frustrations. Sadistic and ignorant, they mocked the refugees and invented contradictory rules and orders. In accordance with the rule governing the exportation of capital, it was forbidden to leave France with more than five thousand francs, not including cheques from the Banque de Martinique; Castaing's troops, however, demanded a security deposit of six thousand francs from French citizens, and ten thousand from foreigner travellers, an iniquitous measure that condemned everyone to poverty or forced work. There was no real selection, since almost everyone was sent to the Lazaret, a former leper colony in Pointe-Rouge. The only people spared were Lévi-Strauss, Smadja the Tunisian, who presented a safe-conduct pass, and the Békés who lived here – the captain's guests, in other words. The ship sailed on to the Lazaret, a building impossible to distinguish in the inky darkness. There were no sounds save for the shouts of the lieutenant's men. Lifeboats were lowered into the water and, by lantern light, the convoy was guided to the shore at Pointe-du-Bout, where some thirty black soldiers were waiting, sentries guarding a camp filled with Polish prisoners of war and emigrants waiting for another ship.

Pointe-du-Bout
Night of 20–21 April 1941

The lifeboats shuttled between the *Paul-Lemerle* and the Pointe-du-Bout. Dozens of bewildered passengers could be seen being transported from the ship to the former leper colony, nobly dubbed the Lazaret. Aube was asleep in her father's arms, a rag doll pressed against her neck, lulled by the water lapping against the lifeboat. She was dreaming of three rabbits dancing in a forest glade on a spring morning. When she opened her eyes, Breton was cradling her in one hand and carrying a heavy suitcase in the other as he stepped out of the boat. As he set down his daughter, still half-asleep and swaying slightly, exhausted and confused, she burst into sobs. It was a month since they had last set foot on terra firma, a deceptive term given that the ground beneath their feet – a rickety jetty of warped timbers – swayed alarmingly. Breton was concerned, as was Jacqueline, while Aube, finding herself plunged into darkness, woke to a nightmare. Just imagine, all around her, the glowing pinpricks of a thousand fireflies, the shrill cries of a thousand cicadas, with every step, the clatter of huge insects colliding with the jetty and the vast orchestra of animals. Now imagine a child's nightmare. Remember the terrifying monsters that once lurked beneath your bed, were they any more terrifying than those that, in this moment, Aube senses in the waters, glimpses in the distant mangrove swamps? A black phalanx marched past, three guards, a mixed-race lieutenant who turned to her father, lit by the glow of a paraffin lamp. He gave orders for the passengers to go into the building, escorted by sentries armed with bayonets. 'We're being treated like prisoners!' Breton protested for the sake of form. They groped their way through the dimly lit courtyard of the Lazaret; even the soldiers seemed overwhelmed, they shouted at the tops of their lungs, bridled at the slightest sign of reluctance. They were simple men of no great value, a Basque officer was collecting his pay, a boy in an oversize uniform from the nearby town of Le Diamant was brooding. It began to rain, a brief downpour, everyone ran for cover. Jacqueline nodded to one of the ramshackle huts at the far end of the courtyard, she walked over and, through one of the windows, saw that the floor was strewn with mattresses where children slept next to the elderly. She wondered how much longer they could endure all this. After twenty-seven days at sea, the dream of a hotel in Fort-de-France, a porcelain bathtub and fresh sheets on the bed had been transformed into a seedy garrison where people slept on the floor with only their folded clothes as a pillow. She could have wept. Aube was sitting on a suitcase. In the fearful crowd, one woman suddenly lost her head. Sobbing and swearing, she scooped up handfuls of gravel and threw them. When she had finished, she opened her trunk, took out a thick tattered blanket and carefully laid it on the ground. Trembling, panicked, overcome, she lay down next to the wall and fell asleep, oblivious to the rats that scurried past from time to time. No point getting into a state about things, said a respectable old woman wearing a tartan dressing gown, all we can do is grin and bear it, she muttered, platitude following platitude, but what would not have sounded out of place on the boulevard Saint-Germain here sounded like an insult. What good would it do? None. What good would it do if they meekly accepted things? No good whatever. In which case, it hardly mattered what anyone did.

In a curious gesture, the guards admitted that they were at a complete loss. They repeated their apologies. The young Basque officer said: 'It was only at three o'clock this afternoon that we were told to prepare the place for sixty people. We only have twenty beds, so we put them in one of the huts for the elderly and the children. We salvaged the straw mattresses from the ship and have put them in the other two huts. There's no drinking water in the Lazaret except for the rainwater we collect in the tank, and that's not enough, so with two hundred people ...' He was a good lad who clearly felt a little lost in the barracks. He took orders from a lieutenant he despised, he would happily have chucked the uniform, but there was a war on, that would be classed as desertion ... he would be thrown in jail. Two of the other guards on duty were draining a bottle of cheap red wine.

Some hours passed. Breton stood watching over his sleeping wife and his daughter as a swarm of mosquitoes droned overhead. What, in the darkness, had been a simple outline framed against the moonlight gradually filled in as dawn broke. As the clamour of the forest died with the sun's first rays, he studied the Lazaret in the light of the new day. He was reminded of tales of treasure, of pirates, and his exploration began to feel like an adventure. As his eyes adjusted, he saw a patch of waste ground ringed by crumbling ramparts. Scattered here and there, like the debris from an explosion, people wrapped in coats lay on the ground. They all looked dead. He stared at them in wonder. The sun beat down, waking them, one by one. He walked over to the walls, which were no taller than half a metre, trying to get an overview of the scene. Below was a beach of black sand; in the darkness it had been no more than a smell of silt and seaweed. From the peak of Fort-de-France to the isthmus of Pointe-Rouge the lush coastline undulated like a child's scrawl. The leper colony had been built near the village of Trois-Îlêts, on a headland called the Pointe aux Pères, in the parish of Cul-de-Sac-aux-Vaches, where, in the neighbouring village of La Pagerie, Joséphine de Beauharnais, the woman who would become Napoleon's bride, was born. If chance exists, then it is mischievous. But Breton knew little about chance and would not have seen this as a coincidence. Apart from the fact that, at the age of ten, Joséphine consulted a Creole fortune teller from Croc-Souris who predicted that she would become 'greater than a queen'. Rising from the savannah, the fort loomed over the bay. Perched on a low wall, Breton turned around, his suit rumpled, his face gaunt, his expression defeated, and watched these lost men and women go about their business, the tricolour being raised. A concentration camp that faced the Americas. The surrounding jungle seemed to team with creatures, he recalled a painting by Douanier Rousseau. The image, though hackneyed, perfectly expressed the scene before his eyes: *the snake charmer*. There are men for whom words alone can reinforce what they see. That morning, the sky was violet.

LETTER FROM LIEUTENANT CASTAING
CHEF DE LA SÛRETÉ
TO A FRIEND IN SWITZERLAND

21 APRIL 1941
FORT-DE-FRANCE

Currently, I am dealing with the travellers flocking here in search of a new homeland...

Most have chosen the United States, where they are awaited by other members of their tribes. I find it particularly pleasing to have to deal with 'the vermin of the human race', as the Duke of Orléans dubbed them long ago. I exult when I see them disappear behind the last bastion of the world's democracies ... There, they will doubtless sow debauchery and infirmity ... Poor Americans doomed to become the cesspit of the world. [...]

In the past months, I have made great strides in the Sûreté Coloniale et Navale du Haut-Commissariat de l'État Française for the Antilles, Guiana and Saint-Pierre-et-Miquelon.

If I have not succeeded in arresting all the political bastards who helped to put France in the situation in which she finds herself, I have had the great satisfaction of eliminating many, all of whom claimed to be pillars of the new government and the Révolution Nationale.

Clearing out the higher echelons is an excellent start, but it is not enough to have a decent Governor when the whole corrupt administration is still in place. Here in the colonies, it is impossible to recruit adequate local personnel. We need healthy men from metropolitan France in every key post ... It is taking a long time for them to get here. The reorganisation of the Municipal Councils has allowed me to create a reasonably good image, as our teachers back in Solange used to say. I was a ruthless intelligence officer (more than once considered in high places to be a 'bloody pain in the neck'); I judged the men I appointed purely by the values work-family-fatherland... Poor Martinique is a monument to Republican obscenity. Such corruption, such shoddiness (customs, climate, rum)!...

Imagine the battle I have been waging and the disgust I have felt. Alas, it is far from finished! Too many people still fail to embrace the Révolution Nationale and I am beginning to believe that a cudgel is the only way to teach the shiftless and the riff-raff. For the moment, I am distressed and disappointed (for them) to see even relatively decent men behave like blackguards, and I'm beginning to think that a beating might not do them any harm, either.

Pointe-du-Bout
21 April 1941

According to the communiqué sent on 17 March by Yves Nicol, Governor of Martinique, to the colonel, Commandant Supérieur of the Antilles troops of Fort-de-France, the thirty-nine Czech and Polish soldiers lately arrived on the SS *Charles-Louis-Dreyfus* were to be taken to the Lazaret. There they would be housed and placed under the supervision of the military authorities, with the following provisions: they would be subject to a twice-daily roll-call and forbidden to leave the site.

In the morning, the camp commandant, a young Creole lieutenant, demanded that all prisoners gather under the flag. Having mangled the names of the Czech and Polish prisoners, he called the summoned passengers and ticked off the list of two hundred and twenty-two names drawn up by Castaing aboard the *Capitaine-Paul-Lemerle*. The roll-call lasted almost half an hour. Everyone had to respond and introduce themselves to the camp commandant. With despotic authority, he gave a welcoming speech about the situation in the Antilles, about Admiral Robert and respect for the *France éternelle* of Maréchal Pétain. He mocked the emigrants, these so-called refugees, cowards who had wanted this war and were now running away ... It was an astonishing, ill-disciplined gathering, children were clambering over the walls, the soldiers on guard had put down their weapons and were dozing on the cannon. Standing alone, the lieutenant barked. He listed the rules that applied within the Lazaret, the schedule, the morning and evening roll-calls. He announced that all suitcases and trucks would be inspected later that day, and all writings, magazines and printed matter in French would be prohibited, letters would be returned, envelopes confiscated together with all cameras and rolls of film. Roll-call would take place at the same times every day. He informed them that they would remain in the Lazaret until the departure of the next boat for New York or South America. He did not sound very optimistic, and gestured to the navy warship patrolling the bay and blocking the admiralty's access to Fort-de-France. When he had concluded his litany, he pointed out the canteen, one of the shacks down on the shore, and, to the joy of the faithful, announced that coffee was being served. There followed a great commotion, the passengers having not drunk coffee in a long time – real coffee, that is, not the dishwater they had been served in Marseilles or the tasteless substitute sold every morning on the deck of the *Paul-Lemerle,* but genuine, freshly ground black coffee.

As they had aboard ship, the crowd split into various factions, the Spaniards in one group, the Germans in another, the economic migrants, and the intellectuals. The previous night, in the former leper colony, there had been reunions with German refugees who had arrived on other ships. Anna Seghers and the Kantorowiczes had bumped into Robert Breuer and Kurt Kersten, the former a journalist, the latter a historian. Together they had escaped from a camp in northern France and made it as far as Bordeaux. They had managed to get aboard the last ship that left the port before the armistice. They described the swift crossing to Casablanca, the crowded decks, the end of the old world, the ministers and members of parliament desperate to escape, the businessmen and industrialists trading worthless stocks and deeds to confiscated properties. From Morocco they had decided to head to America via the Antilles, aboard one of the ships repatriating demobilised Martinican soldiers. In Fort-de-France, they had been sent to this camp, where they had languished ever since. They had written to their friends in the United States, to Thomas Mann, Ernst Lubitsch, Albert Einstein, but every reply had brought fresh disappointment, no one was in a position to help them get a visa: the American government considered that, having crossed the Atlantic, they were already safe. For the past nine months, they had been prisoners in the Lazaret, a former hospital, they were told. Over time, they were joined by quarantined sailors suffering from typhus and other diseases and, later, by prisoners brought from Papua New Guinea. Today, it was the turn of the undesirables newly arrived on the island whom the reactionary government billeted here for the duration of their stay.

Blocking the view, affixed to the beach by madrepores and visited by surf

– at least the children had the playground of their dreams to romp in all day long – a ship's carcass in its very fixity provided no respite to the exasperating impossibility of moving about other than with measured steps in the space between two bayonets.

He seated himself with his back against the wall of one of the shacks and his sketchpad propped against his knees. The leaves were of rough, sturdy, off-white paper that allowed transparencies to spread. At his feet, a small oak box lay open, twenty-five tubes of paint, five brushes of varying sizes, a sponge, a rag and an eraser. A small porcelain bowl filled with water was set on the edge of the lid. With a single brushstroke he applied his blue, then suddenly added black, creating subtle shades from azure to cornflower blue, ultramarine to petrol blue, which floated, suspended in the water, then clotted as he directed the rivulets by tilting the pad. Like the sediment swept along by a river in spate, the pigments naturally settled into the tiny hollows of the rough surface, hugging the imperfections of bumps and ridges, imprinting a vibration, a faint trembling, into the strata. He wetted the paper or dried it, blending flat-wash technique with the more vigorous wet-on-wet which demanded the artist work in swift, agile, unbroken strokes, like a freehand drawing. At first the paper would become engorged with water, absorbing without tearing, a matter of proportions. When he decided the moment had come to intervene, he would take the squirrel-hair brush from the box, a slender brush whose handle he had carved so that he could hold it in the palm of his hand and move it over the surface like a fine sponge. Brushwood colours, not entirely clear, not entirely smooth, in dark patches on the paper. While he waited for them to open up like suns, he worked on another area of the sketch. He moved from one side to another, the landscape before his eyes, two islands, a log cabin on the left blocking the view, the water, dark green near the shore, glittering and blue out to sea. He began with the sky, which he painted white before adding a little cerulean blue, then dabbing the surface with a rag to reveal the white of the rough paper that formed a layer of cloud. He moved down, creating a different, clearer blue for the waters of the bay, translucent and preternaturally brilliant, electric blue, that was the word, this he mixed with a dark green somewhere between sage and spinach. He waited for a moment, the layer dried, and in the patches of white he added red ochre tones, a line of bulbs planted along the streak of vegetation to create the roofs of the houses in the neighbouring village. He moved on to the foreground, the camp kitchen a skin-tone beige with openings in stark black, the fallow land a military green, and the rocks on the shoreline. Carl Heidenreich set the sketchpad at his feet and waited for the paper to dry before closing it.

LETTER FROM THE FRENCH HIGH COMMISSIONER
OF THE ANTILLES AND FRENCH GUIANA
TO ADMIRAL ROBERT
COMMANDER-IN-CHIEF
OF THE NAVAL FORCES
WEST ATLANTIC THEATRE

22 APRIL 1941
FORT-DE-FRANCE

*Re: French and foreign Israelites
residing in Fort-de-France*

In response to your letter No 62 AC, I have the honour to inform you that of the 222 passengers from the SS Capitaine-Paul-Lemerle who arrived on 20 April 1941, only three plan to settle in Martinique.

1 – the French citizens SAINT, André, and MERCAN, Albert, demobilised soldiers returning home.

2 – a Spaniard DE MIGUEL Y LANCHO, Jésus, born 9 October 1905 in Badajoz (Spain). An industrialist arriving from Casablanca, where he is ordinarily resident on rue Lafayette. This foreigner is travelling as a tourist and has been given leave to remain according to authorisation No. 60 dated 11 March 1941, by the Governor of Martinique.

He is staying at the Hôtel de la Paix, 39, rue Schoelcher, Fort-de-France.

All other passengers are being held at the Lazaret Camp, or have been given temporary leave to stay in various parts of the island while awaiting onward travel.

11

Here Be Dragons

—

Hôtel de la Paix
Fort-de-France
23 April 1941

Though the situation in metropolitan France was chilling, though there was talk of captures, round-ups, assassinations, of enemies and undesirables being arbitrarily arrested and interned in camps, of the Crémieux Decree being amended to drastically curtail the rights of Jews, who were now scrupulously registered, France was still some months away from revoking the French citizenship of Jews, forcing them to fall back on a religious identity that most had long considered secondary. In Martinique, police officers in the uniform of shorts, boots and *kepi*, befuddled by the heat and the rum, fluctuated between hatred of the British, the Americans, the Jews, the wops, the Negroes, considered themselves the vanguard of the Révolution Nationale, and classified Jews according to categories of Israelites. Lévi-Strauss, by his own admission, moved through this darkness with the same lack of concern as an animal bound for the slaughterhouse, and so, as he liked to recount, after the bucolic summer of the French defeat, he went to Vichy to request authorisation to travel to Paris to take up a new position as a teacher at the Lycée Henri-IV. He had come forward, he added, in a *sedentary spirit*, as though to absolve himself of his reckless undertaking. The person in charge of secondary education, who, as it happened, was sitting behind a teacher's desk, was dumbfounded and saved Lévi-Strauss from making a mistake, from throwing himself, as they say, *into the lion's mouth*. 'Go to Paris, with a name like yours? Are you serious?' he had said. And so, when he was insulted by Capitaine Castaing, when he heard his nationality being denied because he was a Jew, he realised that from being *potential fodder for the concentration camp*, he was now considered a *scapegoat* by the authorities on the island. Isolated from the rest of the world, and closely patrolled by American warships, Martinique at this precise moment in history was a locus for every evil of a civilisation pervaded by deviancies and poisonous ideologies, a mixture of French spirit and colonial barbarism that, on the pretext of its mission to civilise, was attempting to reinstate the orders and castes of the Ancien Régime.

As the heat subsided, Lévi-Strauss headed into the city. The roads were tortuous, little more than dirt tracks or forest trails, they drove blindly, looking up from time to time to catch a glimpse of the bay and use it as a guide, as one might the shore of a lake, *while the old Ford was churning its way up steep tracks in bottom gear*. The cloudy sky gradually turned the ground into puddles of mud, the road into a raging river, the soil into liquid. It was Lent, they said, the dry season that even here was unbearable. And yet it was raining. Behind the steering wheel, Lévi-Strauss drove as best he could, dazzled as he was by this landscape that reminded him of the Amazon, or the outskirts of São Paulo, surprised to find himself on these roads that felt so familiar, knowing that he owed his salvation to transatlantic journeys made before the war, to friendships idly struck up. A Jew and academic, half-explorer and half-scientist, married and single, stateless or almost, with his leather knapsack stuffed with papers and his imposing trunk held at the customs offices, Lévi-Strauss – whose name, even more than his doubtful curriculum vitae, was like a red rag to the young lieutenants of the colonial forces – paradoxically found himself well off compared to the other passengers of the *Pôvre merle*. As he drove away from the former leper colony, he thought about those who were still being held prisoner in the Lazaret, shocked by conditions in the camp at Pointe-du-Bout. The humiliations, like the degradations they had suffered aboard ship, the insufferable arrogance of rookie captains and sergeants taking orders from tinpot second lieutenants, like picaros or self-proclaimed kings of this no-man's-land, a patch of waste ground at the end of a trail, an arsenal sitting atop the gold reserves of the Banque de France whose governor spent his nights dreaming of shelling the warships in the bay. How many bastards and hypocrites dreamed of reigning over their own penal colony a thousand leagues from their crimes? *Here be dragons*, as cartographers wrote on unknown or dangerous lands in the Middle Ages. The Napoleon complex, so common in our world, took on a different dimension here, where abuse and arbitrary power fused with racism and religion, affording anyone with a rank, a uniform and a medal almost complete impunity. It was hilarious to watch the theatrics of the Creole captain bellowing at the camp inmates, hilarious and tragic. Passengers told Lévi-Strauss about the preposterous morning and evening roll-calls, the confiscated books and letters, the fee of fifteen hundred francs prisoners had to pay for their internment, and their security deposits. They told him about the terrible food, the sweet potatoes, the stew of frozen meat and orange peel like a salted punch. With no showers, and water tanks that were empty, the more daring dived into the sea to wash, the others, fearing sharks or some other beast, rubbed themselves with eau de Cologne. In less than two days, the elegant men, already bedraggled after the crossing, had taken to rolling their trousers up to their knees and their shirtsleeves up to their shoulders, while the women wore long dresses smeared with dirty oil whose hems caught and tore and were stained red by the strange flowers that hung from the ferns. All were so tanned they would pass for *darkies*. The passengers of the *Capitaine-Paul-Lemerle* shared the space with other exiles who had washed up here, while the Czech and Polish soldiers bummed around and befriended their gaolers, decent soldiers who shared the shacks and the mess hall. The bravest, it was said, managed to evade the sentries guarding the gate by swimming two hundred metres before emerging from the sea and heading to the market at Trois-Îlets to buy provisions. For everyone else, the black-market canteen, the Lazaret delicatessen, sold tins of sardines, cigarettes and bottled water at swingeing prices. Elegant ladies of the sort who had been seen playing bridge and sipping cocktails with the captain in the Champs-Élysées of the upper deck now paced the camp like sentries, half-crazed, their complexions yellow, their hair dishevelled, talking to themselves. Anyone crossing their path would hear the same few words uttered like cries of indignation: 'Impossible ... Impossible!' 'Disgusting ... Disgusting...!' Some felt that the supreme humiliation was having to take orders from a mixed-race officer. The same militant socialists who had preached equality at the Montparnasse meetings aboard the *Capitaine-Paul-Lemerle* now argued that the skin colour of the lieutenant in charge of the Lazaret was a deliberate snub by 'that twisted bastard Castaing'. Ill at ease with this unexpected power, and driven by an inferiority complex, the Creole officer vacillated between punctilious politeness and brute rage. Breuner and Kersten, friends of the Kantorowiczes and the Radványis, who had been here for months, made life easier for the German exiles. Both had been granted permission to leave the camp. Every day, they would go into town with a list of errands, they would collect the money orders sent by the community in the United States.

Lévi-Strauss had spent the night of his arrival soaked and sweating, wandering along the jetty of the Société des Bateaux à Vapeur in the shadow of the Saint-Louis fort. Having crossed the manicured gardens bizarrely known as La Savane, he stopped at the Hôtel de la Paix on the corner of the former rue de la Liberté and the rue Victor Hugo. The third-floor room had simple wooden furniture and a fan whose blades brushed the ceiling as they turned, like a bicycle wheel. He had fallen asleep fully clothed, woken up two hours later sweating, his mouth dry, his clothes rumpled and the ridges of the sheets imprinted on his face. He had opened the shutters, put on his spectacles and stepped out onto the wrought-iron balcony, still disoriented, to see eight palm trees and a white marble statue of the Empress Joséphine on a pedestal carved with scrolls and Corinthian pilasters. Perhaps it was in that very moment, with the honking of car horns and the calls of street hawkers, that he watched the parade of colonial khaki helmets as he might the comings and goings of Descartes's spectres – *but what do I see other* than hats and coats that could conceal automata? It was not to kill the spineless characters beneath the pith helmets, but hunger and curiosity that prompted Lévi-Strauss to go down at midnight and stroll among the sandbox trees and tamarind trees, where he found a hawker selling roasted pistachios by the bandstand, then wandered past the Maison des Sports, the scene of shameless goings-on, a whore turning a trick with a sailor who was later seen pulling up his trousers behind a statue of the Comte Belain d'Esnambuc.

When he disembarked, Lévi-Strauss had left his trunk at customs. He had been cunning. This was the amusing explanation he offered the engineer. Having been volubly insulted on board ship by the lieutenant from the Sûreté, he had been convinced that, on land, he would encounter customs officials, police officers and soldiers of the same ilk, and feared that, having inspected the documents chronicling his travels and expeditions, they would subject him to lengthy interrogation, ignorantly mistaking his notes for proof of espionage.

Linguistic and technological card-indexes, a travel diary, anthropological notes, maps, diagrams and photographic negatives – in short, thousands of items. The suspicious load had crossed the demarcation line in France only at considerable risk to the professional smuggler who had agreed to transport it. From the reception I had received in Martinique, I concluded that the men, the police and the naval intelligence officers must not be allowed even a glimpse of what they would inevitably interpret as instructions in code (the notes on native dialects), or diagrams of fortifications, or invasion plans (the maps, sketches and photos).

Even though it was clear that a spy would be ill advised to put all his information in a trunk bearing his name, Lévi-Strauss was not prepared to gamble on the intelligence or the discrimination of the authorities, with their stupidity and their pig-headedness, but rather, like a broker faced with a falling stock market, he had declared his trunk to be in transit, which meant that, to avoid it being opened or abandoned, he would have to leave Martinique on a ship flying a foreign flag, which, given the demands of the Germans and the suspicions of the Americans, would be extremely complicated. He kept with him only a leather suitcase, and wanted for nothing except reading matter and work. And what is a scholar with no field and no papers but a free thinker?

Sitting on the terrace of a café on the corner of the rue de la Liberté, staring out to sea, Lévi-Strauss looked at the *Paul-Lemerle* moored at the jetty and at the procession of men carrying baskets, the coal merchants walking along the pier between the park and the ship. 'Now, if the island were British,' the engineer said, 'it would be a very different matter – the empire would have organised reprisals in the Caribbean. Here we have taken a joker from a pack of cards and shown it everywhere, like a safe-conduct pass. Everything people dreamed of, summary justice, a purge of the administration, the dismissal of mayors and elected representatives, has become reality through the magic of the Révolution Nationale. This is the dream of the great plantations, a rural society entirely governed by a corporate hierarchy.'

The engineer had been transferred to the island, a punishment disguised as a promotion, he claimed. He enjoyed discussing literature with Lévi-Strauss, whom he had taken under his wing and helped with administrative processes, explaining the little things that might make his stay more pleasant or hasten his departure. Over lunch, they would sit chatting on the terrace overlooking the bay, protected from the sun by tall buildings and the large balconies. The engineer was a laconic, sullen man who found life on the island terribly boring. In their conversations, one might describe the Nambikwara or the Tupi-Kawahib tribes, and the other might discuss life under Admiral Robert, the bay about to go up in flames, two thousand five hundred soldiers sweltering on the quay, two hundred and eighty-six tons of gold from the Banque de France hidden in the surrounding hills, the unarmed ships, the American cruisers and German U-boats out at sea, the foreign spies, the officers of the Sûreté Générale, a visiting naval observer, all this on an island like a tarnished pearl. Add to this the fact that Pétain was feted as though he were Father Christmas, and the Monroe Doctrine hailed as gospel and you get the picture. Radio Martinique constantly broadcast the message: 'Citizens of France, in the course of your history you witnessed a miracle, the miracle that was Joan of Arc. Now, you have witnessed a second miracle, the miracle of Pétain!' In the harbour, ships came and went, a merry-go-round that nothing could stop. Oil was once again in short supply, and now and then the newspapers would print the misadventures of ships that sank during the crossing, or were rerouted or becalmed, like the *Fort-Royal*, a banana boat which had been seized on 27 March by Royal Exchange, a New York insurance company. Among the harbour workers and the officials working for Messageries, no one seemed to know when the next ship was to set sail. There was talk of the *Duc-d'Aumale*, currently in the dry docks at Saint-Louis for repairs, but though men were working on it, it looked unlikely to put out any time soon. Those interned in the Lazaret were to be its passengers, and the ship was scheduled to stop at Santo Domingo before heading on to New York.

The merchants on the rue Saint-Louis, together with the proprietors of the hardware shops on the rue Antoine-Siger and the restaurants in the covered market, railed against the government's decision to intern the passengers who were in transit. Prisoners on the island were like manna from heaven, they argued, set them free and we can fleece them! Prisons do not help the local economy. Nor were they backward in pressing their point: Fort-de-France chamber of commerce sent its president to discuss the matter with Governor Nicol. A double penalty and a provocation. Not the destitute, perish the thought, keep them in the prison camp in Trois-Ilêts, no, they were referring to the rich travellers – perhaps some sort of selection process could be put in place, they could be asked to pay a security deposit, whatever it takes, but please be reasonable, think of the livelihood of your citizens, this represents a devastating loss of income for the bars, the shops, please give the idea some thought, Governor. Never forget that money is a magnificent engine of progress.

Fort-de-France
24 April 1941

The street was deserted, a patch of waste ground haunted only by shadows. The night was drawing to a close. A strapping, bare-chested man was rummaging in the rubbish bins and sucking on an extinguished cigarette end, he staggered between the closed kiosks.

Other tramps began to stir, they headed down to the shore to dive in, to wash, to wake themselves. The sky brightened, unfurled, clawing streaks of light onto the darkness. A tiny moon no bigger than a star disappeared behind a thick bank of cloud. Lévi-Strauss, who had woken before daybreak, was already down by the ships at their moorings. He walked down the pier, stopped at the far end and sat, legs dangling in the empty space.

The blue of the sky intensified, this was the coming of the light, a slow, inexorable battle, lost before it had begun, the darkness struggled, or sought refuge behind the folds of the horizon. The sea did not yet have the scale it has at midday – nothing was visible save for the slender beams of beacons and fog lamps. In the leather bag was a folder marked 'Novel', three sheaves of paper, twenty-seven notebook pages, a text written in pencil with the title 'The Sunset'. It described a grandiose spectacle, and highlighted our inability to distinguish and differentiate in our minds between two moments, dawn and dusk. The preamble preceded a series of minute-by-minute notations – five pages written on the deck of the *Mendoza*, on the crossing back from Brazil.

For scientists, dawn and twilight are one and the same phenomenon and the Greeks thought likewise, since they had a single word with a different qualifying adjective according to whether they were referring to morning or evening. This confusion is a clear expression of the predominant interest in theoretical speculation and betrays remarkable neglect of the concrete aspect of things. It may well be that any given point of the earth oscillates with an indivisible movement between the zone of incidence of the solar rays and the zone in which sunlight misses it or returns to it. But in fact no two phenomena could be more different from each other than night and morning. Daybreak is a prelude, the close of day an overture which occurs at the end instead of the beginning, as in old operas. The face of the sun foretells the immediate nature of the weather; it is dark and lowering if there is to be rain during the early hours of the morning, but rosy, buoyant and frothy if the light is to be clear. But dawn is no guarantee of the nature of the rest of the day. It starts the meteorological process and declares: it is going to rain, it is going to be fine. Sunset is quite a different matter; it is a complete performance with a beginning, a middle and an end. And the spectacle offers a sort of small-scale image of the battles, triumphs and defeats which have succeeded each other during twelve hours in tangible form, but also at a slower speed. Dawn is only the beginning of the day; twilight is a repetition of it.

In the hotel lobby, he ordered a coffee. In the pile of old newspapers on the low table was a copy of the *Courrier des Antilles* dated 3 February 1941 and, a month and a half after the fact, he was able to read that Paul-Émile Victor had come to give a series of lectures.

**The explorer
P. E. VICTOR
will give a second lecture
on the subject of Eskimos
on Monday 3 February**

Monsieur Paul-Émile VICTOR, the young explorer who headed the 1934–35 French expedition to Greenland and who, in March 1936, returned to spend an entire winter living with the Eskimos, is currently on a brief visit.

A lecturer at the Collège de France, head of the arctic section of the Musée de l'Homme, Reserve Naval Lieutenant and a scout of twenty years' standing, Monsieur Paul-Émile Victor kindly agreed to give a lecture for the people of Martinique. This took place on Wednesday last in the Parochial Hall. For the intellectual elite of the island to hear a lecturer speak here is a rare opportunity. But to hear the account of a remote and difficult expedition from the explorer himself is truly an astonishing occasion.

Monsieur Paul-Émile Victor, an eminent scientist, gave account of his travels and his studies in the polar Arctic regions in terms understandable to the layman, enlivened by anecdotes about Greenland and its fine, intelligent inhabitants. The lecture was illustrated by slide photographs, which in themselves represent a valuable document.

Admiral Robert and Governor Nicol honoured him with their presence.

The speaker was introduced by Colonel Achille and, following an enthusiastic ovation, was thanked by Monsieur Jean de Laguarigue.

Since many who wished to attend the lecture were unable to secure a ticket, Monsieur P-E Victor magnanimously agreed to speak again on 3 February.

Tickets, costing 10 francs – 5 francs for schoolchildren – are on sale at the Parochial Hall and at bookshops.

The Lazaret on the Pointe-du-Bout
25 April 1941

Commercial law prevailed over the martial law. After three days' internment, the passengers of the *Paul-Lemerle* were authorised to go into the city each day until 5 p.m. The shops in Fort-de-France celebrated the victory over the authorities by hiking the price of every product on their shelves that same morning. All's fair in trade and war. Shopkeepers waited for liners to dock so they could fleece the passengers, just as the washerwomen by the harbour waited for huge bundles of dirty laundry they could scrub clean on the smooth stones of the river, dry in the sunshine and fold, all for ten sous.

Castaing showed up at the Lazaret early. He set himself up behind a desk in the officers' hut where, scanning through the list, he met with each of the internees. He ticked off their names, collected their passports and issued permission slips. Sometimes, he would linger over a name, and check it against a list of agitators and undesirables – drawn up in Marseilles or aboard ship, no one knew – given to the Sûreté by the captain of the *Paul-Lemerle*. Predisposed to refuse all permissions, he read the recommendations and ignored the comments. Those who had been unable to pay the security deposit of nine thousand francs were forbidden to leave the Lazaret. There are limits to humanism that even the commercial world accepts. If he came across a Jewish name, of someone he did not like the look of, he launched into a tirade of jeers and insults and then came up with some spurious pretext to deny him permission to leave the camp. He cared nothing about the prisoners' protests and their indignation – in his eyes, they were cowards, deserters, so-called intellectuals, writers, self-professed philosophers, academics, they were rabble, they were vermin, they were a disease to be protected from – he delighted in the notion that they had been quarantined in a former leper colony – oh yes, Jewry and communism were the plague of the century. Located as it was in the shelter of a cove, the Pointe-du-Bout was a furnace. As aboard the *Paul-Lemerle*, it was possible to move around only at dawn and after dusk. The fort and its surroundings were insalubrious, the shacks dilapidated and overcrowded, pervaded by the smell of death, and the rusty hulk of a ship lay rotting near a bed of sea urchins. As darkness fell, the air was thick with mosquitoes and the short, shrill calls of tiny frogs created an unimaginable cacophony in the twilight. Breton found himself waking up at three or four o'clock in the morning, he would go and sit down by the pier where the roar of the sea drowned out the noise of the forest; blind night calmed him for a time before plunging him into a profound melancholy. *In prison I would die*, he had written in Marseilles. And what had his life been since then if not incarceration? Floating, shifting prisons, from a boat in the harbour, to a ghost ship to a military camp in the midst of some fantastical jungle, with hope constantly thwarted by a gunwale, a wall, a rampart, and beyond the moat, the sea. Breton had the extraordinary ability, some might call it a blindness, to assess events entirely in terms of his own perceptions, ignoring anything that might disrupt that view. He saw things as the relentless fury of fate. What he did not see was the incredible inadequacy of surrealism and of war. He had known a heroic period, and the world had foundered, it was no more now than faded memories. Like all those of an ironic bent, Breton liked to believe that waiting, that expectation, was merely a pause orchestrated by malicious fate in which it would pen episodes of some greater story. In subscribing to material mechanism, he walked in the footsteps of catastrophe, and so he could confidently go forward to meet ordeals and initiations, could embrace the indirect route, the only road worth taking.

The morning was drawing to a close. The lush grass shattered into splinters beneath the sun's battering. It was Breton's turn to be interviewed. Castaing recognised him, he remembered their conversation aboard the *Paul-Lemerle*, remembered Breton's infuriating manner, arrogant, aristocratic, a poet and a wastrel, he did not even trouble to look up but ticked the name and noted his summary judgement: *Breton. No.* No, what, no permission to leave, no, never, no for the time being? At length he gave his cruel answer: *The security council is opposed to your setting foot in Fort-de-France.* What security council? An officer grabbed his arm and led him out, gasping, distraught, raising his voice, Breton insisted he would lodge a complaint. Which he did, that same day. A friend delivered his letter to Governor Nicol.

He found himself standing, lost, in the middle of the camp, saw Aube, and suddenly his face softened.

LETTER FROM CLAUDE LÉVI-STRAUSS
TO HIS PARENTS

25 APRIL 1941
FORT-DE-FRANCE

Dear both, this brief letter will not tell you much, I am sending it simply to shorten the time that will pass before my first letter from New York. They are very strict here about letters, so we have to stick to generalities. My cable will have let you know that I arrived, and now I have to wait, at least a little longer, before I can carry on. But I will certainly be with Aunt Aline in time to celebrate your wedding anniversary. On my arrival, I found a letter from her waiting, she is very optimistic about my situation. She is talking about a two-year extension to my contract, which seems to indicate that my situation with the New School has been settled, and of a possible post at Yale which would, of course, be wonderful. The crossing went well, the delays and the discomfort were mitigated by the warmth and the intellectual qualities of many of the other passengers. By the end, it had almost become a little university: lectures, debates, conversations, etc.

Martinique is magnificent, it reminds me of the Brazilian coast north of Rio (around Victoria). I am staying in a simple but clean hotel with a group of very pleasant companions: two young couples involved in film-making (German refugees), who are going to Hollywood, and a Tunisian art collector who knows Édouard. We spend the time we have to wait here as pleasantly as possible, swimming beneath the coconut trees and gorging on tropical fruits – which are more plentiful here than in Brazil. Europe already feels so far away! And, when I think of you, I feel ashamed of all this abundance.

I have also got in touch with local archaeologists and think I may do a little work with them, or at least get a sense of what there is to do here. I have not written to Pierre since I cannot go into details, but could you let him know 1) I am afraid I will not be able to deliver the message in the way that he had hoped and 2) that I received a warm welcome from Monsieur Sussfeld, the friend of Jean Valabrègue, to whom I am grateful. Here, I have also met a Commandant Halpren, who owns land in Loiret. Do you know him?

I have heard very little of what is happening in the world over the past month, and what little I do know does not make me want to learn more ... I hope to have news from you when I get to New York. Please don't worry if my next letter is a while in coming since I will probably wait until I have arrived before writing again, and we are unlikely to sail any time soon.

In the meantime, I am allowing myself to live a little,
All my love,
Claude

12

Snake Charmer

—

Offices of La Paix
Fort-de-France
26 April 1941

'A saintly man. You should meet him, you don't often find a priest with a fascination for archaeology. You would be a great help to him. He is rector at the cathedral and editor of *La Paix*, who knows, he might even be able to sort out the situation with your luggage and your visa,' the engineer advised. Lévi-Strauss knocked on the door of the presbytery after morning service. He was invited to wait in a narrow hallway of which every wall was lined with bookshelves. Books about religion, about the agriculture of the island, travellers' tales. Having spent two hours reading the morning papers, he looked up and glimpsed a figure in a black soutane with a long bushy beard, the figure of a chaplain to natives lost in the forest, ready to put them to fire and the sword. It was Jean-Baptiste Delawarde. He ushered Lévi-Strauss into his office. On the desk were stacks of books, an earthenware vessel, a pile of documents. Lévi-Strauss introduced himself. He began by talking about his travels, explained that he had taught in Brazil and returned to France, that war had put an end to work on his thesis and to the exhibition he had been preparing for the Musée de l'Homme. Delawarde offered to share his breakfast, a bowl of black coffee and thick slices of pineapple. Lévi-Strauss had not eaten pineapples so delicious, so juicy, since Brazil, the ripe flesh trickled over his fingers and he laughed. From the delighted smile on Delawarde's face, he realised that he had happened on an enchanting man who had wound up in Martinique by dint of chance and serendipity. Through providence. The priest was overjoyed, and immediately began to talk about his discoveries, the earthenware vessels and hollow cylinders of pre-Colombian civilisations, Saladoid vases and spatulas, the excavations in Mitan cove and the Lorraine. It was like finding a fellow lepidopterist in the middle of the jungle eager to show you his collection of butterflies. Delawarde was working on a book about magic in Martinique, the healers, shamans, fortune tellers, witch doctors, snake charmers and sorcerers. He was collecting stories from every village. In his large black notebooks, he kept a methodical account of his research, with numerous sketches and captions. He gave Lévi-Strauss copies of the articles he had published in the *Journal de la société des américanistes,* his crowning achievement as an archaeologist. Accounts of the vestiges of the first Christian movements in the New World and Christopher Columbus' foundation of Santo Domingo; another concerning his expedition to Dominica, a survey of the territory and its indigenous peoples. Lévi-Strauss paused while reading a story about Sésé, a young woman who lived in a small hut with her brother and mother. Every night, Sésé was visited by a lover, though, in the darkness, she could not tell his identity. One day, seeing that her daughter was with child, the mother decided to confront this mysterious visitor. When next he visited, someone posted in a corner of the hut smeared the lover's face with the inky black juice of the jenipapo fruit so that they would know who he was. Come morning, the mysterious lover was revealed to be none other than Sésé's brother. The whole village of Le Carbet was incensed and ashamed, according to the tale, the guilty party decided to flee and to live in isolation. He scaled the heavens and became the moon, on whose face black traces of jenipapo juice can still be seen. Lévi-Strauss was amused by the ending, the recurring trope of a cursed childhood to be found in Ivan Turgenev's tale of an enchanted violin. The child of this union was named Hiari and, in memory of her lover, Sésé asked a hummingbird to soar into the sky and take the babe to see her father. This the hummingbird did, and was rewarded for its pains by bright feathers and a crown upon its head. Hiari was the father of all the Caribbean peoples. But even today, women are fearful of the moon and, waxing or waning, it no longer visits them.

The conversation turned to Brazilian expeditions. Lévi-Strauss talked about the hand paintings of the Kadiweu tribeswomen, about the scientific material he had brought back to the Musée de l'Homme. He talked about the enigmatic symbols the Kadiweu painted on faces and hands, arabesques like Christian illuminations, a sophisticated decorative art. Before they parted, Delawarde showed Lévi-Strauss his collection of indigenous objects sprinkled with creosote before being wrapped and stored in crates in the basement of the offices of *La Paix*. Lévi-Strauss promised to return the following day and make an inventory of the pieces.

Fort-de-France
27 April 1941

Give me the name of your hotel, but be warned. Surrealist, hyperrealist poet, we have no need of that in Martinique. Remember that you have no one to see here. Above all, avoid the coloureds. They are big children. Anything you say they are bound to misinterpret. You can write all the books you like after you have left here.

On one particular day – though no one truly knows which one – Breton stopped in front of a haberdashery owned by Madame Ménil. He had come to buy a length of blue ribbon for his daughter. It was a tiny establishment on the corner of the rue Victor Hugo; in the window, amid the spools of ribbon, the rolls of pompadour, tartan and Liberty fabric, of Tarare poplin, soft khaki, gingham and linen, his eyes were drawn to an incongruous object, a magazine whose simple cover bore the words *Cultural Review* and a title, *TROPIQUES*, with the letters D.M.C. stencilled in the background. Of this moment, there are many accounts by witnesses that embroider and inflate the incident until it almost becomes a novel

– accounts that for all their embellishment cannot capture the splendour of the moment. Perhaps we should leave Breton standing before the shop window, lost in thought, since he himself will relate this moment, back it up with words, with language honed until it is as sharp as a sword, construct a frame for this coincidence, decorticate its symbols, whittle it down to Aube's blue ribbon, the inciting incident, bending the tale to his perceptions, relegating the people around him to mere automata governed by his whims, moving with the stilted gestures of fairground marionettes. History is a statement, the future a blank page. A story reorders chance into a neat, tidy structure. And this is what everyone did, they embellished something that resulted from a momentary boredom. Beware stories, they offer the semblance of truth, but it is mere semblance – gibbous interpretations that are instantly erased by other gazes.

What of René Ménil's sister, what does she think? After all, this is her shop, she is at home behind the counter and behind her sewing machine. And she does not care tuppence about literary history. From inside the shop, she probably could not see Breton standing on the pavement, hazy in the sun's reflected glare; perhaps she was chatting with customers who – having come in to ask for a piece of advice, a length of fabric to finish a suit, a few minutes with the handsome pedal-operated Singer sewing machine in the back to adjust a pair of trousers, affix an elbow patch – are chattering away like the garrulous men in La Savane, the washerwomen bent over their tubs down by the river or the fishermen at the fish market at dawn, joking as they lay out the morning's catch on the zinc counter. Perhaps Ménil's sister did not even look up, did not witness the entrance of this beanpole of a man whom history would wreath in mystery and dub a great poet. Perhaps – and this is something we have never read – she saw him come into the shop, did not say hello, scorned him in spite of his air of elegance, and returned to her conversation, laughed loudly at a joke in a Creole that to Breton sounded like a soft melody from which he might have fashioned a sound if he could but master the instrument and which the women heard only as a word with no melody beyond that which takes the swiftest route to the intended meaning. Perhaps, the women thought, he would leave as quickly as he had arrived, entering and leaving in a single movement; would they be irritated if he should run a hand over a bolt of indigo fabric and ask them about the colour, as though it were something rare, something other than cheap fabric for making overalls? Or perhaps Breton did not speak to her, but simply sat on one of the stools we can easily picture by the door, picked up a magazine from the pile left by her brother, Ménil the schoolmaster, magazines that for the most part sat gathering dust though, sometimes, to her great surprise, someone would buy a copy without quibbling over the twelve francs – the price of ten metres of fine woollen fabric. Naturally, she had glanced at the magazine, had read the preamble like a cry she would have echoed, though in different words, but as for the rest, she was suspicious of the philosophy and the flights of fancy, and amused to see her brother with his grand Parisian manner, his pauper's bow ties. And so, here was this tall, lanky fellow perched on one of the stools, who delicately plucked the creases of his trousers, hiking up the cuffs to reveal immaculately polished shoes in fine tobacco-coloured leather. He picked up a copy of *Tropiques* from the pile as yet unsold, studied the indicia with a jaded eye, perused the contents and then plunged, as he tells it, into the first pool of words – the editorial written by Aimé and Suzanne. Let us assume that this is how it happened, that he immediately experienced what we call a *revelation*; that, cynically expecting to find mothing but a nosegay of moronic, bourgeois words, a twittering from the islands, he encountered a text, something genuine, something darker and more striking, scathing and surprising, something that prepared to dig deeply.

Wherever we look, the shadow is encroaching, wrote Aimé Césaire. *One after the other, the home fires are extinguished. The circle of shadows closes in amid the cries of men and the howls of beasts. Yet we are those who reject the shadow. We know the world's salvation depends on us, too. That the earth needs its children, whosoever they be. The humblest.*

For the rest, history relates that Breton questioned the haberdasher about the people behind the magazine, and that her response was clear and simple – the magazine was edited by her brother, René Ménil, he was at school that morning, he taught philosophy at Schoelcher secondary school. Breton wrote a note for her to give to him. What history does not relate is that he already knew Ménil, he had rubbed shoulders with him in Paris on *Légitime Défense*, a magazine with a single Issue, 01 – seized as soon as it appeared, created in reaction to the Exposition universelle and its market of colonies – and indeed that he had invited Ménil to his apartment on the rue Fontaine. But this would have entailed presenting the discovery as a reunion, and while the reunion resulted from the purest happenstance, it would have seemed less dazzling, so he allowed himself to gloss over this fact.

The Martinican haberdasher, in one of those flukes that typify the most auspicious moments, took little time before introducing herself as the sister of René Ménil who, together with Césaire, was the driving force behind Tropiques. Her intercession would facilitate the conveyance of the few words I hastily scribbled on her counter. And in fact, less than an hour later, having combed the streets to find me, she returned with an assignation on behalf of her brother.

Balata internment camp
28 April 1941

The cabin boys who had been so polite and helpful during the crossing, attentive to the slightest request, were recognised by the passengers as agents of the German secret police. *Such a futile act can be seen only as the mindless, routine, disinterested prolongation of the systematic policy of demoralisation and disillusionment which has become the most fearsome weapon in this war.*

Standing by the guardrail with one of his two sons, André Masson was listening to the story of Ludger Sylbaris, one of only two survivors of the 1902 eruption of Mont Pelé, a prisoner saved by his cell walls. Left with burn scars that covered his face and body, the poor man later became a freakshow attraction in the Barnum and Bailey circus. Having set sail a week after the *Paul-Lemerle*, the *Caminaré* was now approaching the island from the other side.

Imagine, André was saying to his son Diego, the seas trickling away, the oceans left dry and the land like towering peaks. I have often dreamed about it, the waters vanished, inexorably drawn to the centre of the earth through a fissure acting like a giant siphon. First, the rivers run dry, it is a slow process, the fury of the wind subsides, it is an unwholesome, alien swell, birds wheel in circles, disoriented flocks dropping from the skies; meanwhile the waves grow bigger as they ebb, in a terrible roar of clattering pipes. The surging backwash hugs the shore and the fish, caught unaware, lie flailing in the mud, with the sea already far away ... Like a bathtub draining out to leave a ring of scum, the retreating oceans leave clumps of seaweed like greasy hanks of hair, huge whales beached, belly up, cargo ships run aground. Within a week, the water has disappeared, millions of fish, great white sharks and squid wriggle deep within the canyons; the ground that has been home to mankind is now an upper storey, this is a new world to which people must adjust, a world of three dimensions, of three storeys. After two weeks, the wind from what was once the high seas brings the smell of putrefaction. There is no sea now, only a murky pond, one that men would willingly clean and scour if they only had the tools. At this point, he explains, people would go about their lives wearing gas masks, or with clothes pegs on their noses. Volcanoes would be extinct, the lava in the bowels of the earth doused, from time to time sponges swollen with water would splutter, sending up huge geysers where once searing cauldrons belched thick smoke.

They spotted a town and, almost immediately, the military truck carrying them headed up a steep hill. As they climbed towards the peaks, the forest grew darker. A lush, dense jungle sprang up on either side of the road, a long corridor thick with heliconia and ferns. They passed a church with a cupola of white stone like some ghastly replica of the Sacré-Cœur; at the top of the hill, the truck turned onto a dirt track. Far below, they saw the entrance to a military camp. This was Balata. It was at this moment that they woke from the long crossing and realised – as the passengers of the *Paul-Lemerle* had before them – that they were in hostile territory.

In the upper districts of Fort-de-France, the evening wore on. Aube lay sleeping on a bench; sitting around the table were René Ménil, Aimé and Suzanne Césaire, Breton and Jacqueline. There was laughter, there was joy and considerable wit, there was no judgement, no aloofness. Breton praised the magazine, admiringly quoting various passages. He questioned his three new-found friends about the situation in the Antilles, the administration under Admiral Robert and the state of siege. Suzanne recounted their arrival in Martinique aboard the *Bretagne*, a ship that sank on its return voyage, like a warning sign of bonds that had been broken. Their discovery of a sleepy country and a vengeful colonial administration. The establishment of a regime that put an end to rights and freedoms. She talked about the empty bookshops, the ships massed on the quays, the appropriations and the rationing. About the fanatical speeches: Pétain as saviour of the plantations, the treasure of the Banque de France, the golden calf, and Hitler as the second coming of Jesus to expiate the sins of the old world, the Békés as a master race, a whole island in the grip of madness. *Tropiques*, she said, had been the only possible response, to write, to publish, to fight and not surrender, to face down the darkness of the mind. To use cunning, to play at being naive exotic poets, delicately planting bombs beneath the worthy gentlemen of Governor *Robé*, smiling all the while. Deceiving whenever possible, she said, you can just imagine these demented, deranged burghers playing the *crazed Negroes*. Perhaps Suzanne had told them to be wary of pretty names, of *doudou literature* – it was important to reimbue the landscape with its violence, the beasts their savagery, the mangrove swamps their ravaging incantatory power, only then would it be possible to reappropriate language – the title, *Tropiques*, was mere camouflage; seemingly inoffensive poets and folklorists spreading dissidence and a call to action.

Suzanne was mysterious. A girl born in Poterie, in the district of Trois-Îlêts, she had gone to study in Paris and returned some years later, the wife of a four-eyed professor from Basse-Pointe and the mother of four small children. She cultivated an exaggerated air of exoticism, reinvented herself every morning, weaving her hair into a long plait or into little-girl pigtails, wearing a light print dress or the long skirt of a schoolmistress. She loved to laugh, to read out in the open air, to dance, while her husband, whom she claimed had two left feet, never dared. They shared those things that were essential: life and writing. They were bound by such deep mutual admiration that one never criticised the other, and to those who knew them as a couple, Suzanne was the soul, the driving force. She provided *the material needs* of the magazine, she sourced the paper, the authorisations from the Information Service, negotiated with the printers and organised distribution. She also wrote. A scholarly article about the Africanist Leo Frobenius, an impartial study of the meaning of civilisation in which she explored what she called the *grandiose conceptualisation* of paideuma, a life force that exists within all things. A former pupil of Alain, she thought in terms of philosophy, though from time to time she exchanged rigorous axioms for a powerful lyricism, flirting with the poetry she loved, trading Socratic dialogue for an astounding howl, a call for revolution. *It is now imperative to dare to know oneself, to dare to admit our nature, to dare to consider what we want to be. Here, too, men are born, live and die. Here, too, the entire drama is played out. The time has come to gird our loins like valiant men.* Suzanne was less naive, less susceptible; whereas Césaire was dazzled by Breton, her peremptory side, her Saint-Just side, was wary.

They said he was an extraordinary teacher, with his bottle-green suit and his lisping Latin verses; the pupils were quick to nickname him Césaire *the green lizard.* He did not care, after all he was the one who claimed that at any moment he might transform into *a flying gecko, suddenly a fringed gecko.* He stalked the school corridors with his hurried gait, remonstrating with those who massacred Rimbaud by reciting his verse in the flat tones of good pupils. The schoolyard was a vast patch of waste ground that the children invaded during lunchtime recess while the teachers took shelter in the shade. At noon, Suzanne would come down from Bellevue, from the avenue Saint-John-Perse, taking one of the steep paths that wound between the buildings. Schoelcher school overlooked the bay; above the roofs splayed like a concrete fan, above the warren of alleyways, from here one could see all the way from Balata to Lamentin.

The evening ended towards midnight. Césaire offered Breton an off-print of *Notebook of a Return to the Native Land,* and in return was given a copy of *Le Revolver à cheveux blancs.* They promised to meet again for dinner at the Césaires.

Fort-de-France
29 April 1941

They cleared the table, left the crockery and cutlery to soak in a sinkful of soapy water. She sat in the wicker chair on the veranda. The wind slipped through the shingles. She went on sitting on the porch. She was reading in silence. The children, having screamed and hurled themselves at her, tugged at her dress, sweaty and red-faced in their pyjamas, were now sleeping soundly in their room. The reeds swayed with a strange shrill sound. Suzanne liked nothing better than to read at bedtime, she did not hear the river, nor the hummingbird on the windowsill – a hunk of stale bread hung from one of the thick branches of the calabash tree – nor did she hear the chickens scrabbling against the wire fence or the creak of the gate below. But she heard some mongrel barking and pulling at its chain in the alley. So she set down her book and went into the kitchen to fetch her pack of Royal Navy and her cigarette holder. Following a precise order, as though she were at Mass, a ritual to dispel this noise that was troubling her life. She planted her bare feet on the grass, the breeze whipped away the cigarette smoke and she continued to read as the thick night engulfed her. In the house, Aimé was correcting homework, he came outside, kissed the back of her neck, his spectacles pressing against her skin. She fell asleep in the chair and woke in the early hours. There were different noises now, the sounds of birds and daybreak.

Valley of Absalom
30 April 1941

There are certain places and certain meetings that can change a world. We all know the story of Caesar and the River Rubicon, but who knows the story of Césaire and the valley of Absalom? The river marked the boundary between Roman Italy and Cisalpine Gaul, and Caesar, *freely determined*, crossed the Rubicon, that is the lesson according to Leibniz. Is there a possible world in which, in the midst of war, on an island in close proximity to the Americas, *objective chance* does not stage-manage the meeting between

Breton and Césaire and all the subsequent events that followed the hike to the Absalom valley? That morning, crammed into two ramshackle Ford cars, Aimé and Suzanne Césaire, Helena Holzer and Wifredo Lam, Jacqueline Lamba and André Breton, and André and Rose Masson were heading up the hill towards Balata. Along the way, Breton mocked the ghastly replica of the Sacré-Coeur, that public expiation for the Paris Commune. Aimé guided the group as they hiked down the steep trail into the valley amid the towering trunks of mahogany, torchwood, gum and kapok trees. A tree of twined liana and epiphytes, a vast emerald-green wall pierced by shafts of light that illuminated anthurium and wild orchids, here and there purple heliconia glittered like garlands. The thermal spa down in the valley overlooked the river next to a stone arch. This was the beginning of a trail that Aimé particularly liked, known as the Route de la Trace, which wound along the slopes of the Pitons du Carbet. From the woods of Grand'Rivière and lush hillsides to the simmering junction of the twin gorges, Césaire acted as guide, naming the plants and explaining that the route known as La Trace had once been called the great road of the river and the highlands, a name they came to understand when they reached a steep path that led up the foothills of the mountain, half-hidden by dense tree ferns that lined the ridge. To either side, stretching away, were undulating waves of dense foliage of a green that seemed phosphorescent in the sunlight. In the distance, the bay of Fort-de-France and the Piton du Carbet, a landscape that was nine-tenths sky. Here, thought Masson and Breton, nature was imitating art, emulating the jungles of Le Douanier, surpassing the surrealist imagination. *Yes, crags, chasms: this splendid sylvan forest is also a well. And everything exists under the sign of the humid. See, those explosions of bamboos are wreathed in vaporous steam, and the summits of the peaks are beturbaned with clouds of such heft [...] the canna flower, exquisite as the blood circulating in the lowest and the highest life forms, its chalices filled to the brim with the marvellous lees. Let it be the heraldic expression of the conciliation we seek between the visible and the boundless, between life and dream – it is through a maze of canna flowers that we pass so that we can continue our advance in the only valid way possible: through the flames.* And the rain beat down. They found shelter beneath the vaulted branches of Bois-Verts. For a moment, the surrounding foliage created a rustling cascade. Water streamed through the tree ferns in a fine drizzle, rose from the source of the volcanoes, dripped from the leaves of the Forest of Pythons, releasing the petrichor. We do not know whether Lam saw the explosion and heard, in the reflecting silence of water and hummingbirds, the clatter of pipes and organs, the outline of masks. Plunged into this verdancy, Lam reconnected with his childhood, the Jungle was leading him to the Gate of Hell.

Fort-de-France
1 May 1941

Breton and Lévi-Strauss were entertained by the curious antics of the plain-clothes police officers. Having met in the bar of the Hôtel de la Paix, they talked about the surveillance they were subjected to, laughing as they described the techniques of these rookie spies. They classified them according to categories, on one side the *benchmen of the gendarmerie*, on the other the *gallant Martinican inspectors.* Breton mocked two men who had been sitting on benches in La Savane park and were now having lunch at the next table, heedless of the fact that they might be spotted, leaning back in their chairs the better to eavesdrop on the conversation, Mr Spook and Mr Ghost. 'You know,' Breton was saying ironically, 'we've made a couple of staunch friends on the island, unfailingly helpful and friendly ... The morning the police captain set me free, or, rather, allowed me to move around under strict surveillance, in a little bar where we were looking at the machine they used for extracting juice from sugar cane, two people from the boat suddenly appeared and with them two mulattos of about twenty, decent fellows, Monsieur Blanchard and Monsieur de Lamartinière, who, curiously finding themselves at a loose end, offered to guide us around the island. And there they were, driving us around with a generosity and an eagerness to please so extraordinary that they pre-empted any questions by saying, "Martinicans like to be helpful" – but those who had been helpful guides one day soon became a cumbersome escort to our every outing, they could often be quite disagreeable, trotting out dull racist generalities, "Martinicans don't know what they want, they're just big children! They shouldn't be given a choice, it would be a catastrophe, besides, they'd only refuse it, etc." Over time, they became aggressive and easily offended. After a trip to Saint-Pierre in the north of the island, one of them – we had excluded him from our walks – didn't even trouble to hide the fact that he was a member of the secret police.' What Breton found surprising was that he was still under strict surveillance. The banning of *Fata Morgana*, the search of the Villa Air-Bel, being confined aboard the *Bouline* during Pétain's visit to Marseilles – the relentless determination had carried on into the tropics.

The Lazaret
2 May 1941

He could constantly be heard talking about his wealth. Affectionately, gruesomely, meticulously. He ran an accounting service for wealthy merchants, speculated on his confiscated properties and his worthless shares. Madame, his plump bourgeois wife, also liked to boast. In the wash house, she talked about her former life, looked down on other women. Though now penniless, filthy, tanned and stinking prisoners of the island, they still thought they belonged to a superior caste and kept themselves apart. They were so infuriating that everyone in the Lazaret longed to teach them a lesson. It was the young people who did so. In a parody of protocolary language, they drafted an official invitation to the Governor's Palace for a dinner in honour of Admiral Robert. Though they were the only people from the leper colony to be invited, this illustrious honour did not strike the Galician couple as bizarre or suspicious. They washed as best they could with seawater, donned their best clothes, the gentleman borrowed a mirror from the lieutenant and shaved in the latrine. The invitation stated that a boat would collect them from the pier by the Lazaret at 5 p.m. to take them to the dinner. They waited, elegantly sweating in their party clothes, the boat was late. It grew dark and still they waited for a little while then sheepishly made their way back.

The map of the island
3 May 1941

La Jambette, Favorite, Trou-au-Chat, Pointe La Rose, Sémaphore de la Démarche, Pointe du Diable, Brin d'Amour, Passe du Sans-Souci, Piton Crève-Cœur, Île du Loup-Garou, Fénelon, Espérance, Anse Marine, Grand'Rivière, Rivière Capot, Rivière Salée, Rivière Lézard, Rivière Blanche, Rivière La Mare, Rivière Madame, Les Abîmes, Ajoupa-Bouillon, Mont de la Plaine, Morne des Pétrifications, Morne d'Orange, Morne Mirail, Morne Rouge, Morne Folie, Morne Labelle, Morne Fumée.

In the café, in turquoise ink, Breton wrote a poem on the back of a colour postcard depicting 'The Cane Fields and the Mill' and dedicated it to Aimé Césaire.

Pointe-du-Bout
4 May 1941

The other cook, an aide-de-camp called Vlady, washed vegetables in seawater, laid them on a flat rock in the sun to dry, and then, in huge, dented copper pots, he made the feast. Red snapper simmered in broth with scraps of leftover chicken. Remembering that she liked white wine and sea urchins, someone bought a half-bottle of cheap plonk in Trois-Îlets and wedged it between two stones in the sea to chill, while someone else used a knife to slice open the half-dozen sea urchins speared that morning by someone hunkered in the tide, with one arm below the waterline. Tipsy and dozing on a chaise longue, through narrowed eyes it was possible to see Pointe-Rouge beneath Pointe-du-Bout. It was still early, the boat would not cast off until evening, so they decided to swim to the nearby bistro, laughing and joking. There are some joys that have no other name than fraternity – this lunch was one such. They kissed Germaine and she disappeared into the night.

Fort-de-France
5 May 1941

We know that there were many departures, and drawing lines on a map from point to point would create a spray like a hose – from north to south. Mail destined for the penal colony in French Guiana left from La Rochelle or from Marseilles and stopped over in Martinique before sailing on to Cayenne and its final destination, Saint-Laurent-du-Maroni. Germaine Krull kept a notebook in which she meticulously noted the names of every ship she saw or photographed, worried about having to invent captions for harried editors. In that notebook, one can read: *At last, a miraculous day – there is a shortage of rice in Martinique and a French ship is sailing to Brazil to bring back rice. So I am leaving with a few friends who are also headed for South America. The Saint Domingue, a handsome cargo ship of several thousand tonnes, is sailing to Pará-Belém via Guiana. I am leaving the Lazaret with its guards and its officers wondering how this can be possible, right under the noses of the American warships. I am also leaving the Creole people who are tuned to radio stations in London and New York, hoping for their salvation.*

LETTER FROM CLAUDE LÉVI-STRAUSS
TO HIS PARENTS

6 MAY 1941
GRAND HÔTEL DE LA PAIX
FORT-DE-FRANCE

Dear both, I am writing this message which I hope will reach you sooner than it would by aeroplane since it will be brought back by the ship that brought me here. I am enclosing receipts for the two parcels I sent you this morning. One, weighing two kilos, containing chocolate and cigarettes, the other, weighing two and a half kilos, containing green coffee beans and tea. It is something people routinely do here, I hope that they will arrive safely. My sojourn is beginning to become tedious and I hope it will be over soon. Aunt Aline seems terribly impatient for reasons I do not understand, either she urgently needs me there or she is worried about my situation. Truth be told I know very little about my situation except in broad outline, and that alone worries me greatly. But from a personal point of view, I cannot envisage any major problem arising. That said, and in spite of Aunt Aline's advice, I did not take the aeroplane; I would have been obliged to leave all my luggage behind, something I am loath to do under any circumstance. It is currently being held at customs, because keeping it with me would have required dealing with the sort of bureaucracy I had to deal with in Brazil. In fact, you would not believe how much I feel as though I have travelled back in time – precisely three years and six months. I hope you manage to work out which point in my history. Right now, everything suggests that I will be on my way again soon. But obviously, it is impossible to know what to believe with so much 'advice' being bandied around.

Here, I have more or less exhausted the pleasures of the exotic and truly magnificent markets, especially the fish market: lobsters at preposterous prices, fish of every colour, huge shellfish that are grilled like beafsteaks [sic], etc. There are also many more types of fruit than there were in Brazil. I have just spent two days in the countryside, at 1,000 metres altitude, in the foothills of Mount Pelée. A glorious break, and so different from the sweltering heat of Fort-de-France day and night. Yet despite everything, it is best that I stay here, to be aware of any news, but if my stay here goes on much longer, I will commute between the two. The countryside is extraordinarily beautiful, bewilderingly mountainous like a Chinese painting: the cliffs, the peaks, etc. But on a much smaller scale. There are whole forests of tree ferns, and numerous sandy beaches with huts, bread-fruit trees and coconut palms; everything here looks charming, friendly, almost childlike, much more reminiscent of the Pacific Islands (at least as I imagine them) than the Americas. Brazil is much less pleasant, but it has a tragic grandeur.

As I have already said, I have adopted two young couples who work in the cinema as my travelling companions; with them, the time passes agree-ably enough; we go for walks, we go bathing on the nearby beaches. We are constantly running into people we know, directly or indirectly; just now, I bumped into the sister-in-law of my former boss (G.M.), who gave me news of him. He is now living somewhere near Bordeaux. A few days ago, I received the letter you sent to Nemours. You can tell Dinah that I met Monsieur Goldschmidt, a friend of General Wibié. Apart from the socialising and the ice-cream sodas that play a crucial role here, I have been engaged in a little local archaeology with a Reverend Father, a colleague from the Society of

Americanists, and I wait for the time to pass. That's all I have to tell you, I think. All my love,

    Claude,

    P.S. Don't forget to let me know about any material concerns. Is the stipend being paid regularly, etc.?

Part Three

———

Are There Cows in America?

*It is the events that have accommodated themselves
to the book, not the book to events.*

Victor Hugo, *Bug-Jargal*

13

The Goose Game

——

Aboard a Swedish banana boat
8 and 9 May 1941

He who lands on thirty-one, there will find a deep, dark well, and must wait his turn until he can clamber out of hell. A journey such as this has to be imagined like the Goose Game, thought Lévi-Strauss. As with the board game, there is only the illusion of skill, of strategy, the traveller is like a player blowing on the dice, he must trust to chance and uncertainty, must grope his way along a path strewn with traps and pitfalls, joys that are quickly disappointed, plans that fail or, on the contrary, succeed by a stroke of luck, finding an unexpected solution at the expense of other travellers who cannot move. Bridges, wells, hotels, prisons, or death, eeny, meeny, miny, moe, out you must go. The player advances his counter along the board, slides back, leaps the cliff by throwing a double six, but just as he is rushing towards the finish, he stumbles and falls into a labyrinth and finds himself back at square one. Having spent their time in Marseilles playing Tarot, the passengers who boarded the leaky tub on 24 March were once again throwing dice, playing a game of Goose or Snakes and Ladders, hoping to throw a double so they could reach their destination more quickly. The Gulf of Mexico, for instance, is a snake that ends up in French Guiana, at the mouth of the Orinoco, a group of islands adrift in the Caribbean Sea, an archipelago mimicking a route from the tip of Florida to South America; it is a tortuous route in which every island is a square on the board and the Americas represent the finish line. You throw the dice and move from square to square; some may interrupt your journey, others bring you closer to your goal. *He who lands on fifty-two, there will find a prison cell, and must wait his turn until the throw of dice lands well;* one of the prisoners could have chalked these words on the walls of the fortress at Pointe-du-Bout as he waited for the *Duc d'Aumale*, a ghost ship that never came. 'If Christopher Columbus had had to deal with so much paperwork, he'd have given up on discovering America!' people joked as they once again found themselves forced to obtain unlikely visas, to pay exorbitant guarantees, *a throw of nine will take you far, if you should throw a six and three go to twenty-six, if you should throw a four and five race all the way to fifty-three* could have been stamped on their passports with three counters to pay the security guarantees. To reach a destination, the passengers had to trace routes entirely at odds with elementary geography, a wild scribble on the map with countless dead ends. *The first to land on sixty-three, the fabled garden of the goose, shall win the game and shout with glee. But he must land precisely there, if he do not, back he must count, the remaining squares to remount.*

One by one, Lévi-Strauss said his goodbyes to all those who had welcomed him during his time on the island. He packed his bags, checked out of the Hôtel de la Paix and headed for the quays and the offices of the Compagnie Transatlantique. On the deck of the pristine Swedish banana boat sailing swiftly towards Puerto Rico, he may have thought that the simplest route is never what one might imagine, the obvious route is inevitably a detour, a trap masquerading as a short-cut, a calculated risk. *The accidents of travel often produce ambiguities such as these,* he wrote in his diary. Of the prisoners aboard the *Paul-Lemerle*, he was the first to reach the continent. And perhaps within ten days he would be strolling along the broad avenues of Manhattan, giving his first lessons at the New School. Having been convinced that declaring his luggage in transit would cause delays, since this meant waiting in an embargoed port for a ship flying a foreign flag, he had been saved by the collection of drawings and notes he had amassed during his expeditions, the very documents he had feared some zealous, ignorant official would mistake for some secret code. He was on the move, his counter sliding across the board, he could pick up the cup, throw the dice, and land on another square which might be a hotel or a labyrinth; in the meantime, his companions had to miss their turn, while he would take a chance card from his pocket: the Nambikwara.

The boat was new, *immaculately white*. There were eight passengers on board and the crew were friendly and attentive. It was some time before they pulled out of the harbour.

Aboard the Saint-Domingue
10 May 1941

On every ninth square, and in the four corners of the gameboard, were symbols relating to the Dreyfus Affair (the broken tablets of the rights of man, a soldier's *képi* in the scales of justice, masks swept away, the *état-major* rolling the dice of the law) and, in the centre, not a goose, but *naked truth*, an allegorical figure holding aloft a shining beacon – this was The Game of The Dreyfus Affair and the Truth, a parody of the Goose Game created by Dreyfus' supporters. The rules of this version, where prison was the Devil's Island penal colony, read: 'Do not stop on the squares marked TRUTH (naturally, since all the truths presented so far are pure humbug)'. A player had to avoid landing on *The Military Stockade of the Pont des Invalides* or *The Minister for War* and instead head for *Le Mont-Valérian*, armed with a handful of counters and a playing piece shaped like a cannon or a fort. Along the way he might encounter Émile Zola, the gaoler at Cherche-Midi prison, Verpillon, who takes the prisoners' mugshots, Clemenceau, Colonel Picquart, Esther Vas-Y and the editor of *L'Aurore* ... Some routes are simpler than others, but it is easier to take the route to Cayenne than tempt fate by heading directly for America.

He who lands on fifty-two, there will find a prison cell, and must wait his turn until the throw of dice lands well. She was the only woman aboard, not that this bothered her. Next to her, two non-commissioned officers, a captain from the Polish Embassy and Jacques Rémy, a screenwriter who was never without his dog, both of whom were heading for Argentina via Saint-Laurent-du-Maroni, Cayenne,

Belém and Rio. One of the other passengers was a special emissary sent by Maréchal Pétain to visit the French overseas territories, just as, on some other ship, there was probably an emissary from de Gaulle telling a very different story. And every evening, all these fine people were guests at the captain's table. Their host had the good grace not to talk politics but instead, as though the pomp and ceremony of the Belle Époque were still in fashion, he would quote the poetry of Saint-John Perse and hum an aria from an opera. 'They tell me you're a photographer. How fascinating!' he said, turning to Germaine Krull and suggesting, as a fitting end to the dinner, that she take a series of group portraits during which the captain learned how to frame a shot, closing one eye and pressing the other to the viewfinder of the Ikarette in which he could see the travelling companions of the *Saint-Domingue* in the instant they were captured on the film.

Saint-Laurent-du-Maroni
11 May 1941

A sailor hailed the captain to say that the *Saint-Domingue* was approaching Saint-Laurent-du-Maroni and to request orders. It was 11 a.m., but in a half-light that made it impossible to see one's hand in front of one's face, it felt as though it were five hours earlier or ten hours later. The entry to the penal colony was via the Maroni, a river wide as a black pool whose banks would have been indiscernible but for the animal cries that rose from either side. The river roared, tearing at its banks, ripping away roots as large as dugouts and mangroves that looked like giant forks. It carried huge quantities of mud and, like a hydraulic pump, spilled floating debris in rotting piles on its banks. They encountered another ship which gave them a wide berth, moving away to hug the far bank, belching smoke and a miasma of oil and petrol that mingled with the suffocating low cloud, the morning mist. Germaine Krull gazed at what was still no more than a cloud of barely dissipating smoke that veiled a secret of which there existed no images, a place where Delescluze, Duval and Avinain had been imprisoned, where wanted men still languished. And it was because of this detour that the authorities had, unwittingly, sent her to this shameful strong-hold *as though to cover a story*. It would have been folly, or at the very least unprofessional, not to take advantage of this twist of fate, which, like a canny editor, had organised this tour of intern-ment camps, from Sanary to the Lazaret on Pointe-Rouge, and now to Devil's Island and Saint-Laurent-du-Maroni. Having read Albert Londres's account of his visit, Germaine Krull imagined it as a verdant hell, *water above and water below*, cyclones and boats skimming like pelicans over the water, prisoners in the sweltering heat of this scrap of Amazonia. In her diary she wrote: *At the mouth of the river, for the rare ship that calls in, sit huge mooring buoys that give off a mournful, plaintive sound.* As they came alongside, she leaned over the gunwale and watched the ship's engine struggle against the current and, further off, the prisoners, in bizarre uniforms of red and white stripes bleached pale pink by the tropical sun and the rains, attaching the hawsers to slimy green floaters barely teth-ered to the wooden jetty. It was like stepping into a forgotten world; here where a leader had rallied an army of fanatics, or had wound up with his head on a stake. The mail and the supplies were quickly unloaded. The captain confined passengers and crew to their cabins for the day, and probably the night.

San Juan, Puerto Rico
12 May 1941

Such is the way of the world; sometimes the very thing that saves you holds you back. What was there in this trunk that Lévi-Strauss could not throw away, other than a form of initiation? The indi-genous dialects and various books in German that had so riled the Vichy authorities in Fort-de-France that they had accused him of being *a Jewish freemason in the pay of the Americans*, here, on another island, in a different context, raised fears of a fifth column, of boats filled with refugees, damning proof that he was a spy and a very strange man. This was not an era of half-measures; Lévi-Strauss was held in custody until it could be verified that the notes of his expeditions, glossaries of Nambikwara vocabulary, sketches depicting the social structure of the Bororos and Kadiweu body paintings did not obscure codes, invasion plans, or other encrypted messages. He attempted to explain, babbling in confused English that these were notes from his years of work, that he would be sorely tried if he were to lose them, but it was futile, hardly had he managed to explain his itinerary and the reason for his stopover in Puerto Rico than a customs officer held up the typewriter with its German keyboard as another damning piece of evidence. Worse still, American immigration rules had been tightened since he had obtained his visa earlier that year, this visa, which was supported by his employer, the New School for Social Research, was merely temporary, and now required that the university supply additional documentation to the authorities. After a farcical interrogation in which Lévi-Strauss was forced to justify both his service record and his work as a teacher, and after difficult negotiations whose details we need not go into, though they would have provided both the reader and the writer of these lines with a precise ethnology, a short guide to Hispano-American grammar and an introduction to the laws concerning immigration featuring cameo roles from Dr Monroe and Charles Lindberg, Lévi-Strauss was placed under house arrest in a hotel in San Juan until, he was informed, an FBI agent able to read French (and, he hoped, the dialects of indigenous Brazilian tribes) could be dispatched to the island ... On square sixty-two, a single roll of the dice from the finish line, Lévi-Strauss made three bad throws, moved back ten squares, and was interned at the expense of the Compagnie Transatlantique in Puerto Rico. Two police officers escorted him to a hotel room in the centre of San Juan, and took turns standing guard. On the second day, on the terrace of the hotel, he encountered one of the passengers he had briefly met on the Swedish banana boat, a young chemist who seemed as lost as he was. His name was Bertrand Goldschmidt and, at the age of twenty, he had joined the Institut Curie as a laboratory assistant. Goldschmidt told him how, during the war, he had been seconded to work in a military laboratory in Poitiers, then captured and interned in a German camp from which, to his great astonishment, he had been released. Then, out of boredom, in the way people find themselves confiding in strangers, one thing having led to another, he began to talk about nuclear fusion, about what would be the atomic bomb, and *revealed that the major powers had embarked on a scientific race, the winner of which would be sure of victory.* Later, having talked no more about what, at that time, was merely a scientific dream, they discovered that they shared a mutual passion for Ravel. There followed a bizarre moment where a young ethnologist studying the indigenous tribes in Brazil and a post-doctoral chemist with expertise in nuclear fusion, both Jews, both exiles, both heading for America, stood on the terrace of a hotel in Puerto Rico and discussed the Piano Concerto for the Left Hand and the finale of *Bolero*. Such is the way with war: sudden, unexpected coincidences facilitate anything, save everything.

Saint-Laurent-du-Maroni
13 May 1941

She took his picture. He ran a bar in Maroni, in what might be called the centre, a clutter of shacks and cabins just past the penal colony. He sold coffee and huge turtle's eggs. He was a former prisoner, a *libéré*, one of the *freed*, to use terminology that has no meaning beyond the banks of this river where prisoners, exiles and soldiers rubbed shoulders and lived according to the law of exceptions. He took the time to explain the status of the *freed*. 'When you've served your sentence in the penal colony, a second sentence begins, you're freed but you have to stay here for a period equal to your original sentence. If you were sent down for ten years, you have to spend ten years more as one of the *freed* – with only a patch of ground and a spade by way of reward.' Those who did not die from the gruelling forced labour might still die of a surfeit of freedom. He described a number of scenarios, from the most common to the most daring. Some ran off into the sugar plantations and ended up God knows where, swallowed by the cursed river that gave up nothing. Others headed for Cayenne and worked as servants for the families of army officers. Little more than slaves (at best), they traded their freedom for a bowl of slops and a glass of rum, they clapped their own feet in irons. Lastly, there were the men who tried to escape, to make it through the jungle. They all died. Nothing was worse than the jungle. He also talked about the *banished*, those with life sentences who were ostracised from society.

'You see them in Cayenne, they all end up there, they've got jobs, but no one has anything to do with them, they're pariahs that no self-respecting prisoner would talk to.' This is the penal colony, a collection of small muddy islands reclaimed from the forest and the river where free men, prisoners and the banished are rotting away. The ship pulled out of Saint-Laurent at dawn, all that was visible was the shadowy pink outline of the prisoners against a vast backdrop of deep saturated green, as though an artist had hurriedly squeezed out a whole tube of paint and spread it over the canvas. It was terrifyingly banal, this human solidarity in the face of suffering. Germaine Krull wrote: *Goodbye, Saint-Laurent-du-Maroni, with your spiders big as hands that bite and kill, your grasses that blind, your river which meanders and sweeps along prawns of every colour that can also kill. And goodbye to the men of this society that makes no sense.*

Fort-de-France
14 May 1941

He who lands on the square number one, there will find an erect penis, does not wait his turn for help. It was in July 1929, on the Île de Sein (square number two shows an outline of a breast), Breton and Tanguy were bored and so, with India ink and watercolours, they set about creating a surrealist version of the Goose Game without changing the rules, the spiral structure or the key squares, they simply filled the squares with images from a different bestiary. The *Surrealist Manifesto* appeared on square forty-eight, square twenty-six featured Josephine Baker's banana skirt, square sixty-two depicted a deep-sea diver and twenty-one the island's lighthouse.

Having negotiated the buying of the paper and scheduled the print date for 20 June, Suzanne was working on the draft of an article about Alain, the philosopher, which she hoped would be in the next issue of the magazine. *And here we are, at the threshold of art, the human alone, almost detached from the obstacle. And it is in the drawing that we find artistic expression in a face-to-face conversation with itself.* She described Breton in one paragraph as 'the authentic poet', surrendered to the dark forces of his mind: *Through a curious encounter, Alain in his System of the Fine Arts and Breton in his Mad Love propose the same example to readers: Da Vinci advising his students to create a coherent painting from the contemplation of stains on an old wall.* From their meeting came echoes of other readings, the conviction, if not the belief, that the alliance between the artist and the world can occur only with a total relinquishment of self, whether through the audacious daring of games such as Exquisite Corpse, but through any method that cast you onto the far shore. It was so strange that a man as brusque and often curt as Breton could inspire curiosity, affection, courage in her. Even the alchemy of these conversations remained obscure to both of them, such that talking about 'methods' seemed entirely at odds with the free association that governed their days. *Objective chance* was the most apposite phrase – the evidence of the encounter, even the choice, as far-fetched as it might seem, secretly fashioned a necessity behind the scenes. Both Aimé and Suzanne seemed convinced that it could not be otherwise. There is no providence that goes unfulfilled, and just as in fairy tales, where the wizard awaits the chosen one, never doubting the time nor the place, so the encounter with surrealism rang out like a rallying cry of the revolutionary force of poetry: *So, far from contradicting, diminishing or diverting our revolutionary feeling for life, surrealism shored it up. It nourished in us an impatient strength, endlessly sustaining this massive army of negations.*

Waiting for the Duc-d'Aumale
15 May 1941

Some said there was trouble with the engines, others that it was the threat from British warships. The night before, the longshoremen had opened the sluice gates of the dry dock where the *Duc-d'Aumale* had lain for several weeks, having arrived, listing heavily, about to sink. It was moored between the *Émile-Bertin* and the *Presidente-Trujillo*, a vessel from Santo Domingo, opposite the Compagnie Générale Atlantique. In the morning, the patrol boats from the Sûreté had shuttled between the Lazaret on the far side of the bay and the jetty. In the former leper colony, the *Duc-d'Aumale* was on everyone's lips. The Germans and the Poles amputated the leading consonants, *U-Aumale*, as though it were the name of an American submarine. No one recognised the name of the former governor-general, leader of the Orleanists, fifth son of King Louis-Philippe, save for a few old men who had one foot in the previous century and the other in the grave, those who had been ten years old in 1870, in their fifties at the outbreak of the First World War, and were now destined to die in exile, plagued by sunshine and mosquitoes, at the age of eighty. Breton had come across the name in the *Journal* of the brothers Goncourt, though he would have had difficulty remembering it now: *There is but one way to describe the Duc d'Aumale: he is the epitome of the elderly colonel in the light cavalry. He has that svelte elegance, that ravaged appearance, the greying goatee beard, the balding pate, the voice worn hoarse from barking orders.* The *Duc* now being readied to cast off was a French Line vessel, high on the water, measuring about a hundred metres from bow to stern. Among the passengers were two hundred from the *Paul-Lemerle* and fifty from the *Carimaré*, for now people talked about their voyages as they did about their lineage, proudly or shame-facedly. All were gathered by the rear hold hatch, which on this ship was called the 'court of miracles'. After several hours' waiting, Commandant Jacques de Fromont de Bouaille, a tall man with a loping gait, addressed the travellers: the ship was not putting out. All tickets would be reimbursed or would be valid if the departure was merely rescheduled. Tempers began to fray. One of the watch officers informed those who were desperate for an explanation that the news from New York was not good. Another liner, the SS *Normandie*, had been seized by the US authorities. The shipping company was not prepared to risk another vessel without a guarantee that it would not be seized.

He who lands on thirty-one, there will find a deep, dark well, must wait until another player also lands there and takes his place in hell. 'His Excellency Generalissimo Dr Rafael Leónidas Trujillo Molina, President of the Dominican Republic, Benefactor of the Nation and Restorer of the Republic's financial independence invites you to come to Santo Domingo aboard the *President-Trujillo*, a magnificent ship that will set sail tomorrow.' The short, stocky man who introduced himself as Consul for the Dominican Republic in Fort-de-France scanned the gangways and the upper deck as he made his call. Instantly, there was a rush of passengers, some of them overjoyed to hear that they were wanted somewhere, others happy to be leaving Martinique. President Trujillo had launched a vast pro-White immigration programme intended to repopulate the country, and, though fiercely anti-communist, anti-Semitic and pro-Franco, the dictator had decreed that Spanish Republicans, European communists and Jews were welcome.

He fostered the hatred of his own people. Three hundred Haitians had been slaughtered on the Haitian–Dominican border and the president had vowed to eradicate 'dogs, hogs and Haitians'. It was not unusual for the hunted to become the hunter in the countries that were referred to as 'sanctuary countries', and of these, the Dominican Republic became a beacon.

14

Trojan Horse

———

According to legend the Goose Game was invented during the siege of Troy. Palamedes, king of Euboea, student of the centaur Chiron and inventor of the games of dice, draughts and jacks, is said to have invented it to occupy the idle soldiers. The spiral course invited players to follow the path of Theseus through the labyrinth of the Minotaur while the Gods and the Fates determined each player's advance according to the throws of the dice. The game instilled in the Achaean troops a tenacity and a bravery that was proof against any ordeal. But sometimes, patience and tenacity were not enough; one had to load the dice, kick over the table, rig the game, disguise the goose as a horse.

LETTER FROM CLAUDE LÉVI-STRAUSS
TO HIS PARENTS

16 MAY 1941
PUERTO RICO

Dear both, by the time you receive this letter, my travails will be over though I confess that, as difficult crossings go, this has been particularly successful. Until now, I have not been able to tell you anything about what happened before; suffice it to say that it was only through luck and exceptional protection (particularly that of the ship's captain) that I managed to avoid the internment camp where my fellow travellers were confined. As for morale, you can easily guess. Since finding a direct sailing to New York was very problematic, I was fortunate (but was it fortunate? The rest of this story might leave you doubtful; however, the speed at which events have been moving has convinced me that I was right to take the first available ship, regardless) to get a place with a dozen other people aboard an ultramodern banana boat heading here to collect cargo. A calm, comfortable crossing of a day and a half; it was only afterwards that the problems set in. Firstly, we were kept on board for four days without any explanation whatever. Then, since the ship was scheduled to leave, we were transferred to a hotel in the city and kept under house arrest, with two guards assigned to watch us, while customs have kept my scientific documents, which they consider highly suspect. Eventually, we appeared before the immigration authorities but, while everything went smoothly for my fellow passengers, I was beset by problems: a four-hour interrogation (in English) under oath while a stenographer recorded my statement; I had to give every last detail of my life, where I went to school, how much I earned teaching at the lycée in Mont-de-Marsan, etc., after which it was decided that the whole thing was decidedly suspect (perhaps the New School does not exist, or, if it does, perhaps there are no students, or, if there are, perhaps it invited two professors to take up the same post, etc.) and that my case had to be referred to Washington.

So, here I am, holed up in my hotel, I have the two guards all to myself now, and they follow me every time I want to go and have an ice cream soda! It happened two days ago. The day before yesterday, I was summoned so that a specialist [sic] could examine my documents, after which he gave them back to me: that's something at least. But no news about my case. Obviously, I immediately sent a cable to Aunt Aline and it was only yesterday, after two days' silence during which I worked myself into a terrible state, that I received a heartening response from Johnson himself, telling me that he is sending me $200 and a new contract, that he is personally in touch with Washington, and not to worry. I have to say that there was something strange about the contracts, since the one I had was for only one year, as a 'visiting professor' when I already have an immigration visa. In this, the New School has behaved tactlessly, and I suspect they now feel a little guilty. As for the money, it will be very welcome because I arrived here with cheques in dollars drawn on a New York bank which no one will cash (people have little faith in French banks) and for the past week I have not had a penny.

It is not very important since, until and unless I am granted admission, I am considered to be aboard ship and the responsibility of the Compagnie Trans-atlantique, thank God Aunt Aline specially recommended me, which made it possible for me to catch this boat and embark on this adventure! The hotel I am staying at costs $2 a day, all inclusive. It is an extraordinary mixture (like everything else here) of sordid Spanish and American influences. In the morning we are given grapefruit, cornflakes, etc., but for lunch and dinner we have 'arroz y feijão'; similarly, the bathrooms are immaculate, but the water is cut off between 8 a.m. and 6 p.m. Life is much like in São Paulo, but on a smaller scale. It is a strange feeling to be once again surrounded by opulence and abundance, but I feel a pang of anguish when I think about France and about you.

As for the cost of living, I get the impression that calculating at 40 francs for the dollar you get a rough equivalence. I've just realised that writing on the other side of the paper makes my letter illegible. So I will stop. My case will definitely be sorted out in the next few days and I hope to arrive in New York, a hero and a victim, towards the end of next week. Have you noticed that I left the last patch of French soil on the same day the Vichy Conseil National, chaired by Lucien Romier, met for the first time in the house of Grandfather Strauss? How symbolic!

All my love,

Claude

P.S. The water drops are not tears, but sweat. It's very hot here!

Pointe-à-Pitre bay
17 May 1941

A tiny, distant point hove into view, a strange bird-like craft with no sail, no mast, whose oars, moving on the waterline, were like huge sweeping wings mirrored in the iridescent sea. The boat came alongside and a man in shirtsleeves and waistcoat appeared beneath the anchor of the steamboat. He stood up in his canoe, a cigarette dangling from his lips, waved his arms and shouted: 'Ahoy, there! Ahoy, Captain!' He looked for all the world like an oarsman in a painting by Caillebotte, but here he was in the middle of Pointe-à-Pitre bay, beneath a sun hot enough to boil the brain. Worse still, he was not wearing a hat. No one knows whether

Breton spotted him, or whether he was elsewhere, in the dining hall or the cabins, only that he was not particularly surprised. We think of war as a long silence, but in fact it was quite talkative – people wrote so frequently that no one was entirely lost, this was an era of letter-writing, mail arrived at its destination in a parcel tied with string, to be forwarded from phantom address to poste restante. People wrote so much, included so many clues, that it would have been possible to find Friday on the other island. So much so that people could trace their tortuous routes, map out their crossing from island to island, thanks to the Post & Telegraph service. As surprising, unlikely as it may seem, was that the curious man approaching from the shores of Guadeloupe in his dugout canoe was Pierre Mabille, a friend of Breton they had left behind in Salon-de-Provence. Since finding refuge in Basse-Terre, he had been overcome by boredom, working as a doctor for a military regime he called more stupid than evil. Breton had telegraphed to tell him about the stopover, and when Mabille realised that, for diplomatic reasons, the *Presidente-Trujillo* would not be allowed to dock at Pointe-à-Pitre, he had rented a skiff from a fisherman and rowed out to meet the ship. A rope ladder was lowered down to him and he was welcomed like a brother, Masson and Breton laughed heartily, Jacqueline threw her arms around him. Mabille hugged Aube, and, hunkering down to speak to the child, paused for a moment and looked at her: 'Hello, Aube, I saw you being born, did you know that?'

US Virgin Islands
18 May 1941

At Sainte-Croix, the *Presidente-Trujillo* was not allowed into the harbour. The people here feared dissidents, the ship docked in Dominica, but the passengers were not allowed to go ashore. The women and children slept in the cabins while the men sprawled in deckchairs and the boys lay on mattresses on deck. In Barbados, a captain of the US Marine Corps came aboard. John A. Butler, a handsome American naval attaché of about thirty, had been tasked with the mission of interrogating Victor Serge. The intelligence service, having been alerted that a leading figure of the Revolution was aboard, feared that he might be on a mission from the USSR. The interview took place in the ship's dining hall, beneath an imposing portrait of Generalissimo Trujillo decked out in his military medals and his presidential sash, which a steward dutifully dusted morning and evening. The room had a farcical air about it, exacerbated by the interrogation, or rather the conversation. The young officer occasionally glanced at a counter-espionage file open on the desk, feigning a familiarity with Russia that Serge, who held his tongue, found amusing. Serge suddenly heard himself being referred to as a member of the *Red General Staff*, as someone who had openly stated that 'Trotsky's party disappeared after Trotsky's death'. Serge gleefully confided fake secrets, determined to blacken his own name in this biography that some academic would doubtless dig out in Washington one day and be puzzled by the notes from this interrogation carried out aboard the *Presidente-Trujillo*, or perhaps find in it material for a spy novel in the style of Graham Greene. He would read Butler's notes, his observations about the subject: 'a brilliant, well-trained observer, whose first thoughts are against Stalin though he is for democracies'. The mention of Lucien Vogel as a double agent, the allegation that 'Without doubt Krivitsky was killed by the OGPU', the possibility of 'bacterial warfare'. Butler, who lived in Louisiana, attempted to conclude the conversation in French, and wished him *bon voyage*. The two men warmly shook hands as they parted. That evening, sitting in the same dining hall, Serge regaled his comrades with an impersonation of the captain. Then, setting mockery aside, he spoke of the man's firmness, the frankness of his expression and his intelligence.

In the stern of the ship, Wifredo and Helena, who were watching the sunset, saw a green ray flare between sea and sky on the horizon. It is a green that does not exist, they said.

Belém, Brazil
19 May 1941

The feeling of danger is intoxicating to someone who knows that they are safe. The marble tiles petered out, the facade of the seventeenth-century palace gave way to glimpses of a corrugated iron shanty town, a wooden shelter, a red-brick chapel. What at noon had seemed like a street during the siesta was transformed by twilight into a ghost town. Life had fled, hanged barons, mad widows, deserted theatres, a liveried hotel bellboy with no guests. The only inhabitants lived in an intermediary zone with no houses which was at the far end of the main street, on the edge of the forest, preferring their ramshackle shelters to the stately buildings in the centre which they claimed were haunted. In a pincer movement, the jungle encroached on the white buildings, moss grew in the half-open doorways, on the windows, in the dimpled chins of statues and the bas-reliefs; threads of liana-like Virginia creeper covered the walls and the courtyards; in doorways and on window sills a confusion of plants rose from floor to ceiling, shattering the cupolas and the glass domes and, lounging like great boa constrictors, creating a canopy. Further off, in the dark street, having stopped at a casino and a brothel run by a French madame, Germaine Krull and her companions were sitting round a table in the great dance hall. Here, ten-year-old girls forced into prostitution twirled and pirouetted with sailors and planters.

They ordered a bottle of champagne.

San Juan, Puerto Rico
20 May 1941

Though he had not fallen into a profound state of lethargy like Professor Tarragon in the Sanders-Hardiman expedition, Lévi-Strauss nonetheless spent much of each day lying on his bed leafing through magazines while the two sentries guarded the door. And just as Tintin breaks the curse of Rascar Capac and prevents his friends from being burned on a pyre in the Temple of the Sun by discovering the date and time of the solar eclipse on a scrap of newspaper Captain Haddock is about to use to light his pipe, so Lévi-Strauss owed his salvation to the daily newspapers. Only war offers the – doubtless inappropriate – illusion that the world is simultaneously shrinking and expanding, and, like a black hole, bringing together two distant points. André Breton was reunited with Pierre Mabille in the bay of Pointe-à-Pitre, while, from a brief newspaper article, Claude Lévi-Strauss learned of the arrival of Jacques Soustelle, a former colleague at the Musée de l'Homme, an expert on pre-Columbian civilisations who was *touring the West Indies in order to persuade the French residents to support Général de Gaulle*. Meeting up again with this man who, as soon as he got his *agrégation*, had run off to Mexico to study the Otomi people and the Mayan languages was like being transported back to before the war, crossing the Trocadéro bridge, climbing the steps up to the Musée de l'Homme and shaking hands with the curator. The two former disciples of Paul Rivet met up again on the far side of the world, in a hotel in San Juan, where they recounted their journeys – Lévi-Strauss, the crossing aboard the *Paul-Lemerle* with its impromptu university on the top deck; Jacques Soustelle, his journey in a convoy of torpedo boats, his stints in New York, Montreal and later Mexico. Eyes shining, he confided the message telegraphed to him by de Gaulle: 'Come to London, but first create a support committee for Free France.' He explained how, between February and April, he and Gilbert Médioni had assembled the Mexican Free France delegation. How, without a penny, he raised money by playing the lottery until the first funds arrived from London, and gathered together the expatriate Resistance fighters. In the middle of his story, he told Claude about his role, his work with the British ministry, his dinner with Général de Gaulle and his mission as the general's personal representative in Latin America to rally partisans and dissidents throughout the Caribbean. He talked proudly about his most recent convert, Philippe Grousset, First Secretary to the Vichy Embassy in Cuba, who agreed to head up the local movement after his visit to Havana where he had been received by General Batista with great ceremony. He had just come back from the Dominican Republic, now under the dictatorship of Trujillo, and had come to Puerto Rico to make sure that Admiral Spruance's fleet did not plan to seize the French Antilles, and to request the support of his government. They probably did not talk much, if at all, about the museum, or the network, about which Lévi-Strauss knew nothing; perhaps, after having talked for a long time, as in a whodunnit where the action stops so that the detective can recap the plot and finally reveal the guilty party, they simply thought that one of the most striking things about war is that, unless people recounted their stories, no one would believe it, they would find this unexpected reunion implausible. Perhaps they even decided that their stories deserved to be told in order to bear witness to this chance, and amused themselves at the thought that their journeys might form the basis of a far-fetched novel. Lévi-Strauss talked about his situation, the trunk seized by the immigration authorities, his visa and his contract with the New School which was about to expire. Jacques promised to pull some strings in New York and Puerto Rico, to make it clear to the American authorities that Lévi-Strauss was not a spy – it would not take more than a day.

They talked about their misfortunes, about how chance invariably involves violence, a stroke of luck, a lucky break, a fighting chance. Lévi-Strauss talked about another lucky break, *my career was decided one day in the autumn of 1934, at nine o'clock in the morning, by a telephone call*, which had seen him leave the École Normale Supérieure for the University of São Paulo. He talked about reading the article in the newspaper, that stroke of *fate*, and, like Tintin in an Inca dungeon, peering at a scrap of newspaper and muttering, 'How very odd … What an extraordinary coincidence!', how he jumped for joy and cried 'Captain! Captain! We're saved!'

LETTER FROM THE SECRETARY
OF THE GOVERNOR OF MARTINIQUE
TO THE DIRECTOR OF THE
COMPAGNIE GÉNÉRALE TRANSATLANTIQUE

21 MAY 1941
FORT-DE-FRANCE

Monsieur le Directeur,
In response to your letter No. 41/57 of 20 May. I have the honour of confirming the agreement reached between us in the presence of Rear Admiral BATTET, Commander PELTIER and the Captain of the Gendarmerie concerning the stay of the passengers aboard the 'Duc d'Aumale' in transit from Martinique, who were previously held in the Lazaret.

> *In accordance with this agreement, the costs of the passengers' time on*
> *board will be settled by the Director for Public Security in the amount of*
> *twenty-five francs per person, per day.*
>
> *Respectfully yours,*
> *Signed: Yves Nicol*
> *Certified Copy: The Secretary General*

Off the coast of Puerto Rico
22 May 1941

In his journal, Lévi-Strauss kept a chart comparing the different rums of Martinique and Puerto Rico. He based his assessment on the excellence of the craftsmanship and the ancient traditions versus the crudity of the technique and the profitability, *wooden casks encrusted with dregs* versus *white enamel barrels fitted with chrome spigots.*

Ciudad Trujillo Harbour
23 May 1941

People grow accustomed to being mistreated; not knowing when such mistreatment will end can feel doubly perverse. Inevitably they expect malice, they hear themselves addressed as Monsieur, offered a hand as they step off the gangway and then, *bam*, they are tripped up. They patiently wait for the blow to come. So, when it does not, they are almost annoyed and certainly unsettled. If there is one thing war teaches you, it is that you cannot be too cautious. Already, as they disembarked, the passengers were annoyed that the controller was stamping passports feverishly, without so much as a surreptitious glance. A principled lady decided to make a stand, shouting that her papers were in order. Some journalists who had come aboard earlier were chatting deferentially to the illustrious passengers, all of whom, they claimed, were ambassadors for their respective countries. It was ridiculous. A grotesque farce, they were fake journalists, perhaps even spies, or plain-clothes immigration officers, informants. Wifredo Lam fell into the arms of

Eugenio Granell, a surrealist painter and friend of Benjamin Péret, a comrade-in-arms from the Spanish Civil War, a Republican in exile. At the foot of the gangways, a crowd of onlookers had gathered and were greeting every passenger. The passengers split into two groups, the first left without any further ado, the second group sat on their suitcases and sent one of the boys off to fetch the immigration authorities. An hour later, the helpless child returned to say yes, all necessary formalities had been completed. Standing against the white wooden wall, frustrated that they had been allowed onto the quayside with no military escort, a somewhat smaller group decided to wait for the customs office to open. But no one came. Nothing had been arranged. There would be no quarantine, no isolated internment camp, not even an interrogation. Nothing but the deserted quays, the street beyond the barriers, the unaccustomed freedom. Men in blue striped uniforms appeared at the other end of the harbour; they were prisoners out walking. And while a hardcore group remained on the docks, convinced that their patience would be rewarded, Breton was on the terrace of a hotel bar giving an exclusive interview to *La Nación*.

Ciudad Trujillo
24 May 1941

The ship's arrival in the harbour of Ciudad Trujillo made the front-page headlines of the 24 May issue of *La Nación*. The whole page was devoted to a list of the passengers, the names, nationalities and occupations. And those who, just yesterday, had been considered pariahs, deserters, cowards saw their names and their professions restored, in black and white, printed in the most important newspaper in the country; the list was a testament to the untold riches of the ship's cargo, a frozen image of a vanished world, the Europe of the 1930s. A Viennese urologist, German writers, a Belgian industrialist, Spanish ministers and ambassadors, a Cuban painter and a Czech engineer, their titles presented with admirable pomp, in capital letters: *Profesor, Excelentísimo, Don y Doña, Doctor*. In the inside pages, sandwiched between the daily transcription of the President's speech, and before the sports results and details of the celebrations for the Feast of the Virgin, one could read an article about Stalin by Victor Serge, and a digest of the interview Breton had given to Eugenio Granell.

ANDRÉ BRETON NOS HABLA
DE LA ACTUAL SITUACIÓN
DE LOS ARTISTAS FRANCESES

'André Breton talks to us about the current situation of French artists.' The interview, translated from the French, was printed over several columns with a photograph of the two men looking dapper, in smart blazers; cigarette in one hand, Granell is clutching a folded piece of paper, presumably to disguise his nervousness. From the picture, one can almost sense the light breeze, the heavy sky, the scent of evening after a long, hot day. There is a cloud in the sky; is it about to rain? Will they have to seek shelter from a brief tropical storm, finish the interview in the hotel bar? By way of pre-amble, Breton is presented as 'a man who is well known in artistic and intellectual circles around the world', one of the editors of the magazine *Minotaure*, a friend of Picasso, of Diego Rivera. He talked about the atmosphere of *withdrawal*, about the nebulous sense of national recovery and, strange as it might seem, he addressed himself to well-informed readers, though, were he to read the rest of the newspaper, he would have discovered it was futile to expect anything other than Dominican shopkeepers and doctors. Breton used the interview to settle scores: with Drieu La Rochelle, for his abject collaboration with the Nazis in the pages of the *Nouvelle Revue Française*, about the banning of books, particularly his own, he mentioned *Fata Morgana* and *The Anthology of Black Humour* ('humour that does not make you snigger but *shudder*, envisaged as a way for the *id* to overcome the trauma of the outside world'). He attempted to defend the idea of an international revolutionary surrealism in the pages of a rag loyal to a Caribbean dictator: 'to dialectically resolve all antinomies that hinder man's progress, reality and dream, reason and madness, objectivity and subjectivity, perception and representation, past and present, even life and death'. Later, on the subject of the surrealist troops, Breton gave news of his comrades: Benjamin Péret, Tristan Tzara and Jacques

Prévert had remained in France, Max Ernst was about to go to New York via Spain, André Masson, who was waiting on a transit visa for the Dominican Republic, had stayed behind in Martinique. On the subject of Picasso, in a testament to his admiration for the man and the painter, he said that if worst came to worst, he would still have a pencil, and if he did not have that, he would still be able to scratch the walls with his fingernails. More dangerously, the interview ended with an encomium to the island and its President Generalissimo. Whether it was sincere or not we cannot know, it is possible that the fulsome welcome had blinded this most Republican of Spanish Republicans from the ship. Every word was carefully weighed. Breton had written, as always, in green ink.

> *I can offer, unfortunately, only an impression, but it could not be more positive. I am happier still to say that the Dominican Republic is currently the hope of all those who, like me, are longing to once again find what they consider to be their raison d'être and of those many, back in France, who are not out of danger. In granting passengers a transit, the government of the Dominican Republic has added lustre to the ritual hospitality of which France, justifiably, has long been proud, and which its current puppet leaders have gravely offended. I was also aware, and have now seen with my own eyes, that my Spanish Republican friends have received a warm and fraternal welcome. They know that they owe the cheering and magnanimous welcome of the populace first and foremost to General Trujillo, who, in transforming the ruined Santo Domingo into the magnificent city that it is today in the space of ten years, has shown the right example and proved that there is no matter or morality so twisted that a determined man capable of embodying the will of others cannot master.*

Cuidad Trujillo
25 May 1941

In the report, he set down the conditions of the horrendous crossing and the internment at the Lazaret – Victor Serge was determined to leave a trail of clues along the way. Truths exist as documents; without proof, without trivial details, dates, names, they fade, they sputter out, or worse, other reports seek to stifle them, to snuff them out, and what prevails is the meticulous, bureaucratic authority of fear. He typed up a report, and filed away in a folder the only statement as witness, victim and judge, a biographical note on the *Capitaine-Paul-Lemerle* and on the Lazaret.

REPORT ON THE PASSENGERS
OF THE *CAPITAINE-PAUL-LEMERLE*

25 May 1941—Embarked in Marseilles on 25 March, 35 people recommended and protected by the IRA: Kuno Brandel, Hans Tittel, Carl Heidenreich, 3 Krizhaber, Alice Fried, H. Czeczwieczka, E. Bersch, K. Braeuning, 2 Oresch, 3 Osner, I. Reiter, H. Langerhans, M. Flake, 3 Barth, J. Weber, 2 Pfeffer, Capari, F. Bruhns, F. Caro, all in possession of danger visas or immigration visas for the United States; several visas have expired en route (Alice Fried). In addition, sent by the American Committee of Marseilles: the André Breton family (3), the Jacoby family (2), the Wilfredo Lam family (2), Kibalchich, Victor and his son.

In addition, about a hundred passengers, mainly Jewish businessmen (a few intellectuals) of bourgeois background. (Several businessmen had danger visas.) Almost all for the United States. Voyage in unsanitary conditions with insufficient nourishment, makeshift toilets on the deck across from an animal stable.

Upon arrival at Fort-de-France on 20 April most of the passengers were interned at the disused quarantine barrack at Pointe-du-Bout on a peninsula isolated from the city. Forty-five minutes on a launch to get to town. Officially 'lodged' under the control of the military authority which delivered 'leaves' to go to the city to see to administrative procedures. Guarded by black soldiers, excellent fellows, under the command of a (mixed-race) officer cadet. In town, closely guarded by Naval Security, Immigrant Services, the admiralty, agents of the 'Secret'. Conditions of internment: large huts with neither furniture nor bedding; straw mattresses to sleep on; no lighting; no fresh water; no medicine; tropical climate. Mineral water was sold for one franc a bottle and there was often none to be had. Upon arrival the authorities had seized all or almost all the passengers' money, according to each case, as a 'security deposit' 'to pay for your departure or repatriation'. They demanded 10,000 francs' security from stateless Russians for their eventual repatriation. This deposit also served to pay for lodging at the rate of 25 francs per day. Unspeakable and filthy food, more often than not tossed into the sea so that it was still necessary to pay 25 francs for corned beef and sardines. We protested and refused to allow ourselves to be robbed in this way, which resulted in conflicts and threats. Young Belgians were threatened with being 'returned to France and handed over to the Germans'. Others (myself) with being 'deported to Morocco'. Correspondence tightly censored, many letters disappeared.

The Transatlantic Company was repairing a steamer that hadn't sailed in some time, the Duc d'Aumale, *in order to send it to C. Trujillo and New York with its passengers as well as those of the* Carimaré, *who arrived three weeks later and are interned in the mountains at the camp of Balata, which is said to be better (among them several nationals of the EMERSCUE). Departure set for 17 May, tickets sold the 15th and 16th. On 17 May the departure 'postponed' because of international situation. Nevertheless, on the 18th all the internees from the quarantine station embarked aboard the* Duc d'Aumale, *where they found cabins and clean food. On 18 May those who had obtained a Dominican visa (2 Jacoby, 3 Breton, 2 Lam, 2 Kibalchich) left for Ciudad Trujillo aboard the* Presidente-Trujillo. *The others, about a hundred people, including thirty-five from the IRA, are interned aboard the* Duc d'Aumale.

The words of Lieutenant Castaing of Naval Security: 'We'll make those who have no more money work to pay for their lodging.' 'They pass under the control of the naval authorities.' 'The Duc d'Aumale *will depart but won't go to New York' – 'to an unknown destination'. It's believed among the passengers in C. Trujillo that the* Duc d'Aumale *did, in fact, leave for 'an unknown destination' with its passengers for the United States. According to a rumour, the admiralty is supposed to have requested authorisation to disembark them in C. Trujillo or Haiti, but we don't have any precise information.*

Ciudad Trujillo
26 May 1941

At sea, to restore their morale people talked about what life would be like afterwards, about what they would do on the other side. They imagined Manhattan, the streets of Chinatown, the Jewish neighbourhoods in the Bronx, and Fifth Avenue. Of all the stories, one sounded like a cock-and-bull story, a fairy tale for overgrown children. It described a strip of hostile jungle on the northern shores of the island of Santo Domingo, where the uninhabited land had been converted by a Jewish mutual-aid association into a prosperous farming community with a medical clinic, a synagogue, a theatre, a library and a school. A sliver of paradise set on a sweeping beach where everyone spoke Yiddish. Among the passengers of the *Paul-Lemerle*, one group, supported by the Jewish migration association HICEM, intended to travel to the settlement from Ciudad Trujillo. When they came into harbour, they were assured that Sosúa did indeed exist, and was in the north of the island, a two-day trek away. About fifteen kilometres from Puerto Plata, having followed a dirt track through the dense forest, the group emerged onto a shore of the Yassica river, and from here they could see the village of Sosúa in the hills. They were greeted by James Rosenberg, a Jewish missionary who was head of Tropical Zion. Each of them was given a deed of property, a bequest from the Great Benefactor – another title Generalissimo Trujillo had given himself – together with a mule, a horse, ten cows and seventy-five acres of land. And the mission to make the desert bloom – or, rather, to clear the jungle undergrowth.

Ciudad Trujillo
27 May 1941

Breton woke up sweating in the middle of the night, and, somewhat amused, he noted down a dream before he could forget it: *With a soaring ambition uncharacteristic of me, while in Ciudad Trujillo, in an anguish of great exaltation, I dreamed that I was Zapata, and was preparing to meet the following day with my army Toussaint Louverture.*

15

Are There Cows in America?

New York harbour
28 May 1941

Just as it was that Lévi-Strauss had heard about the Munich Agreement while in Amazonia, leafing through an old newspaper he
found on the floor in a rubber prospector's hut, so it was that he
was off the coast of New York when he heard about the German
army massing on the Russian border. Another war was about to
begin, another front was about to open. More than two months
after he had set sail from Marseilles, his journey was nearing its end.

First it was a bridge. One skyscraper, then another, a line that
rose imperceptibly into the heavens, blotting out the horizon,
illuminating it in places. It was raining heavily. There was panic,
everyone raced for the bow, as passengers probably did on every
ship, with the hackneyed cry: 'New York! New York!' Lévi-Strauss
felt a shudder run through him, a mixture of excitement and relief.
He had crossed an ocean and two seas, he was experiencing the
limits of a finite world in which extraordinary technological devel-
opment, the dazzling increase in speed and in communications, at
the same time and by the same logic was stifling hearts and diminishing souls. He saw a ray of light move from one shore to the other
and carve a furrow on one of the skyscrapers, glittering in every
window as in a church. Chaos jostling with ambition in a vertical

city. A box of matches about to ignite. *The deck of a ship bound for North or South America offers modern man a finer acropolis for his prayer than Athens did to Ernest Renan.*

New York
29 May 1941

Having left Martinique on 21 May, the Compagnie Transatlantique steamer *Duc-d'Aumale* entered New York harbour on the morning of 29 May. Some hours later, the skipper, Louis Le Guyader, was found to be missing, and quickly dubbed a 'deserter'. André Masson went ashore and wandered the streets of Manhattan.

Ciudad Trujillo
31 May 1941

In the evenings, after dinner, people in Paris or Marseilles would gather in a bistro or a quiet café and wonder, 'What are we playing at?' Sitting on a banquette at the back of the Brûleur de Loups, or standing at the bar in Le Cyrano, they could not hear the rules of the game – whether of war or of exile – being ripped up. People would superciliously judge or haughtily condemn their infantile follies, wax indignant, scorn the childish scrawls of these benighted fools, these *dreamers* – the word says it all; surrealism was born in café society, and there it would remain. Besides, what exactly was so reprehensible? Was it necessary to adopt a serious expression just because the world was foundering, to be panicked by the fighting when one was far from danger, safe, and warm? Seriousness was another of the great maladies of the century. Do you really think that, having survived the Great War only to see fascism blossom over the charnel houses, poetry should have responded with self-righteousness and contemptuous posturing? There could have been no greater defeat. What did the victims matter? Who are we to judge? The study of history frees us from our uncertainties, restores confidence in our judgements, and in our upstanding conduct. Stepping into the lobby of the Gran Hotel in Ciudad Trujillo and seeing Breton sitting there, one might mock the washed-up pope, or listen to him more seriously than ever, realising that, faced with uncertainty, no single voice held sway, that the horror of the blind beast could just as easily be met with boldness and beauty. In the morning he talked with Eugenio Granell, who, unsurprisingly, was an admirer of Breton and who, like many before him, hoped to be sanctified – a certificate of no value beyond the distinction and the pride of belonging to an open order that has no register and issues no diploma. Breton spent the afternoon dealing with his correspondence, gathering together his scattered community. He reread Victor Hugo in the light of his own exile and made plentiful notes in the margins; he began with *Toilers of the Sea*, and then, having discovered that one of Hugo's short novels was venerated in the Dominican Republic, he quickly devoured *Bug-Jargal*. It is a novel based on the historical events (could it possibly be otherwise?) of the 1791 slave rebellion in San Domingo. The edition he read contained a preface by Hugo in which he explained that it was a juvenile work, one that he could not prevent being republished now that he was famous, though he warned the reader that he would prefer that it not be read: *In 1818, the author of this book was sixteen years old; he made a wager that he could write a book in a fortnight. The result was* Bug-Jargal. *At sixteen one is prepared to wager on anything, and improvise about everything.* Breton thought that he could write a book in a fortnight, a book about exile, one page per day, and at the end of his journey he would have sixty, dense pages, a brief *Iliad* on the high seas, the ephemeris of a world engulfed. A ship sailed to the United States via Puerto Rico, he would leave on Sunday from Puerto Plata, in the north, which would give him the opportunity to traverse the island. There was one last chapter to write. With delight, he noted – by a stroke of chance which only a passionate lover of figures would take for irrefutable, not to say scientific, proof – that the warning in Hugo's preface to *Bug-Jargal* had been written on 24 March in the year 1832, the same date as the *Paul-Lemerle* set sail, the first day of his own exile. And so, in green ink, on the onion-skin paper he favoured, like an epigraph for a book yet to be written, he copied out the end of the preface: *As for the author himself, like a traveller who looks back on his journey to try and find in the hazy lines of the horizon the spot whence he set out, he wanted to* make this story a souvenir of that age of calmness, audacity and confidence, when he boldly attacked so immense a subject as the revolt of the blacks of San Domingo in 1791, a giant struggle in which three continents took part, Europe and Africa as the contestants, and America as the battlefield.

51 West 11th Street, New York
11 June 1941

The tortuous Puerto Rican administrative and customs procedures had the advantage of preparing Lévi-Strauss for his arrival in New York. With papers in order, his trunk inspected, and a letter from the FBI agent who had travelled to San Juan only to discover he was unable to offer an opinion, Lévi-Strauss was a man who had been cleared of all suspicion. A room awaited him in a red-brick building located between Fifth and Sixth Avenues. It was early June, the most beautiful time of year, the trees that lined the street were in bloom, huge windows overlooked untended gardens in the middle of Greenwich Village, *the local Montparnasse, somewhere between the Point du Jour and the porte d'Orléans*, a stone's throw from the New School. He set to writing his dissertation, 'Family and Social Life of the Nambikwara Indians'. Above his desk he had hung a map of the Americas, and had begun to paper the walls with drawings, graph paper, a collage of documents and other materials – it looked like the laboratory of a mad scientist or the studio of an artist. Now and then, he would open the window, lean out, and smoke one of the Puerto Rican cigarettes he bought in East Harlem. Down below, on the stoop, were children coming home from school; he waved to them. The mailbox bore the name of another scientist, another man who spent his life racking his brains, another Claude, a mathematician. While Claude Lévi-Strauss was theorising about the elementary structures of kinship, Claude E. Shannon was devising the bases of his mathematical theory of communication. Come on, why don't we cheat a little, the Advent calendar forces us to follow the perilous path of men whose lives are fraught with history, it is a series of blind steps; coincidences and chance encounters are apparent only afterwards. Why don't we imagine that Shannon and Lévi-Strauss bumped into each other in the hall, followed each other up the stairs, that Claude followed Claude to the top floor? In the late spring of 1941, two men lived at the same address, two men lived obsessed with an idea, a shared idea: that the world, though infinitely complex, multifaceted, random and singular, can and must, if one studies certain invariants, be expressed as a series of Ones and Zeros governed by a canonical formula of myth. One would publish *A Mathematical Theory of Information* in 1948, the other *The Elementary Structures of Kinship* in 1949; one would become the father of cybernetics, the other the father of structural anthropology.

Ciudad Trujillo
13 June 1941

He did not leave his hotel, the large, airy, spartan room that opened onto a balcony terrace, the typewriter which seemed nailed to the modest wooden desk, his back slightly hunched while he pounded the keys with feverish excitement. Vlady would sometimes go for a stroll, taking his sketchpad in his bag, he dealt with the shopping and with collecting mail from the post office, expecting news of Laurette. On the 5th, their Mexican visas were renewed for a further six months by the Secretaría de Gobernación. Yet their path seemed blocked: there was a mandatory stopover in Cuba, which demanded a deposit of one thousand dollars to cross the territory, meanwhile, for former revolutionaries, it was impossible to get a transit visa for New York. They had left the soulless, overpriced Gran Hotel, and spent three days living with decent Spanish people in a boarding house. Serge was entirely taken up with writing a pamphlet – the working title *Hitler versus Stalin* made his intentions clear – and an ambitious novel, whose framework he was setting down. He worked like a craftsman, meticulously, imperturbably, considered that his work was done once the sentence, the paragraph, had been carefully shaped and polished. In front of him, sitting at an angle, was a photograph of Laurette taken on the Canebière in Marseilles; Serge had had an enlargement printed in a photography shop in Ciudad Trujillo. She was walking with her head held high, and the more he lost himself in the image, the more he saw the true image of her personality. People constantly attempt to distinguish between the man of action and the man in love. Nothing could be less apt in the case of Victor Serge, a theoretician of the revolution haunted by love and by absence. In his diary, he alternated between the memories of an ageing revolutionary and brooding on his passionate youth. He had started working on his novel, *The Case of Comrade Tulayev*, in Pré-Saint-Gervais, with Laurette by his side, had carried on in Agen and in Marseilles, and – in an irony typical of the times – had finished it in the Dominican Republic. Sometimes he slipped an allusion to Laura into this fresco of the Stalinist purges, a word that only she would notice, a memory in someone else's words, and, being convinced of the power of fiction, he was careful not to say: *This novel belongs only to literary fiction.* In his notebook, he had already written the last sentence of the novel. It was the memory of an evening spent sitting on the rocks in Malmousque, with the strong wind in their faces: *High banks of clouds, gilded by the setting sun, deployed powerfully over the sky.*

Since they were sharing a room, they shared everything, and so, more than he ever had previously, Victor got to know Vlady, the son he always looked on as a distant cousin. Outside, in the company of other travellers, they lounged in deckchairs whose canvas had been worn thin by the salt spray of the Atlantic and the downpours in Martinique. And – the height of luxury – two single beds with mosquito nets! Victor would sometimes agree to go out in the evening. They would go to a cinema that showed American movies – yesterday it had been *Juarez*.

Serge stopped, he opened a copy of *Dersu Uzala* by Vladimir Arsenyev which he read out of a sense of nostalgia, then suddenly a memory surfaced of a morning they had spent at the Calanques de Marseille. He had been writing in his notebook. Laurette, swimming far from the shore, waved to him, her drowned hand appearing above the surface. 'Come in, come in!' she shouted as she caught her breath. The escarpment plunged steeply, creating rocky outcrops and spewing from a shrub bleached white as driftwood a shelter of shadows. He dived in, head first, and swam underwater in broad strokes, flailing his arms so hard he almost dislocated his shoulders. Halfway out, he reached her, floating on her back, the water lapping at her ears. Her floating body stiff as the wooden slats that made improvised diving boards.

This is the fifth time I've found myself randomly writing about you here. The clouds are massing, everywhere things get complicated, and I'm still paralysed by the challenges of getting here. My Mexican visa has finally been renewed, or at least so I've been assured, but that does not help much. I would not feel remotely impatient were I not so worried for you. I am being completely objective, a stark contrast to my neuroses when we were together; what frightens me is simply the complications you are surrounded by; on my journey here, I've seen the ingenious malice that American consuls can use against those who come knocking at their door, so on that subject I would like to feel reassured.

Ellis Island
16 June 1941

A thick fog cloaked the skyscrapers. Here, the glint of a marker buoy eddying the water, there the twinkling lights at the entrance to the harbour. At about eight o'clock, the foghorns on the neighbouring ships grew louder. The passengers were gathered on the foredeck; the previous evening the announcement had been made: tomorrow morning, New York. They opened their eyes wider, trying to peer through the fog to make out a sliver of skyscrapers, wiped the misted windows to see, excited as at the beginning to see something new, to distinguish the peaks, the silhouette of the *skyline*. Then, the sun began to beat down, flattening the layer of fog, melted it away and pierced east Manhattan. For those looking for some omen, the rising sun played the role of 'Easter in New York'. Down below, they could see a fleet of patrol boats from the immigration service skimming across the Hudson, preparing to embark as soon as the ship hove to. An hour later, in the common area of the ship, an officer was checking passports and visas while a doctor examined the passengers. Those whose papers were in order were allowed to go ashore in Manhattan, the others were taken to Ellis Island. André Breton, Jacqueline and Aube were allowed to disembark. At the foot of the gangway, Yves Tanguy and Kay Sage were waiting. Having dropped them with their luggage at the West

11th Street apartment, they arranged to meet them at six o'clock at Brevoort, the only terrace bar *à la française* in New York City – where they drank pastis until midnight.

Ellis Island
17 June 1941

A hall as narrow as a railway platform, queues snaking in every direction, children dozing on wooden benches. This was not a detention centre, this was where borderline cases were considered, where the sick and those immigrants suspected of anti-American activities were refused entry. Passengers were allowed to receive visitors and were allowed free use of the telephone booths at the far end of the room. Netty and László Radványi felt utterly helpless: their daughter, who was extremely short-sighted and when not wearing glasses blinked convulsively, had been diagnosed by the New York Port Medical Officer as suffering from a disease of the central nervous system. As a precaution, she had been sent to hospital for further tests, and since their papers still needed to be checked, they were not allowed to go with her. Their little girl was in Manhattan while they were here on Ellis Island, awaiting the immigration authorities' decision. They were waiting in the hall. Netty had made a number of phone calls, to the League of American Writers and to F. C. Weiskopf, a writer friend, who had not answered. Late in the morning, she called again, shouting into the receiver: 'It's Anna!' 'I'm so delighted!' Weiskopf said. 'Where are you? Ellis Island? I'll be right there! I've got some amazing news for you, just hang on there. I have to tell you face to face!' He was a burly man with short, curly brown hair who wore suits that were much too small, and a beige mackintosh he never took off; he was accompanied by a man with glasses and a thick moustache who was puffing on a pipe. Weiskopf threw his arms around Anna, kissed Pierre and shook hands with László. Then, turning to the man next to him: 'May I present Anna Seghers?' – 'Netty, I'd like to introduce you to your American agent and benefactor, Maxim Lieber. I took advice from a number of friends in New York, then sent Maxim the manuscript for *The Seventh Cross*, and I've got great news: Little

Brown in Boston want to publish it next year! Maxim will tell you all about it and he'll give you the contracts. Since we hadn't had any news from you for three months, we nearly accepted without getting your consent!'

Ellis Island
18 June 1941

While all the guards – without exception – were upstairs in a staff room, ears pressed to the radio, listening to the Joe Louis vs Billy Conn fight, the Radványi family appeared before the immigration authorities. Ruth was back from the hospital, the doctors having found nothing wrong, beyond her myopia. Nonetheless, the officer used the doctor's comments to prolong their detention: *The doctor does not explicitly state that she is not also suffering from a disturbance of the central nervous system. As a result, you have two choices: either you can ask that your daughter be re-examined, and she will then be transferred to a hospital in Washington for further tests, which may take as long as a month, during which time you will stay here on Ellis Island, or you leave tomorrow on the first sailing to Mexico, your final destination.* Tired of resisting, and with transit visas in their pocket, Anna and László agreed to sail aboard the *Monterrey.* A roundabout journey that would end only when they reached Veracruz.

Ciudad Trujillo
20 June 1941

At daily meetings at the Escuela Nacional de Bellas Artes, Wifredo Lam and Eugenio Granell found themselves joined by the Austrian portrait painter George Hausdorf, the sculptor Manolo Pascual, the Spanish artist Josep Gausachs and various Dominican artists including Yoryi Morel, Jaime Colson, a friend of Picasso and Braque, Darío Suro, a student of Diego Rivera. They began to dream about a community of artists, about organising collective exhibitions.

New York
21 June 1941

And the last shall be first. 'Are there cows in America?' Chagall asked Varian Fry when he came to the town of Gordes and suggested leaving France. On 7 May, because seven was the artist's lucky number, they agreed to leave. Mute, unable to paint, Chagall was writing poems in Yiddish.

> *How shall I tell you my last word*
> *You when you are lost*
> *I have no place on earth*
> *To go.*

On the evening of the summer solstice, Chagall and Bella disembarked in New York. Pierre Matisse, the artist's son, was there to greet them on the quay. In their apartment, the couple huddled next to the radio and listened to news from the Russian front. At the far end of the hall from their apartment was a Christian Science reading room.

And the first shall be last. After a journey that lasted five long months, René Hauth finally arrived. He had told his wife and his brother he was leaving in late July, 1940. A former intelligence officer who had worked on the Luxembourg border, and later in the Balkans, he had embarked on the SS *Wyoming*, one of the ships leaving Marseilles for the West Indies. He arrived in Fort-de-France on 24 February, where he spent four months waiting to get an American visa. Let's assume that, a month later, he met Lévi-Strauss, Breton, Serge, Masson and the other passengers who had arrived on the *Capitaine-Paul-Lemerle* and the *Carimaré*. On 17 June he got a place aboard the *Alcon*, a modern ship that traced an arc along the islands of the West Indies as far as New York. At night, he wandered the city, losing himself in the Manhattan streets. At a street corner like every other, he saw the lacework cowl of a skyscraper so tall he had to crane his neck. Looking more closely, he decided it looked like the bonnet of Père Ubu, twinkling in the darkness. Following in the footsteps of harried businessmen, he stepped inside a building: Grand Central Station. He looked up at the ceiling, a celestial vault punctuated by golden signs of the Zodiac and a silver Milky Way. The boat, the plane, the commuter trains and, in the heavens, constellations painted the wrong way around.

Finchley Fifth Avenue
22 June 1941

The finest suits are at Finchley. The name of the tailor, Finchley, rang a bell somewhere. He happened on the advertisement in one of the American newspapers available in the lobby of the Gran Hotel in Ciudad Trujillo. Then he remembered that the owner, Mr Goodman, was a cousin of his grandmother. His American uncle. While on Ellis Island, it occurred to him that he might as well try his luck. He sent a letter to the store. 'I am the grandson of your cousin Hulda Alexander from Berlin, Alfred Kantorowicz.' He put his New York friends' address on the back of the envelope. By the time they got to the apartment, there was a card waiting from the uncle, inviting them to the Finchley Fifth Avenue store. It was a glorious day. The delighted Uncle Goodman presented Alfred with a tuxedo, a Sunday suit, a three-piece work suit, a black velvet blazer and a pair of shoes.

LETTER FROM VICTOR SERGE
TO LAURETTE SÉJOURNÉ

23 JUNE 1941
CIUDAD TRUJILLO

Darling, tomorrow it will be three months since I watched as your silhouette grew smaller on the quay in front of Hangar 7. I have had to accustom myself to not receiving letters from you. I know you have written to me often, but I receive nothing. Only one of your letters arrived, though I get dozens of letters from France, I know Marceau writes to his friends, he told me about you. I like to think that your letters are piling up somewhere along on the way and I will suddenly get a whole bundle, but I try not to hope, because disappointment is too painful. I carry on writing to you like a man casting bottles into the sea, and I will carry on. All my hope is now focused on the telegram telling me of your departure. Do not doubt my patience, or my confidence in fate, we must be determined. I find it frustrating that I have still not arrived anywhere, since, if I were settled, I could do something to help you, here, my hands are tied.

Slowly, the complications are being resolved, I am still waiting for a Mexican visa that was renewed but has not yet arrived, I'm making plans to try and get a Cuban transit visa without having to pay a thousand dollars I don't have. If the worst comes to the worst, we might have to travel by air. All my own worries would mean so little if I felt easy in my mind about you, if I had some positive news. Our friends have sent you a little money, write to them if your departure has not been postponed again (God forbid!). I would so much love to know what life is like for you, how you are holding out and fighting back ...

Vladi and I are experiencing what is happening in Russia as though we were there, we can picture the faces and the land, we can see clearly what is, and what will be. This is going to be the most terrible war, there will be countless victims – the defeat, the collapse, the painful renewal, we find ourselves transported to the most extreme conclusions, much more quickly than we anticipated.

Spent all day yesterday writing about this, in a kind of fever. The little town was filled with sunshine and military music, flags, people joining in the festivities against a backdrop that looked like something from a film by René Clair. As for me, I was filled with an Apocalypse, one that your photograph on my desk could not assuage. In the evening, I took a walk along the deserted quays where the waves crashed like distant cannon fire as they hurled themselves onto the rocks ... This morning, all the sirens in the city trumpeted the news. –

I have just met some people who received a letter dated 30 May by plane from Marseilles, I immediately went to the post office; nothing. I don't even know how to talk to you in these circumstances. Have you had news from Liuba, from Jeannine, from René? Why am I even bothering to ask? –

And yet I can accept all the frustrated expectations that fill my gloomy days, if only you have been able to leave. I think of you constantly, all my love.

Veracruz
30 June 1941

'The thing is, if we asked every passenger aboard ship to keep a diary of the crossing, what would we read?' Anna asked her two children, Pierre and Ruth. 'What is a diary but a witness statement? We are all experiencing the same events, the plot is the same, though our perception, our interpretation, is inevitably different, what's left beyond a canvas, a skeleton frame of dates and notes – as for the rest, details, which are our great wealth, change things completely. A multitude of fragmentary, scattered, twisted, blind observations allowing us to grasp the whole. What do you think we would find in such a diary other than slivers of a fractured whole? *We never see things only from one side.* Our journey is coming to an end; what will we say when we narrate it, what will we forget, what will we retain that is valuable, or painful? Our journey, children, is like Odysseus returning to Troy. I read the *Odyssey* to you last year: at every stage of our exodus we have encountered unforeseen obstacles, faced new challenges and new ordeals.'

Veracruz at noon. Three months and one week after setting out from Marseilles, they were coming into *safe harbour*.

LaGuardia Airport
14 July 1941

A PanAm seaplane from Lisbon landed at LaGuardia airport after a stopover in the Azores. On board were Peggy Guggenheim, her ex-husband Laurence Vail, her current husband Max Ernst, her two children and a biologist travelling with a cargo of laboratory animals. The following morning, the *New York Times* ran the headline: 8 GUINEA PIGS HERE BY CLIPPER TRAVEL.

Havana
10 August 1941

Having no visa for the United States or for Mexico, Wifredo Lam

197

had returned to his homeland. With him was his wife, Helena Holzer. *What I saw when I returned was like hell,* he wrote. Havana was American – *with its white capitol, the mark of America, its banks, its palaces, its luxurious European shops.* It was no longer the Spanish city he had left when he was seventeen. He was reunited with his mother Serafina, his sisters Eloísa, Teresa and Augustina. His father, Lam-Yam, was dead. After a long detour that had taken him from Madrid to Barcelona, from Paris to Marseilles, from Martinique to the Dominican Republic, he had finally come full circle, back to his *native land.* He was approaching his *tropical period,* one different from the astrophysical term referring to the interval between two alignments of the Earth's rotational axis with the Sun. The Route de la Trace and the spectacle of the Absalom valley had set him on his path, it was there he had discovered the feeling of a jungle matrix, the unfurling of violent nature, and he now dreamed of furious frescos. Jungles, waterfalls, hills and peaks, the eyes of the moon hidden amid the assegais, canes that looked like feet, the sable black of their handles, the pleading hands of mangroves in the swamps and the savage coupling of twined liana, all orchestrated and choreographed as a macabre dance – *the strict parallelism of a boundless cemetery* – the bluish green of gentle dawns, the moment that follows the massacre and the shadows of the treacherous night. His subject would be the jungle, into this he would conjure the maelstrom of war and oppressions, finally at peace with himself.

In the mailbox, a letter from Breton announced that the art dealer Pierre Matisse was planning an exhibition of his work the following year.

In the skies over Mexico
4 September 1941

The propellers whined, revving at full throttle. The engine roared and the aircraft took off, nose up. The cabin and the seats juddered in the blustering wind. Sitting up front, Serge and Vlady gripped their seats as they watched the runway fade into the distance, saw the roof terraces of Havana melt into the surrounding landscape and the ochre line of the sierra rise up, framed against a shoreline flecked with foam. As the plane gradually rose into the air, the endless blue down below shifted towards darker hues, a colour swatch like a length of painted canvas stretched away in stripes that ranged from *bleu de France* to cobalt, from Mayan blue to Prussian blue, royal blue to smalt, *bleu charrette* to ultramarine or lapis lazuli. When they reached cruising altitude, Serge, his face pressed to the window, thought about this vanishing era, about the slow death of revolutions, and the many men, born at the close of the previous century, who had lived through something no previous era had known: the extraordinary density of years, the isthmuses of movements and, flanking their forced march, the lunatic proliferation of technologies that had transformed a boundless world into an earth that was too small, darkening the heart even as it illuminated, opening the doors to a paradox on which modernity would greedily feast, gorging until it was sated. They landed at Mexico City aerodrome to find Julian Gorkin waiting for them on the runway. At the hotel, Victor hastily wrote down his impression of the flight for Laurette. The revolution of the machine and the machines of the revolution, Léon Gambetta's hot-air balloon soaring above the city walls of Paris, the railway lines of Adolphe Thiers, the outsize Soviet trains, the aeroplane, man's dream of flight made real, turned into a *machine for killing* other men.

Epilogue

—

The Lesson of the Unicorn

Events without any apparent connection and originating from incongruous periods and places, slide one over the other and suddenly crystallise into a sort of edifice which seems to have been conceived by an architect wiser than my personal history.

Claude Lévi-Strauss, *Tristes Tropiques*

16

Was You Ever Bit by a Dead Bee?

———

Pointe-du-Bout
December 2016

According to what I had read, on the former leper colony on the Pointe-du-Bout, a small tourist town had sprung up, centred on two attractions, the marina and the sand and shingle beaches of the bay, which developers had turned into private beaches for their guests. I had been determined to visit all the places on the island described by the passengers. The Lazaret, or what remained of it, was top of my list. I would be arriving a day earlier on the 5 a.m. flight, would collapse in my room at the Hôtel l'Impératrice, at the corner of rue de la Liberté and rue Victor Hugo, overlooking the gardens that lined the street, what had once been the Savane. Browsing through an online photographic archive, I had happened on a postcard from 1930 depicting the Lazaret, Pointe-du-Bout. It was a view of the building as it had been at the time, you could see the ramparts, the jetty, headland and beach, two military buildings and a shack which was probably the mess hall.

The Pointe-du-Bout, I was warned, is a mecca for tourists, an example of town planning where developers have taken over a five-kilometre strip of land and built a concrete promenade with modern hotels, nightclubs, water-sports facilities and artificial beaches. This was high season, the hotel owners kept saying. I took one of the early morning boats shuttling between Fort-de-France and Pointe-Rouge. I sat at the front, gripping the guardrail, as we crossed the bay and hugged the far shore at Anse-Mitan. At the entrance to the marina, the launch sailed past a mangrove swamp separated from the road by a corrugated iron fence and detritus washed up by the tide. Next to the harbour, a cluster of small houses formed a fake village by the roadside. Further off, facing out to sea, was a derelict building, the former Meridien Hotel, which had been renamed the Kalenda Tourist Complex, which had also collapsed, and now mechanical diggers had begun demolishing the serpentine building. I walked over to it. From a distance, it was impossible to see that the ruin masked what looked like the cove of the Lazaret, a kind of capital P jutting into the sea, cloaked by thick vegetation: the gun battery of the Pointe-du-Bout. There was no one around except for the labourers working on the building site and a tramp who had wandered in from the forest, a dubious character. I asked him about the ruins of the Lazaret. 'I've just come from there, you follow the dirt road a hundred metres, go past the first gate and there's a squat, the guy who lives there is friendly, further along, you'll see, there are steps leading up to the fort.' The fort had never been demolished, he explained; in the 1970s a concrete building had been erected to the north, which housed an open-air cinema with concrete terraced seating. The old facade of the Lazaretto served as the screen. Movies were shown there on Saturday nights, French comedies starring Belmondo and de Funès, and American blockbusters. Business had boomed. There had been a restaurant on the site, too, and the upper part of the building had been tiled. Then developers bought up the land and built a huge monstrosity that had collapsed, not once but twice; now nature had reasserted itself, and with it the old leper colony. I walked through a diminutive jungle, a fifty-metre stretch of weeds and liana that twined around buildings and covered the porticos. First the main arch of the guardhouse, a magnificent tree leaning against the crumbling facade, spanning almost three metres, its branches pressed against the brick and rubble, like a stake planted in a broken flowerpot. All that remained of the perimeter wall were sections of the south-west corner and a part of the eastern parapet that had been restored. Taking a concrete path that was cracked and warped by the roots snaking underneath, I came to the cinema. From here, I could look down through one of the arches at the concrete terraced seating and the graffiti-tagged wall that had served as a screen – and, below, the wreck of an over-turned car. A rusty metal framework sketched out the missing roof of the Lazaret, but gave no sense of its former glory. On the ground, around the derelict hulk, were broken bottles and piles of corrugated iron sheeting. On the ground, around the derelict hulk, were broken bottles and piles of corrugated iron sheeting. A contemporary ruin of steel and plastic merged with the vanished Lazaret of remnants and rubble, towers and parapets, archways and, to the north-west, the gun battery, like something from a story by Robert Louis Stevenson, with two 90 mm cannon.

I remember, as children, my brothers and I were fascinated by ruins. Not hilltop castles or the dry-stone *bories* up banks of scree, not pools of water, no, what fascinated us were abandoned buildings, melancholy ruins whose walls still dripped with their faded past. I am thinking of the roadside grocery shops, abandoned Belle Époque hotels or villas forgotten by heirs and estate agents. The game involved getting inside and groping our way through the darkness with only a torch, encountering tramps and potheads. I believe that we cultivated a taste for the old junk that, over the course of our sorties, we collected and piled up in garages: American chrome oil stoves, beautiful wooden wine racks, military equipment, gas masks and bullets from a revolver. We had to survey the buildings, peering over the wall to gauge the topography, find the hole in the fence or scale the wall, once inside, we would move slowly, covering each other's backs, as though this were a kind of secret mission, fired by a slightly preposterous excitement and a genuine nervousness. It was always an adventure. My brothers were skilled at this game and, like my father, they had an innate sense of the architecture of such places, they could effortlessly break locks, throwing open the doors to cellars and attics. There often were hidden wonders, family photo albums, porn mags or fascist trinkets. In our rucksacks, we carried our burglar's tools, a crowbar and a jemmy. The joy of discovery was followed by a curious uneasiness, a role play in the ruins, chasing each other down the hallways of derelict palaces, engaging in sword fights with rusty iron bars. I think we got our taste for decrepitude from holidays spent in a vast property my grandparents owned in the Camargue. It was a farm where they grew pears and soya beans. Behind a huge storehouse where crates were piled in bizarre formation, and where my uncle had set up a badminton net, there was a remnant of the 1960s, a vestige of the years of post-war, five-year plans and the Common Agricultural Policy: a village built for seasonal workers, like miners' villages near a pithead. Two or three families still lived there, but for the most part it was a series of derelict cottages. Huge clouds of wasps swarmed above the beds while the garden was strewn with broken glass and upturned furniture. I remember an old car in the backyard of one of the houses that we would take apart piece by piece, joyfully kicking holes in the bodywork. Strange as it may seem as I write this, ruins remind me of my childhood. This is a life-size film set, ghosts are lurking here, people once lived here, and we are allowed to take over the place. And on this morning, in the middle of the mangrove swamp, feeling a little lost, immersed in this past that has haunted me (or that I have haunted), I think about my brothers, about how I would like to visit this ruin with them, to laugh with them at the sight of the car wreck down below, to marvel with them at the act of resistance being waged between the buildings, the creeping liana and the huge stands of bamboo gradually enclosing the ruins, incorporating them into a reinvigorated nature. In short, the atmosphere of childhood mingled with that of praying in an artificial place of worship. In this moment, it feels as though all the notes I have accumulated, *the preparations for the novel*, this catechism in the form of an investigation, come to life. Learn as much as possible and read as much as possible so as to be able to move nimbly through these ruins, anticipating a present as it has transformed this past – coming face to face with it and discovering the overgrown backyards. And beyond the tales of ghosts, why this story belongs to us, to us more than to anyone else. What ties bind us to our ghosts? To attempt to describe what was, what has vanished, what can no longer be heard, yet what, for those prepared to listen carefully, continues to tell a story in books, in memoirs, in archives and microfiches, sometimes even in the stones themselves, is to decide by an unreasonable assumption that what we see before our eyes is worth saving. For it is not the nature of the archive that matters, but what it contains: a past.

This is doubtless the lesson that Breton teaches us: *Who am I? If this once I were to rely on a proverb, then perhaps everything would amount to knowing whom I 'haunt'. I must admit that this last word is misleading, tending to establish between certain beings and myself relations that are stranger, more inescapable, more disturbing than I intended. Such a word means much more than it says, makes me, still alive, play a ghostly part, evidently referring to what I must have ceased to be in order to be who I am. Hardly distorted in this sense, the word suggests that what I regard as the objective, more or less deliberate manifestations of my existence, are merely the premises, within the limits of this existence, of an activity whose true extent is quite unknown to me.*

I was waiting for the motorboat. A child was screaming and yelling at the sea, threatening the waves. He hurled pebbles into the water, pumped his fist in the air, yelling at the tide, racing forward only to immediately retreat. A moment later, he was sitting on his backside in the sodden sand. In the back of the boat, I watched as the shore grew fainter, cloaked by the mangrove swamp, the fort, the old jetty of the leper colony where the rowing boats had docked one evening in April 1941. In my mind, the landscape before my eyes telescoped, the green horizon and the spume on the water, the fantasy image of the lifeboats from the *Paul-Lemerle* merged with a sequence of images from *Prisoners of the Sun* in which Captain Haddock and Tintin peer through binoculars at the cargo ship, the *Pachacamac*. The extraordinary chase from Marlinspike Hall to La Rochelle and by seaplane to Callao, Peru, on the trail of the men who have kidnapped Professor Calculus. I would find it difficult to recreate the panels of the comic book, first a panel showing the harbour, then maybe a pennant being hoisted, the Quechua doctor's skiff, the police refusing to allow the ship to be inspected. Then, under cover of darkness, Tintin, having swum from a rowing boat midway between the shoreline and the ship, climbing the knotted anchor rope. And the knife thrower with the tattoo of the great Inca sun. Then, other panels, the runaway train coach in the Andes, Snowy being snatched up by the condor, the Peruvians' refrain, '*No sé*', the spitting llamas, the Phrygian cap worn by the young Zorrino, the front cover with its mummies lying askew among the stones, and Tintin's final ruse while he is tied to the stake in the Temple of the Sun God. Then, by superimposing three panels and a false memory, we could create a new story, Captain Haddock on the shore near the Lazaret, drunk on whisky, hurling insults at the distant ship, at Sagols and the Vichy regime. In the background, the Lazaret drawn in Hergé's *ligne claire* style, in the foreground a full-page image of Captain Haddock shouting himself hoarse, screaming his lungs out, and in the speech bubble taking up half the page we could read the list of insults being hurled at the *Capitaine-Paul-Lemerle*.

The motorboat pulled into the jetty, next to a taxi rank and the main bus station of Fort-de-France. Earlier that morning, before leaving the hotel, I had made a note of the timetables, and the stop closest to the Public Records Office on the rue Saint-John-Perse, near the college, atop one of the hills of Fort-de-France. The records office, a modern building high above the city, offers a ready target for the stiff sea breeze. In the reading rooms, the sheet-metal roof creaks like the mast of a ship, mixing with the rain clanging on the roof like a peal of church bells. Armed with Reader Card 8504, I went to the lending department to pick up the documents I had reserved, only to be told that, because some of the letters, newspapers and documents were fragile or difficult to track down, they would be given to me in dribs and drabs, so I would have to come back regularly. The archivist behind the desk wheeled out a double-decker trolley on which were piled numbered boxes and folders. The librarian handed me the documents one by one, carefully making a list of the document numbers and signing the slips. One of the box files contained a listing of all documents relating to the Lazaret, meticulously inventoried and indexed by number. By way of introduction, we can read: *The naval service has a number of infirmaries or lazarets. Between 1841 and 1929, the Lazaret located at the Pointe-du-Bout served as a centre for disinfecting and fumigating ships, for quarantining any passengers who displayed symptoms of contagious diseases. During the governorship of Admiral Robert, it served as an internment camp for foreign soldiers, but also as a holiday resort for colonial officials and youth camps. In 1949, it was converted into an orphanage.* Among the first batch of documents were the records of the maritime police for 1941: those arrested, a list of personnel, treatments given by the health inspectors, letters and memoranda, together with a large cardboard box numbered 4 N 4590/A and 1 M 6766/B.

I am not sure exactly what it is that I love about archives, the rustle of documents being handled, the musty smell of paper that has been stacked and boxed, or the impression of illicitly gaining access to traces of a – private or public – past, to memoranda and official letters that, when written, were filed away as a matter of routine, out of habit, or an obsession with archiving, in anticipation of a roof requiring repair or a patch of land being extended, but certainly not in anticipation of the far-fetched notion of someone trying to write a novel. Every document – the very word takes on the coldness of control, of a dead language – quivers with a hidden presence; a letter, a word, is a distant otherness. The calculations, the words, the detailed pencil drawings resonate, and, by a strange form of reanimation, the simple cross-section of a stone vault or the frontal elevation of a colonial building become living, breathing things filled with stories. Inside the archive of maritime health service, in a yellow folder numbered 1 M 3670, in spidery handwriting written in faded blue ink, 'Situation of Polish and Czech soldiers and of foreign civilians interned at the Lazaret', the accounts of the camp, the price of new beds, the salaries of the guards, and a frayed carbon copy of a memorandum to Admiral Robert written on 22 April 1941, headlined: FRENCH AND FOREIGN JEWS STAYING IN FORT-DE-FRANCE. Sometimes, unaware of our own ridiculousness, we arrogantly think we are in the presence of something unique, something never before revealed, something that can be unfolded, read for the first time, something that has been patiently waiting for us, classified and filed away, attached to the folder with a paper clip. That day, among the relics of the Lazaret, inside a blue folder marked 'Department of Bridges, Thoroughfares and Colonial Buildings', was a cross-section of the Lazaret and a topographical survey that, carefully unfolded for fear that it might tear, gradually revealed the geography of the Pointe-du-Bout. Once unfolded, it revealed the shoreline, then the landing stage, the latrines, the sulphur fumigation station, the ramparts and the water tanks, the watchtowers, the infirmary and the buildings in which some of the prisoners from the *Capitaine-Paul-Lemerle* slept.

That night, back at the hotel I watched *To Have and Have Not* on my laptop. To tell the truth, I had almost completely forgotten the movie, and in my mind, I had mixed up the story with the plot of *Casablanca*. I had fun imagining a character played by Humphrey Bogart popping up in every book, like a cameo. The aeroplane flying to Camp Cazes aerodrome in *Casablanca* transformed into a fishing boat sailing along the shores of the island, Hoagy Carmichael singing 'Hong Kong Blues' or a piano accompanying Lauren Bacall as she sings 'How Little We Know', drowning out the voice of Ingrid Bergman in 'As Time Goes By'. The final line, 'I think this is the beginning of a beautiful friendship', would be answered by 'If you want me, just whistle. You know how to whistle, don't you? You just put your lips together and blow.' The caricatured backdrop of Martinique set against an exotic Casablanca. There is a legend that, while on a fishing trip with Hemingway, the director Howard Hawks, in a last-ditch attempt to persuade the writer to join him in Hollywood, said he would make a film of the writer's worst story. 'My worst story?' Hemingway apparently said. 'That goddamned bunch of junk called *To Have and Have Not*.' Hawks accepted the challenge; Hemingway, convinced that Hawks could never adapt the book, agreed. Hawks simplified the plot, turned the story of the fishing boat and the Cuban cigars into a story of resistance set in the Caribbean, with dialogue written and rewritten before each take by William Faulkner.

'Was you ever bit by a dead bee?' Eddie, the perpetually drunk ship's mate, asks everyone. The riddle of the bee is like a ritual of initiation. Most people say: 'I have no memory of being bit by any kind of bee.' But Slim and Steve – Bacall and Bogart – give what Eddie thinks is the only valid answer: 'Were you?' 'I bet I been bit a hundred times that way.' 'You have? Why don't you bite them back?' 'That's what Steve always says. But I ain't got no stinger.'

17

The Lesson of the Unicorn

Paris
July 2017

A quest cannot be accomplished unless, in its epilogue, it offers a solution to a mystery. As I finished writing, I hoped to solve at least two mysteries. The first was to track down the painting Henri Smadja brought aboard the *Capitaine-Paul-Lemerle* wrapped in shirts – whether a Manet or a Degas, I still did not know. This entailed finding a portrait of Berthe Morisot that would have been sold in New York in the summer of 1941. Two years after the war, Smadja bought a fifty per cent stake in *Combat*, the newspaper founded by Camus in 1941. At the end of his life, having bankrupted the newspaper and destroyed its editorial policy (what had been the mouthpiece of the Resistance had veered sharply right-wing), he holed up in his castle in Médan which he had converted into a printworks. The house had been left to him by the widow of the Nobel Prize winner Maurice Maeterlinck. Heedless of the cornices and the parquet floors of this castle that had once welcomed François Villon, Ronsard and Paul Cézanne, Smadja installed the printing presses, drilled holes in the walls to run pipes, poured a concrete floor over the hundred-year-old tiles; the workers slept up in the attic, they hung their laundry on the linotype presses to dry. On 14 July 1974, Henri Smadja committed suicide; six weeks later, on the night of 29 August, the last issue of *Combat* was printed; on the front page, the headline: SILENCE, WE'RE SINKING!, and on the back, facing a blank page: *Having come from nowhere ...* Combat *is going back.* It was reading the morning paper that Claude Lévi-Strauss, now sixty-six, learned of the death of a man whose name and face were familiar. This was Smadja, the man with the painting, the man who shared his cabin, *a curious character who claimed to be Tunisian. One day he showed me a Degas he kept in his suitcase. He enjoyed special privileges and, during stopovers, going ashore posed no problem for him. He came and went as he pleased. I knew his name, Smadja; I found him intriguing. Much later, when the founder of* Combat *died and his photograph was published in the newspapers, I recognised it; it was him. He was probably on some sort of secret mission, though for whom, I do not know.*

'We who joined this newspaper poor are leaving it just as poor. Our only wealth has been concentrated in our respect for our readers,' Camus wrote in his final editorial when he sold *Combat*. Emmanuel Mounier, founder of *L'Ésprit* and a friend of Victor Serge, also left the newspaper. My research into the history of the daily unearthed one of the most far-fetched of many outlandish ideas, a column, first published in 1950, entitled 'At the forefront of *Combat*', which offered a forum to the surrealists: 'Starting in *Combat* this week: André Breton, Julien Gracq, Suzanne Labin, Henri Pastoureau, Aimé Patri, Benjamin Peret, Henri Pollès and David Rousset.' Bizarrely, I remembered that the surrealists had contributed to *Combat* during the 1950s. In Greil Marcus' book *Lipstick Traces*, I had read the chapter 'The Assault of Notre-Dame' (Michel Mourre, a member of the Lettrist movement, went up onto the altar of Notre Dame during Easter high mass and told the sanctimonious congregation 'God is dead!' and narrowly avoided being lynched); he also mentions the columns written by Breton and Nadeau, who interpreted the gesture as highly artistic – *the simplest surrealist act*. You might ask, why this digression ... although the very notion of recall creates the ebb and flow of memories, mingling and confusing one memory with another. This brief but unexpected association (a right-wing editor offering a forum for surrealists) had been Smadja's idea, and the idea for the column, which came to an end after the assault on Notre-Dame – which provoked a clash between the editorial department, outraged by Mourre's blasphemous act, and the surrealists, led by Breton, who congratulated the former Dominican friar for his act of bravery against the deadly power of the Catholic Church – had probably been born aboard the *Capitaine-Paul-Lemerle*. Years later, when Smadja re-encountered Breton, he probably thought that he should thank fate. Such an unlikely alliance could only have occurred on the deck of a ship.

I visited the Musée d'Orsay and talked to the curators, asked them whether they knew anything about a small portrait by Degas or Manet that would have been sold in New York, or one that might have resurfaced years later. I came away empty-handed. Goodbye, Berthe.

Paris
August 2017

The second riddle: did any other photographs of this crossing exist? Pinned up over my desk, in my notebook, the two group portraits from 25 March 1941, one taken in Marseilles harbour, the other perhaps off Port-Bou. The joy of setting sail, of fears allayed, nothing in these photographs hints at the difficult three-month journey between two continents. Browsing the website of the United States Holocaust Memorial Museum, I thought for a moment – the coincidence would have been extraordinary – that the Lowenstein credited with taking these photographs was the same man who, eight years later, would fly to New York aboard an Air France Constellation with the curious goal of marrying his ex-wife. But he was a different man, and his story was one I felt I had read a hundred times before, a German family in the 1930s finding refuge in Paris, only to flee again in 1940, crossing the French Demarcation line, steering a course between the mountains and the sea, knowing that the only escape route was exile.

I followed a different path, the photographs that Germaine Krull had taken of the crossing, and her photo reportage about the prison colony in Saint-Laurent-du-Maroni. In her book *La vie mène la danse*, she tells all those convinced that there must be a copy or a set of negatives somewhere: *I destroyed all the photographs I took there, since a country should not be burdened with such shame.* Perhaps the crossing was fated to be blind, a moment of unreality that passengers would have to relate in the vain hope of being believed, the festival of Neptune, the livestock and abattoir on deck, the crowd of misfits, the names Seghers, which would find worldwide success with *The Seventh Cross*, Claude Lévi-Strauss, the father of structural anthropology, Wifredo Lam, whose painting *The Jungle* is now in MoMA. It was like telling a joke. When I first read her book, I did not notice a name that cropped up in French Guiana and Brazil, and again when Germaine Krull was reunited with Louis Jouvet. The name was Jacques Rémy, a French film-maker or screenwriter, I was unsure. Krull tells the story of how his dog died, having been bitten by a snake in a banana plantation in Brazil. Then she adds: *I had news from Jacques Rémy, but much later.* On that particular day, out of pure serendipity, I had been planning to search for Rémy online. Jacques Rémy turned out to be the *nom de plume* of Raymond Assayas, father of the journalist Michka Assayas and the film-maker Olivier Assayas. Dazzled once again by the wonders of the digital world, I leafed online through the pages of *Assayas by Assayas*, a book of conversations, then searched for 'Lemerle'. I have to admit that I was half-asleep and had to reread the paragraph: *I became interested in it because, while tidying up my house in the country, I happened on a series of photos taken by Germaine Krull aboard the* Capitaine-Paul-Lemerle, *and my father's account of the crossing which, to my knowledge, has never been documented. My father also talked about his visit to former penal colony inmates in Cayenne during a stopover in Saint-Laurent-du-Maroni. Germaine Krull was there also, and I came across her photo report.* There was something utterly absurd about this moment, something thrilling, unsettling and joyful. I managed to find an email address for Olivier Assayas and wrote to him that night. He replied the following morning.

Dear Olivier Assayas,
In *The Death Ship*, B. Traven wrote: 'I have learned that it is not the mountains that make destiny, but the grains of sand and the little pebbles.' Nothing could be less true. I'm writing to you because I've just made an amazing discovery. I'm in the process of finishing work on *Outrageous Horizon*, a book set aboard the *Capitaine-Paul-Lemerle*

in 1941, the story of the crossing and the meeting, on the far side of the world, between Breton and Césaire, brought together by a ribbon in a Martinique ruled by degenerate army rabble. Guided by an imaginary ship's log, the book follows a number of destinations from Marseilles to New York by way of the Lazaret at Pointe-du-Bout, the Absalom valley, the *Duc d'Aumale*, ending with an image of Grand Central Station, beneath the celestial ceiling painted by Paul César Helleu, and its inverted constellations. You know this story, because your father was among the players, together with Germaine Krull, Curt Courant, Claude Lévi-Strauss, Anna Seghers, Victor Serge ... Reading interviews with you, I discovered that there are photographs of the crossing and of a visit to former penal colony prisoners in Cayenne during a stopover in Saint-Laurent-du-Maroni, as well as your father's account of the crossing. My approach may seem a little cavalier, please forgive my eagerness, which is merely a confused mixture of astonishment and joy at this coincidence: I would love to meet up with you and talk about this, and, if you will permit, to look at your father's account and the photographs of Germaine Krull you found. I will be away from Paris from next Wednesday until 16 August. I can be available tomorrow or Wednesday or, otherwise, after I get back. The sooner the better.

Sincerely,

Adrien Bosc

Dear Adrien Bosc

I wanted to write back straight away. I am not currently in Paris, and won't be until the end of August.

But we can talk on the phone or communicate by email.

I have photos documenting the journey by Germaine Krull, which I have identified and annotated, of Martinique, of the Lazaret and the remainder of her journey with my father, first to Cayenne and later to Rio de Janeiro.

I have my father's account of the crossing, as well as a text by Germaine Krull (whom I knew very well) recounting her journey and her travails in Martinique. I transcribed these from a typescript sent to me by Germaine Krull's biographer, Kim Sichel, it probably comes from the GK archive at the Museum Folkwang in Essen.

Regards,

OA

Paris
August 2017

I remember Olivier Assayas' film *Summer Hours*. It is a story of inheritance, of a family house in Valmondois – a veritable museum filled with paintings by Corot, furniture by Majorelle and Hoffmann and panels by Odilon Redon, a legacy from a famous ancestor, the artist Paul Berthier – and of the memories that must be dispersed after the death of the matriarch. Now, I pictured boxes piled with memories, and, in the middle, something that looked to me like a treasure chest, those images that I had tried to comprehend with nothing to rely on but snippets of stories, scattered memories, footnotes, excerpts from archives, snatches of lived moments. To have written a novel in a *camera obscura*, and now to have the hope of seeing those moments captured on film, to be granted access at the end of the story to a *camera lucida* – the magical reveal, frozen, like the photographic plates my father had inherited from his parents, which we would sometimes look at, startled to suddenly find ourselves in the presence of his ancestors, marvellously alive, in relief, captured in a smile, in a moment of suspended time. But I still needed some means of seeing them, these images I had fantasised about so often, whose revelation would be like an *open sesame*, uttered in the clatter of a Super 8 projector.

During our first conversation, Olivier Assayas talked to me about the Germaine Krull exhibition at the Jeu de Paume. At the time, he had approached the curator who had not seen fit to include the photo reportage. I was astonished. We were talking about the exodus of 1941, the friendship between Germaine Krull and Jacques Rémy, a friendship that had lasted half a century. He mentioned two stories by his father, written aboard the *Capitaine-Paul-Lemerle*. Two manuscripts running to ten typed pages. The photographs had been printed in Rio before their paths diverged, perhaps with the intention of publishing a joint account, or so he assumed. They had met up again much later, in Saigon, in the 1960s. Germaine was running The Oriental, the largest hotel in Bangkok, Jacques was doing location scouting for a film about the voyages of Marco Polo. On his return to Paris, they had seen each other often. The photographs had long since been forgotten and lay in a drawer of a cabinet, confused with photographs by Pierre Verger, others taken by his father and snapshots from their holidays. No doubt Germaine Krull had been surprised to see these photographs from 1941, having destroyed the negatives. Olivier told me he had read extensively, and compiled copious notes and stories retracing his father's journey from France to Brazil, the Atlantic crossing aboard the *Paul-Lemerle*, the stopover in Martinique, the last trip aboard the *Saint-Domingue*. About the dog mentioned in Germaine Krull's memoirs, a dog called Mascotte that his father had picked up along the way.

We arranged a late summer meeting at his apartment in Paris, one Monday in September at 6.30 p.m.

Paris
4 September 2017

As I headed to the apartment, I was nervous about seeing the photographs. I felt a mixture of excitement and dread, wavering between the desire to see with my own eyes the *eyes that saw the Emperor*, as Roland Barthes so aptly writes, and the curious desire not to see these images for fear of being disappointed, of puncturing the unreality of the story. I had developed a form of neurosis. The steady accumulation of documents, of books, of clues, had put me in the presence of these men and women. I had spent four years rubbing shoulders with them and my obsession was such that, if I closed my eyes, I could stroll along the deck of the ship, go from one hold to another, recognise the captain and his passengers, address many by their first name and draw a detailed cross-section, like a fanatical archivist. I also feared I might cheat, that I might change what I had written, revise it to contain the unexpected things I *might have seen*. And yet, by the time I reached the courtyard of the building, the anxiety had vanished. It suddenly seemed to me that a piece of a larger puzzle, an unfinished part of the story, had just been given to me. The building was a large town house in the process of being restored, the tangle of scaffolding in the stairwell, seen from below, looked like a bizarre grid. It reminded me of Germaine Krull's *Fers* – photographs of bolts and metal structures. I waited in the living room. Olivier Assayas was running late and had sent his apologies. I felt ill at ease in the huge armchair. I didn't dare move. I scanned the vast bookshelves and the books on the coffee table. *Lipstick Traces* by Greil Marcus. He arrived at seven o'clock. We had talked for five minutes at most when he took out a large folder and opened it on the kitchen table. I listened dazed and unable to move as he commented on each photograph. Before me was a series of astonishing shots, cattle being loaded at Casablanca, laundry hung out to dry, food being prepared in huge saucepans in the canteen, women sunbathing on deck, children balancing between two planks attached to the bow of the ship, the P.45 whaler, the former leper colony at Pointe-du-Bout, the Polish soldiers aboard the *Saint-Domingue*, and convicts from the prison colony in Cayenne; a whole life beginning to stir before my eyes. I recognised the faces of strangers as though this were my family album. Wifredo, standing shirtless in a hut at the Lazaret with Helena by his side. A group photograph taken at the Lazaret, Victor Serge smoking a cigarette in his deckchair with Vlady sitting cross-legged on his left and Germaine in the centre. A string of buoys tethered by a rope and, in the background, the fort of Oran. Here a gang of laughing Spanish children, there a woman writing in a notebook, a board propped against her knees by way of a table, her companion bending to read over her shoulder. The stern of the ship and the foamy wake below. It was exhilarating, unsettling, utterly amazing. The highlight of the show: a dozen shots of the festival of Neptune. Young men in shorts and pointed hats, letting go of a diver who they appear to be holding at arm's length, the ship's chaplain looks as though he has stepped out of a play by Genet or a production of *Ubu in Chains* directed by Max Ernst, Neptune is wearing a fake beard, cardboard sunglasses and a papier-mâché wizard's hat; at the bottom of the photograph, a pair of feet and, out of frame, a body falling backwards, having been tossed into the deep end of the baptismal pool. In the next photograph, Neptune is blessing with a seriousness that befits the farce a young man sitting on the diving board. It was unbelievable. This was no dream: in the mid-Atlantic, survivors from a war-torn Europe shrugging off the misery of exile and the end of a world they had known, in the joyous ritual of crossing the Equator. I stammered, unable to say a word, to comment on what I was seeing. So, I simply took photos of the images with my smartphone. Then I sat down and I read the accounts written by Jacques Rémy and edited by his son, the memories of his time aboard the *Paul-Lemerle* and his report on the penal colony. His style had wit and brio, and there was a profundity to his descriptions. These passages matched up with details I had gleaned from other stories: the organisation of the ship into Parisian districts, the canteen, the stinking holds, the crossing-the-line festival, the suspicious cargo and the escort convoy from Oran. His account of Saint-Laurent-du-Maroni, as harrowing as Germaine Krull's photographs, should have been published as *A Supplement to the Travels of Albert Londres*. A civilian identity card from Martinique dated 2 May 1941, an extract from a baptismal certificate issued by the archbishop of the city, together with a certificate issued by the deputy mayor of Fort-de-France: *The mayor of Fort-de-France hereby certifies that Monsieur Assayas, Raymond Jacques, born in Istanbul on 21 June 1911 and residing in the city, is of good character, and that his conduct has been irreproachable, that he is a citizen of France and has never been convicted of theft, fraud, breach of trust or an offence against public decency. In witness whereof, this certificate has been issued to assert his rights. Fort-de-France, 3 May 1941.* After an hour, maybe, I left the apartment and found myself out on the street, frantic, dazed, confused. I walked aimlessly. When I reached the place Dauphine, I sat on a bench beneath the chestnut trees. I thought about my brothers, about our nights on the rooftops of Paris, climbing the scaffolding at Saint-Sulpice and elsewhere, our daring feats as we scaled the city from bottom to top. I tried to call Jean, but he did not answer. Everything was jumbled together: Krull's *Fers* and the memories of our past life, our wild adventures when we were twenty, and pre-war surrealism. Alexandre, the eldest, dubbed the ancestor, the daring survivor of a fall from a five-storey building. A vast mythology fuelled by surrealism, the writings of Rigaut, Cravan, Vaché, the *three suicides of the society,* the exponents of *black humour* anthologised by Breton, the poems of Cendrars and Apollinaire. The laws of objective chance and the poetry of the streets brought together all these disparate elements, the atmosphere of my childhood mingled with the adventures of other men, as though the past were resonating more loudly, more clearly, than the present, the surreal *coup de théâtre* of a spell in which mysteries and ghosts are revealed in all their beauty. I had a clearer grasp of the whole. And, just as ancient myths from different societies may share the same plots and characters, I was discovering a story that was at once remote and intimately familiar. When Claude Lévi-Strauss was asked about his vocation, he would conjure a bucolic dreamlike scene he had known during the debacle. On the evening of 4 September, as I sat on a bench in the place Dauphine, I felt as though I were sharing that scene. *I think that it was one day, as I was lying in the grass and gazing at the flowers, particularly a dandelion clock, that I became what I did not know was called a structuralist as I thought about the laws of organisation that must necessarily govern a complex, harmonious and delicate structure of the kind I was contemplating, which I could bring myself to believe had resulted from a series of accumulated accidents.*

In the margin of my book, I wrote: *The lesson of the dandelion.*

I got home late. From the Pont Neuf to the place Léon-Blum, I thought about this quest that spanned two hemispheres in search of the remnants of the *Lemerle*. My mind was whirling with the adventures of Tintin, *The Secret of the Unicorn* and *Red Rackham's Treasure*. The discovery of the secret of the *Unicorn* in the basement of Marlinspike Hall. The revelation in the final panels of the comic: to find the hidden jewels you had to press on a point on the globe where the *Licorne* had sunk. The treasure is never at the far side of the world, it is at the far end of the street. The doorway to adventure in the cellars of Marlinspike Hall. Do I even need to mention that the geographic coordinates on the scrolls in *Red Rackham's Treasure* lead to an island off the coast of Martinique?

On a scrap of paper, I scribbled a note that I pinned to the corkboard on the wall: *The lesson of the unicorn.*

18

The Magnetic Earth

———

Le Diamant
31 December 2017

In 1941, when I was thirteen years old, I had the good fortune to spend whole evenings in the company of André Breton, André Masson, Claude Lévi-Strauss. The French intelligentsia fleeing the Nazi armies.

In 1941, Édouard Glissant was thirteen years old. He was a pupil at the Lycée Schœlcher. In the playground, he rubbed shoulders with Frantz Fanon, who was three years his senior. Both of them read *Tropiques* and occasionally had the opportunity to talk to one of the two teachers who edited the magazine, Aimé and Suzanne Césaire.

In 1943, Glissant was fifteen, still too young to follow in the footsteps of Fanon, who had taken one of the boats used by the Maquis to bring dissidents to the Dominican Republic and the Free French Forces.

In May 1943, Suzanne Césaire brought the articles that were to appear in the next issue of *Tropiques* to the offices of Admiral Robert at the Service d'Information to request that the contents be approved and to ask for the paper they would need for printing. The head of censorship, Lieutenant Bayle, usually skimmed the contents page and found only academic and literary articles. This time, he discovered hidden calls to arms, cries of revolt, and, like any panicked civil servant, he cheated, he rectified his mistake, and made up for his earlier tolerance by issuing a ban, which the editorial team received on 10 May 1943:

When Madame Césaire requested paper for the new issue of Tropiques, *I immediately agreed, having no objection – quite the contrary – to the publication of a literary or cultural review.*

I do, on the other hand, have very formal objections to the publication of a revolutionary, racial and sectarian review. [...]

Let us leave aside how shocking it is to see public servants who are not merely paid by the French state but have achieved a high cultural level and a first-rank place in society attempting to issue a call to arms against a country that has been so very good to them. Let us also leave aside the fact that you are teachers charged with the responsibility of educating the young. This in effect does not concern me directly, so let us simply remember that you are French. [...]

Excessive centralisation is an evil suffered by every French province. It risks stifling personality and replacing it with something conventional and standardised, risks killing art by drying up the fountainhead of truth. A man like Mistral symbolises the necessary reaction to such things. In Tropiques, *I thought I detected the signs of a similarly vigorous and no less desirable regionalism. I now see that I was wrong and that you are pursuing a very different objective. [...] You believe in the power of hatred, of rebellion, and you have set as your goal the unfettered expression of every instinct, every passion; it is a return to sheer barbarism. Schœlcher, whom you invoke, would be shocked to see his name and his words used in support of such a cause. [...]*

I therefore hereby forbid the publication of this issue of Tropiques, *whose contents are enclosed herewith.*

The answer from the editorial board of the review came quickly, it took the form of a manifesto, and was nothing short of a declaration of war:

Monsieur,
We have received your indictment of Tropiques.

'Racists, sectarians, revolutionaries, ingrates and traitors to the fatherland, poisoners of minds'; we find none of these descriptions essentially repugnant.

'Poisoners of minds'? Like Racine, according to the Messieurs de la Port-Royal.

'Ingrates and traitors to the fatherland that has been so good to you'? Like Zola, according to the reactionary press.

'Revolutionaries'? Like the Victor Hugo who wrote Les Châtiments.

'Sectarians'? Fervently so, just like Rimbaud and Lautréamont.

'Racists'? Yes. The racism of Toussaint Louverture, of Claude McKay and of Langston Hughes – pitted against the racism of Drumont and Hitler.

As for the rest, do not expect pleas, or recriminations, or arguments from us.

We do not speak the same language.

Signed: Aimé Césaire, Suzanne Césaire, Georges Gratiant, Aristide Maugée, René Ménil, Lucie Thésée. Fort-de-France, 12 May 1943.

Two months later, the arrest of Admiral Robert and the arrival of the Free French Forces in Martinique sounded the death knell for the Vichy regime in the Antilles.

A friend had mentioned a book to me that specialists might consider minor, but one he loved and recommended that I read: *The Magnetic Earth*. This novel, one of Édouard Glissant's last works, had been written by two people, the cover mentioned 'In collaboration with Sylvie Séma'. Now weak and unable to travel, Glissant, who had been commissioned to write a travel piece about Easter Island, decided to send his wife, entrusting her with the mission of collecting information, notes, photographs, film footage and sketches that would make it possible for him to write the book. 'The Visitor' as he dubbed her, set off for the island, while he wrote the book at Le Diamant in Martinique, basing it on the documents she sent, the feelings she conveyed; an *affair* between travellers. *The two of us, Sylvie and I, were like ethnographers of the encounter, one the physical body working at the site, the other, the imagination, soaking up the space, roaming the alleyways of generations and paddling up the rivers of genealogies, except that we were utterly untroubled by descendants or heirs.* The result is astonishing, the writer seems to capture the island as no writer had done before, with a lucidity and a daring that more meticulous explorers had missed. I finished my reading, dazzled by such far-sightedness, convinced that, regardless of the journey, what matters is the account of it. And that there is no vision that is not shared, enriched, illuminated, enhanced by the gaze of a loved one. And so, Glissant was in conversation with Cendrars, who playfully responded to the age-old question, 'So, Blaise have you really travelled on the Trans-Siberian Express?'

'Why do you care, since I allowed every one of you to travel on it?'

On a blank page of my notebook, I jotted: *The lesson of Easter Island.*

When I reached Caffard cove, I took the path towards Le Diamant. Skirting a white sandy beach, I reached the place known as Le Diamant – a village with a covered market overlooking the sea where people take shelter from the tropical rains, not far from a patch of waste ground next to a trunk road, a strip of tall scorched grass, and the roiling sea below. Behind the dock, the village cemetery is made up of about fifty graves, dotted here and there with family mausoleums that look like white-tiled pools washed by a pressure hose. Strolling among the graves I happened on one which was modest, rather simple – humble, one might say. Looking at it, one can read the name of the deceased, Édouard Glissant, and an epitaph engraved on one of the cracked tiles: NOTHING IS TRUE, EVERYTHING IS ALIVE.

I retraced my steps, satisfied by this last maxim. One last aphorism to be deciphered if I was to advance. One final riddle to escape the labyrinth of networks, of half-open graves, the vestiges of a past conjugated in the present, one peopled by the dead, despite the living, the veiled images of another world, of a story written by others, in accounts and narratives, in notes and memoirs, a child lost in the darkness who might reach out towards a wall, might stumble from dresser to shelf, from shelf to wall, grip a door handle, flick a switch, bring light to the dark room. I could close the book, at peace with myself, wiser for one last lesson: *Nothing is true, everything is alive*, this was *Glissant's lesson.*

*

In Martinique, night falls as swiftly as the sea rises, and darkness quickly engulfs the pathways, the jungle clamours with strange noises, pervasive shrieks; fireflies pierce the black sky and tumble by the roadside like shooting stars, like grazing fire. The house was still a twenty-minute walk. At the last junction, I spotted a peeling blue sign, CHEZ ERNEST RESTAURANT, and a track that branched off to the left towards the sea. At the end of the path, nestled between two rocks, sheltered from the sweeping beaches, was a quiet place. I don't know whether it was the music I noticed first, a Billie Holiday song, 'All of Me', I think, or maybe 'When You're Smiling'. The soft, husky voice drifted from a shack in the deserted cove that had a fuchsia neon sign beneath the awning. I remember walking towards it, sitting on the porch. I talked to the owner, who used to work on the rue de Seine, a huge guy with a stoop, not exactly easy-going, but funny and sardonic. I called my beloved. I suggested we have dinner here with friends to celebrate New Year.

We were sitting on the veranda, the meal was almost over, it was balmy; behind me, a light, warm breeze, I kissed my wife, winked at my son, I took my fork and speared a piece of pineapple from my neighbour's plate, raised my glass and proposed a little quiz to the assembled diners: 'Who said: "We cannot know the taste of pine-apple from travellers' tales"?'

Acknowledgements

I have had a number of books with me throughout this journey, like travelling companions, books that with a word or a dialogue have allowed me to get closer to certain characters. These acknowledgements will trace the go-betweens who engineered these meetings, character by character.

My thanks to Emmanuelle Loyer, the author of *Paris à New York, Intellectuels et artistes français en exile, 1940–1947*, whose work was very helpful, especially the remarkable, definitive biography *Lévi-Strauss*, and more especially those chapters devoted to the Musée de l'Homme, his time in the United States, and the writing of *Tristes Tropiques* (the German A.-G. vorm Seidel & Naumann typewriter!). My thanks to Vincent Debaene, whose book *L'Adieu au voyage: L'ethnologie française entre science et littérature* (Bibliothèque des Sciences Humaines), and whose article 'A district of Paris as unfamiliar as the Amazon. Surrealism and ethnography' (*Les Temps Modernes*, issue 628), led me to understand the influence of surrealism on the mind of Claude Lévi-Strauss and on the structure of the embryonic novel that was the original version of *Tristes Tropiques*. I would like to take this opportunity to praise the Pléaide edition of Lévi-Strauss edited by Vincent Debaene, Frédéric Keck, Marie Mauzé and Martin Rueff and the interviews conducted by Didier Eribon for his book *De près et de loin*, which provided the clue that helped me track down the extraordinary Henri Smadja. Before leaving Lévi-Strauss, the man of the distant gaze, my thanks to Maurice Olender, who published *Chers tous deux* (Librairie du XXI Siècle), a collection of Lévi-Strauss' letters to his parents, with a foreword by Monique Lévi-Strauss.

I am grateful to the historian Eric T. Jennings, author of one of the key works on the Antilles route, 'Last exit from Vichy France: The Martinique escape route and the ambiguities of emigration', published in *The Journal of Modern History* and in *Vichy in the Tropics, the National Revolution in Madagascar, Guadeloupe, French Indochina, 1940–1944*, and also an essay, 'Escape from Vichy, the refugee exodus to the French Caribbean', as yet unpublished. My thanks also to Jon Juaristi, author of *Los Árboles Portátiles*, and to the Colonial Archives and Departmental Archives of Martinique, whose incredible conservation work led to extraordinary discoveries; my warm wishes to the archivists and documentary makers, clerks and secretaries whether encountered in Aix-en-Provence or Fort-de-France.

My thanks to Bernard Noël, author of *Marseille New York, 1940–1945*, a boundless source of wonders that first led me to this story; to Alain Paire, the most important historian of the Marseilles period of surrealism whose website fosters a spirit of fraternity and understanding; I would also like to take this opportunity to mention the anthology to which he contributed, *Le Jeu de Marseille: Autour d'André Breton et des surréalistes à Marseille en 1940–1941* (Ed. Daniele Giraudy, Éditions Alors Hors du Temps).

My thanks to two unique publishing houses, Signes and Balises, who published the personal writings of Victor Serge – the correspondence between Serge and Laurette Séjourné, *Écris-moi à Mexico: Correspondance inédite (1941–1942)* provided a crucial piece of the puzzle – and also to Agone, the publisher of Serge's *Carnets (1936–1947)*.

When it comes to Anna Seghers, the greatest introduction is a memoir by her son, Peter Radvanyi, *Au-delà du fleuve; avec Anna Seghers*. My thanks to Annabelle Hirsch for her translation of certain passages from the memoirs of Alfred Kantorowicz.

Thanks to Mark Polizzotti, biographer of André Breton, and to Dominique Berthet, the author of the essay 'André Breton, l'éloge de la rencontre: Antilles, Amérique, Océanie'. Not forgetting Maurice Nadeau, whose *L'Histoire du surréalisme* was a boon companion throughout the writing of this book.

The *Lam Métis* catalogues proved invaluable, in particular those articles by Édouard Glissant, Jacques Dubanton and Jean-Louis Paudrat that allowed me to map the tortuous paths of Wifredo Lam, and Max-Pol Fouchet's monograph *Wifredo Lam*, a mine of information on the artist's time in Paris. My thanks to the author of the chronology of Wifredo Lam, and custodian of certain biographical wanderings.

My thanks to Daniel Maximin, author of *Aimé Césaire, Lam, Picasso, Nous nous sommes trouvés*, which brought me close to several of my characters, and the editor of Suzanne Césaire's *Le Grand Camouflage. Écrits de dissidence (1941–1945)* published by Le Seuil. My thanks to Jean-Michel Place, who published the complete collection of the magazine *Tropiques*.

Reading Germaine Krull's autobiography *La Vie mène la danse* helped me identify the names and people in her photographs, and, more importantly, it gave me a sense of her path through life.

My thanks to my editor Manuel Carcassonne, who also published Olivier Assayas' interviews, without which I would probably never have discovered the photographs of this crossing, from the port of Marseilles to a penal colony in the jungle.

Lastly, I would like to thank Monique Lévi-Strauss, Aube Breton-Elléouët and Olivier Assayas, and also Bernard Chambaz, François Guillaume, Benoît Heimermann, Émilie Pointereau and Kaouther Adimi for their careful and considered readings.

Sources

———

Italicised passages in the book are excerpts from texts, writings, diaries and accounts of the journey by those who sailed aboard the *Capitaine-Paul-Lemerle*.

ix
Walter Benjamin, 'On the concept of history', translated by Edmund Jephcott, in Walter Benjamin, *Selected Writings, Vol. 4, 1938–1940*, Cambridge, MA, Belknap Press, 2003.

4
Nicolas Bouvier, *Le Poisson-Scorpion*, Paris, Éditions Gallimard, 1982.

5
G. W. Leibniz, *New Essays on Human Understanding*, translated by Peter Remnant and Jonathan Bennett, Cambridge, Cambridge University Press, 1996.

7
Victor Serge, *Notebooks, 1936–1947*, edited by Claudio Albertani and Claude Rioux, translated by Mitchell Abidor and Richard Greeman, New York, NY, New York Review Books, 2019.

15
Varian Fry, *Surrender on Demand*, Boulder, CO, Johnson Books, 1997.

22
Hannah Arendt, 'We refugees' in *The Menorah Journal*, 1943.

25–6
Victor Serge, *Notebooks, 1936–1947*, edited by Claudio Albertani and Claude Rioux, translated by Mitchell Abidor and Richard Greeman, New York, NY, New York Review Books, 2019.

27–9, 30, 31–3
Wifredo Lam, Personal archives of Wifredo Lam.

31–33
Wifredo Lam, Max-Pol Fouchet, Éditions Cercle d'Art.

37–38
Manuscrits divers, 1941, Lot 2230, vente 2003, répertoriés et consultables sur le site.

39
Victor Serge, *Notebooks, 1936–1947*, edited by Claudio Albertani and Claude Rioux, translated by Mitchell Abidor and Richard Greeman, New York, NY, New York Review Books, 2019.

40
Albert Camus, *Notebooks 1935–1942: Volume 1*, translated by Philip Thrody, Ivan R. Dee, 2010.

48
Victor Serge, *Notebooks, 1936–1947*, edited by Claudio Albertani and Claude Rioux, translated by Mitchell Abidor and Richard Greeman, New York, NY, New York Review Books, 2019.

64

André Breton, *Nadja*, translated by Richard Howard, London, Penguin Modern Classics, 1999.

65

Claude Lévi-Strauss, *Look, Listen, Read*, translated by Brian C. J. Singer, New York, NY, Basic Books, 1997.

66

Victor Serge, *Memoirs of a Revolutionary*, translated by Peter Sedgewick, Iowa City, IA, University of Iowa Press, 2002.

74–5

Victor Serge and Laurette Séjourné, *Écris-moi à Mexico. Correspondance inédite 1941–1942*, Toulouse, Éditions Signes et Balises, 2017.

75–8

Claude Lévi-Strauss, *Look, Listen, Read*, translated by Brian C. J. Singer, New York, NY, Basic Books, 1997.

81

André Breton, *Martinique, charmeuse de serpents, avec textes et illustrations d'André Masson*, Toulouse, Pauvert, département de Librairie Arthème Fayard, 1972, 2000.

82–4

Claude Lévi-Strauss, *Look, Listen, Read*, translated by Brian C. J. Singer, New York, NY, Basic Books, 1997.

86

Victor Serge, *Notebooks, 1936–1947*, edited by Claudio Albertani and Claude Rioux, translated by Mitchell Abidor and Richard Greeman, New York, NY, New York Review Books, 2019.

89

Victor Serge, *Notebooks, 1936–1947*, edited by Claudio Albertani and Claude Rioux, translated by Mitchell Abidor and Richard Greeman, New York, New York Review Books, 2019.

97
Honoré de Balzac, *La Comédie humaine, III*, 1834.

98
Anna Seghers, *Transit*, translated by Margot Bettauer Demb, New York, NY, New York Review Books Classics, 2013.

99
Victor Serge, *Notebooks, 1936–1947*, edited by Claudio Albertani and Claude Rioux, translated by Mitchell Abidor and Richard Greeman, New York, NY, New York Review Books, 2019.

99
Anna Seghers, *Transit*, translated by Margot Bettauer Demb, New York, NY, New York Review Books Classics, 2013.

101–2
Victor Serge, *Notebooks, 1936–1947*, edited by Claudio Albertani and Claude Rioux, translated by Mitchell Abidor and Richard Greeman, New York, NY, New York Review Books, 2019.

107
Claude Lévi-Strauss, *Tristes Tropiques*, translated by John Weightman and Doreen Weightman, London, Penguin Modern Classics, 2011.

109
Aimé Césaire, 'In Truth ...' from *Ferraments*, Paris, Éditions du Seuil, 1960.

109
André Breton, *Martinique, charmeuse de serpents, avec textes et illustrations d'André Masson*, Toulouse, Pauvert, département de Librairie Arthème Fayard, 1972, 2000.

113
André Breton, *Martinique, charmeuse de serpents, avec textes et illustrations d'André Masson*, Toulouse, Pauvert, département de Librairie Arthème Fayard, 1972, 2000.

117–18
Letter from Lieutenant Castaing to a friend in Switzerland, 21 April, 1941, Archives départementales de Martinique.

119–20
André Breton, from 'A Great Black Poet', his introduction to *Notebook of a Return to the Native Land* by Aimé Césaire, translated by Clayton Eshleman, Middletown, CT, Wesleyan University Press, 2001.

124
Claude Lévi-Strauss, *Tristes Tropiques*, translated by John Weightman and Doreen Weightman, London, Penguin Modern Classics, 2011.

127
Claude Lévi-Strauss, *Tristes Tropiques*, translated by John Weightman and Doreen Weightman, London, Penguin Modern Classics, 2011.

130–31
Claude Lévi-Strauss, *Tristes Tropiques*, translated by John Weightman and Doreen Weightman, London, Penguin Modern Classics, 2011.

133
From a letter from André Breton to Simone Kahn.

134–5
Claude Lévi-Strauss, 'Chers tous deux', *Lettres à ses parents 1931–1942*, ed. and intro. by Monique Lévi-Strauss, Paris, Éditions du Seuil, 'La Librairie du XXIe siècle', 2015.

139
André Breton, *Martinique, charmeuse de serpents, avec textes et illustrations d'André Masson*, Toulouse, Pauvert, département de Librairie Arthème Fayard, 1972, 2000.

141
Aimé Césaire, 'Presentation', from the first issue of *Tropiques*.

142
André Breton, *Martinique, charmeuse de serpents, avec textes et illustrations d'André Masson*, Toulouse, Pauvert, département de Librairie Arthème Fayard, 1972, 2000.

145
Suzanne Césaire, *Le Grand Camouflage, Écrits de dissidence*, Suzanne Césaire, ed. Daniel Maximin, Paris, Éditions du Seuil, 2015.

145
Aimé Césaire, *Cahier d'un retour au pays natal*, Paris, Voluntés, 1939, later re-translated as *Return to My Native Land*, by John Berger, Archipelago Books, Brooklyn, NY, 2014.

147
André Breton, *Martinique, charmeuse de serpents, avec textes et illustrations d'André Masson*, Toulouse, Pauvert, département de Librairie Arthème Fayard, 1972, 2000.

151
Germaine Krull, *La vie mène la danse*, édition établie et annotée par Françoise Denoyelle, Paris, Éditions Textuel, 'L'Écriture photographique', 2015.

151–3
Claude Lévi-Strauss, 'Chers tous deux', *Lettres à ses parents 1931–1942*, ed. and intro. by Monique Lévi-Strauss, Paris, Éditions du Seuil, ' La Librairie du XXIe siècle', 2015, translated by Frank Wynne.

157

Claude Lévi-Strauss, *Tristes Tropiques*, translated by John
Weightman and Doreen Weightman, London, Penguin Modern
Classics, 2011.

158

Claude Lévi-Strauss, *Tristes Tropiques*, translated by John
Weightman and Doreen Weightman, London, Penguin Modern
Classics, 2011.

159

Claude Lévi-Strauss, *Tristes Tropiques*, translated by John
Weightman and Doreen Weightman, London, Penguin Modern
Classics, 2011.

161

Germaine Krull, *La vie mène la danse*, édition établie et annotée
par Françoise Denoyelle, Paris, Éditions Textuel, 'L'Écriture
photographique', 2015.

164

Germaine Krull, *La vie mène la danse*, édition établie et annotée
par Françoise Denoyelle, Paris, Éditions Textuel, 'L'Écriture
photographique', 2015.

164–65

Suzanne Césaire, from 'Alain and Esthetics', in *The Great
Camouflage: Writings of Dissent 1941–1945*, translated by Keith
Walker, Middletown, CT, Wesleyan University Press, 2012.

165

Suzanne Césaire, from 'Alain and Esthetics', in *The Great
Camouflage: Writings of Dissent 1941–1945*, translated by Keith
Walker, Middletown, CT, Wesleyan University Press, 2012.

169

Claude Lévi-Strauss, 'Chers tous deux', *Lettres à ses parents 1931–
1942*, ed. and intro. by Monique Lévi-Strauss, Paris, Éditions du

Seuil, 'La Librairie du XXIe siècle', 2015, translated by Frank Wynne.

176
Claude Lévi-Strauss, *Tristes Tropiques*, translated by John Weightman and Doreen Weightman, London, Penguin Modern Classics, 2011.

176
Claude Lévi-Strauss, *Tristes Tropiques*, translated by John Weightman and Doreen Weightman, London, Penguin Modern Classics, 2011.

180
André Breton, 'Entretiens avec E.F. Granell' in *Alentours I recueilli dans Œuvres complètes, tome III*, Paris, Bibliothèque de La Pléiade, Éditions Gallimard, 1999.

181–2
Victor Serge, *Notebooks, 1936–1947*, edited by Claudio Albertani and Claude Rioux, translated by Mitchell Abidor and Richard Greeman, New York, NY, New York Review Books, 2019.

183
André Breton, 'Entretien avec Eugenio Granell', in *Œuvres complètes, tome III, Écrits et notes de 1940–1942*, Paris, Bibliothèque de la Pléiade, 1992, translated by Frank Wynne.

186
Claude Lévi-Strauss, *Tristes Tropiques*, translated by John Weightman and Doreen Weightman, London, Penguin Modern Classics, 2011.

187–8
Victor Hugo, *Bug-Jargal*, Paris, 1826.

188
Claude Lévi-Strauss, *Tristes Tropiques*, translated by John

Weightman and Doreen Weightman, London, Penguin Modern
Classics, 2011.

190
Victor Serge, *The Case of Comrade Tulayev*, translated by William R.
Trask, New York, NY, New York Review Books Classics, 2004.

191
Victor Serge et Laurette Séjourné, *Écris-moi à Mexico.*
Correspondance inédite 1941–1942, Toulouse, Éditions Signes et
Balises, 2017.

193
Anna Seghers with Pierre Radványi, *Au-delà du fleuve*, Le Temps
des Cerises, 2014.

194
Marc Chagall, 'In Lisbon, Before Departure', quoted in *Marc
Chagall and His Times: A Documentary Narrative* by B. Harshav.

195–6
Victor Serge et Laurette Séjourné, *Écris-moi à Mexico.*
Correspondance inédite 1941–1942, Toulouse, Éditions Signes et
Balises, 2017.

198
Wifredo Lam, Personal archives of Wifredo Lam.

201
Claude Lévi-Strauss, *Tristes Tropiques*, translated by John
Weightman and Doreen Weightman, London, Penguin Modern
Classics, 2011.

206
André Breton, *Nadja*, translated by Richard Howard, London,
Penguin Modern Classics, 1999.

212

Claude Lévi-Strauss, 'Chers tous deux', *Lettres à ses parents 1931–1942*, ed. and intro. by Monique Lévi-Strauss, Paris, Éditions du Seuil, 'La Librairie du XXIe siècle', 2015.

214

Germaine Krull, *La vie mène la danse*, édition établie et annotée par Françoise Denoyelle, Paris, Éditions Textuel, 'L'Écriture photographique', 2015.

214

Olivier Assayas, *Assayas by Assayas*, Paris, Stock, 2014.

220

Édouard Glissant and Sylvie Séma, *La Terre magnétique, Les errances de Rapa Nui, l'île de Pâques, Peuples de l'eau*, Paris, Éditions du Seuil, 2007.

223

Édouard Glissant and Sylvie Séma, *La Terre magnétique, Les errances de Rapa Nui, l'île de Pâques, Peuples de l'eau*, Paris, Éditions du Seuil, 2007.